COTTONWOOD GULCH

COTTONWOOD GULCH

BY CLARENCE E. MULFORD

AUTHOR OF

"Bar 20," "Bar 20 Days," "Bar 20-Three," "Black Buttes," "Buck Peters, Ranchman," "Bring Me His Ears," "Tex," "The Coming of Cassidy," "Hopalong Cassidy," "Johnny Nelson," "The Man from Bar 20," "The Orphan," "Rustler's Valley," etc.

A. L. BURT COMPANY

Publishers   New York

Published by arrangement with Doubleday, Page and Company

Printed in U. S. A.

RESPECTFULLY DEDICATED TO THOSE MEN
WHO CARVED OUT LAW AND ORDER
IN THE MINING CAMPS OF THE
GREAT NORTHWEST

CONTENTS

vii

COTTONWOOD GULCH

COTTONWOOD GULCH

CHAPTER I

THE EXODUS

THE little valley, like many others, had lain unnoticed, almost unknown, since the fur-trade days, when it had yielded up its beaver and straightway joined the ranks of the unimportant. The dead cottonwoods in its cosiest bottoms, killed for their bark to provide winter food for the animals of the trappers, had since then been used for fuel by roaming Indian villages. Now, recovered from that slight spoliation, it lay under the Montana sky, a thing of greenery and beauty.

Two weather-beaten old prospectors paused on the valley's rim, their apathetic pack mules glad of any excuse to stop, and looked down into the velvety paradise with eyes which saw none of its beauty. Their close-lidded gaze followed the course of the rippling stream, the occasional out-croppings of rock, and the shallow enlargements of the sandy and gravelly bed of the creek. They pushed down the gentle slope and unpacked on a low bench at the side of the stream. Hungry as they were, hunger could wait; shovel and gold-pan were the important considerations of these two. Panning a creek was nothing new to them—still, years of failures or mediocre rewards had not dulled the fever in their blood; they attacked the gravel with a partly restrained frenzy, their broad, shallow pans dipping, rocking, and whirling, spilling thin and fragmentary sheets of roiled water over their rims. Simultaneously they bent over the residue in their pans, and simultaneously stared at each other, their tobacco-stained mouths agape. Stunned disbelief was in their eyes, mad hope on their seamed and contorted visages; after all the years of misplaced hope, stubborn optimism, privations, and solitude they had found their reward.

"Great Godfrey!" shouted old Jim Hankins, hopping from one foot to the other. "She's here, Hank! We're struck it at last! Richer'n Alder Gulch, or any find in the last twenty years!"

Hank chewed reflectively, spat with care and precision, and squinted an eye at his old partner.

"Wall, I dunno 'bout that, Jim," he deprecated, but a fire gleamed in his old eyes that belied his cautious words. "Mebby so, mebby so; if she holds out. I've seen it like this more'n onct. Can't prezactly tell about her yit."

Two old backs bent to work again, and remained bent most of the day. When darkness brought their labours temporarily to an end and gave time to think of food they cooked their supper with careless haste and bolted it nervously.

"That there's near the last o' the grub, Hank," said old Jim, anxiously. "One o' us has got ter go after supplies, come daylight." The thirst in his throat had bothered him all day but had been deadened by the excitement of the find. Now it tortured him. He dissembled expertly, and sighed with reluctance. "Reckon it's me that has got ter go."

"Yore turn," grunted his friend, his eyes and thoughts on the little stream purling close by in the darkness. "Mind ye keep yer trap shet," he cautioned. "I'll be goin' East soon. Reckon my darter's married by now; but I'll make out ter find her. A feller don't jest notice the years slippin' by."

"When was it ye last writ ter her?"

"Reckon it must 'a' been that time we follered the Lone Pine rush," answered Hank, defensively.

"Great Godfrey!" exclaimed his partner. "That's nigh ten year back! If I was her I'd throw ye out."

Hank remained silent, realizing that he had nothing whatever to say on that subject; but he looked across the fire and grunted, going on the offensive along another line.

"Reckon *I* better go to town; you'll git drunk an' spit out all ye know. You'll come back with th' hull o' Box Elder on yer heels."

Jim sneered and leaned forward.

"Git *drunk*, will I? Like *you* got, mebby, the *last* time! I felt like shootin' ye when I saw the rush comin' with ye! No, sir, by Godfrey! You'll set here an' hold 'er down; *I*'m goin' ter Box Elder, my *own* self!"

Box Elder had long since grown sedate, as behooved a town that was all of four years old. Grown to its full size in three weeks, it had been steadily shrinking ever since, keeping even step with the shrinking of the placer yield in its vicinity. Had it been able to hold and keep the transient population it had seen in the four years of its existence it would have been a city of dignified size. There had been a time when two coaches a day rolled into it with seats at a premium; when the road and the careless trails were deep with dust that had no time to settle. The result of a strike and magnifying rumours, by the same means it was slowly reverting to the bare hillside on which it stood.

Old Jim Hankins walked down the dusty slope of the hill, two sleepy burros before him, running over in his mind the result of his and his partner's careful scheming. For him to come in alone was to arouse suspicion; for him to come in with two burros was to stamp the suspicion a certainty. They were well known, these two old men, wherever prospectors congregated; Box Elder, hanging to existence with desperate fingers and toes, would melt like a snow flurry out of season and in twenty-four hours be no more than a memory if it got wind of a strike, or a rumoured strike; and for old Jim Hankins to come in without his inseparable partner, and driving two burros for provisions, would be wind enough. He must give a good reason for running so against precedent. He shook his cunning old head as he squinted down on the town and tried to spit, but his mouth was dry, lined with dust; his constricted throat burned insistently, a persistent torture.

"Burn, drat ye!" he growled. "Burn, an' sizzle, if ye wants; ye'll git no likker till I gits back ter camp!" But as he said it, he knew it was a lie. He swung into

orekeeper, wishing he could re-
ccount was paid up. It smacked
cy at this sorrowful moment to go
book. He cursed the shortness of
ften had cursed the shortness of his

memory was as bright as a newly
Hank had told him, carelessly, that
up with Tom Buckner. The artist
touch that puts conviction into the
d Jim Hankins loved it as much.
Hank had in the world he left ter me,"
g his head in sorrow. "'Twarn't much;
st, his mule an' trappin's. I don't want
leave no debts behind. I want he should
d up with them he owes." His voice was
r he was almost beginning to believe, him-
demise of his ancient and beloved partner.
wrapped up in his acting that he began to
e eventual death of his partner; and once
hed that frame of mind he had only to move
ful event forward in the matter of time and
weep with conviction.
orekeeper, eager to relieve the uncertainty of
ining partner, made good time to his book, and
sely over an ink-smeared page. One searching
did not satisfy him, and he went over the
t again. He sighed heavily and turned to face
urner, himself a mourner in lesser degree. At the
nt he could not think of a thing to charge up to the
departed.

the littered, ugly street between the sorry, ugly buildings, his long legs swinging from the hips, his booted
toes turning slightly in, making his four miles an hour
despite his years. It was old Jim's boast that he could
walk down a relay of horses; but it was certain that he
could cover his thirty miles a day if he wanted to,
provided there were no burros to hold him back; and
now the burros, with only a few minutes more to travel,
and scenting water and feed, were as spry as the old
man behind them; but they did not fool him.

"If ye'd hit it up all day like ye do the last mile, drat
ye," he said to them, "a man might git som'ers," and
then he swiftly put the pack animals out of his mind and
gave heed to a pressing need. He sniffled and drew a
dusty sleeve across his eyes, his wrinkled countenance
bespeaking sorrow, which was so deep that he refused
to recognize an old acquaintance who was peering at
him from the Miners' Rest.

The old acquaintance was appraising the solitary
pedestrian and the two burros, his lips pressing and
relaxing, his faded and stained moustache rising and
falling, and in his eyes there swiftly grew a vast suspicion. To his side there stepped the stage-driver, who
was marking time until noon and a waiting coach would
find work for his calloused hands.

"One, an' *two*," said the stage-driver, his brevity
making his thoughts senseless to any one but his companion. "H'm!"

To this cryptic utterance the other made answer by a
grunt, and stepped carelessly forth into the street, his
old face innocent as a Chinaman's.

"Howdy, Jim," he said, careful not to look at the two pack animals, which, strangely enough, refused to stop and rest. They went on briskly toward a well-known stable at the far end of the street.

Jim turned watery eyes mournfully on the speaker, and gently sniffled, seeming to be a little ashamed of this show of grief.

"Howdy," he muttered, and turned his head ostensibly to wipe off a tear, but really to smear the moisture prominently over the dust on his face. The rough fabric of the coat sleeve, dragged cruelly across his eyes, inflamed them and, besides giving them a becoming redness, helped the tears to flow.

"What's the matter, Jim?" asked the acquaintance with a solicitude he was far from feeling. He flashed a quick glance at the bobbing rumps of the burros.

"Hank's gone," came the answer in a strained and hollow voice. Again the old head turned away and the punishing sleeve scraped the watery eyes.

"Gone? Gone where?"

"Heaven, I hopes; hell, I fears," answered Jim, turning away and shuffling on. Under his breath he was swearing.

He should have shuffled sooner. He should have begun it at the top of the hill, instead of down in the street. There had been no signs of a broken heart or weakening sorrow in that long, swinging stride; and Sagebrush Joe was now more suspicious than ever.

He spread his feet and looked after the old prospector.

"'Heaven, I hopes; hell, I fears!'" mimicked Joe, his moustache rising and falling with renewed energy.

"Hank don't owe me nothin'," he said, sighing again. "That is, not nothin' I kin recolleck right here an' now. I s'pose there's a few things standin' out ag'in him; there usually is."

"Then they'll have ter stand, I reckon," said Jim, sniffling again. "You won't see me no more, Tom; I'm pullin' out, soon's I kin load up some supplies. I jest can't stand it up here without Hank. I'm goin' down ter Arizony, where the winter'll be easy on old bones. Pore Hank: we was aimin' fer ter go down together." Out of the corner of his eye he had been watching a shadow remarkably like that of a man's hat, head, and shoulders, which lay on the floor near the back door, and now he saw it move and disappear. He spoke loudly, giving a large list of supplies, which he hoped would last him all the way to Arizona, but reckoned, pessimistically, that they would not.

The storekeeper made no move to fill the order, seeming to be stunned by the passing of Hank Simpson. Arizona was a long way off, and at this particular moment he was greatly interested in cash sales.

"So he left ye a little dust, did he, Jim?" he remarked, consolation trickling through the sadness of his voice.

Jim, too full for utterance, which was the only time in his life that such a condition had existed, nodded and gulped. He dug down into a capacious pocket and slowly, sorrowfully, and reverentially brought to light a dirty and greasy buckskin sack. With fumbling fingers he pulled at the drawstrings, and deliberately up-ended it in the pan of the gold scales, his blundering and shaking hand knocking a quarter-inch wrought-iron nut from a bent claw under the pan. If one had spoken of this nut as being worth its weight in gold he would have fallen far short of its true value, for it was worth its weight in gold multiplied by the number of times it had escaped detection. To have weighed it as a diamond would not have done it justice. Jim thoughtlessly kicked it through the door and into the dust of the street. The storekeeper was discreetly blind to all this, not being in the position to speak about it; and he had several pounds of wrought-iron nuts between him and any scarcity of the supply.

He was, apparently, curious about the colour and quality of the dust and went to poke his exploring finger about in it, after the said finger had explored under the counter and paused for an instant in a can of water; but the sad eyes of the disconsolate survivor of an almost life-long partnership rested on the wet finger to which would stick quantities of the finer dust, and the storekeeper carelessly and thoughtlessly wiped that valuable digit across his sleeve, and even forbore to feel the dust. His weights in the other pan assured him that the old prospector's list of supplies would go with that person as far toward Arizona as they would hold out; and he began to assemble them.

"I'll be back fer 'em, Tom," said the mourner. "Got some business ter attend ter down the street." He reached toward the buckskin sack and the scales pan, but the proprietor beat him to the latter. Deducting the full amount of the needed supplies, he gave the remaining dust to the man with the sack, and nodded his understanding of the arrangements. He was not going to be cheated out of a good cash sale in favour of the Placer Saloon.

Jim shuffled to the street and followed it for a few doors, turning into the false-fronted Placer. At the bar stood Sagebrush Joe with borrowed dust in his pocket and a bottle at his hand. With the entrance of the mournful survivor he gestured invitingly, filled both glasses, and sadly raised his own.

"Ter the mem'ry o' old Hank Simpson, an' may he rest in peace!" he said.

Jim Hankins's throat constricted spasmodically and clamoured for the universal pain-killer, the conqueror of sorrow. His face twitched and his tongue clove to the roof of his mouth. He thought of Hank and his warning; he thought of all the trouble drink had brought upon them both, and of his determination to keep their precious secret. He could see Hank, the picture of health, panning frantically in the creek and pessimistically eyeing the skyline in the direction of Box Elder, every moment expecting to see the gold-crazed mob descending upon him. Yet Hank could excuse an old friend and partner for drinking to his memory: how could a man be a friend and refuse to perform such an honour? He would take just one drink with Joe and the boys and start back, presumably for Arizona. A voice behind him made him turn his head. The stage-driver had stopped, waiting for Jim to step from the door and let him enter. Jim stepped from the door by going through it, and he mechanically walked toward the full glass on the bar, telling himself that he would take no more than one.

"Ter the mem'ry o' pore Hank Simpson," he said, sadly, as his glass went up even with that of Sagebrush Joe.

"Hold it!" hurriedly exclaimed the stage-driver, glancing knowingly at Sagebrush and reaching for the glass the bartender was sliding toward him. "Hold it, boys, an' lemme jine ye. I allus thought a heap o' Hank. Here's ter his mem'ry, Lord rest him."

The solemn rite gone through with, custom insisted that the driver even things by paying for a round. He paid for it, and it was drunk in beseeming dignity. Hank was not to be unmourned. The bartender, not for an instant forgetting his instructions, waved his pudgy hand at the bottle, which Sagebrush tilted and then passed on.

"Have one on the house, which mourns the passin' of a friend an' customer. May he rest in peace." He reached for the bottle and slid it suggestively in front of old Jim.

Jim's throat was beginning to feel so good that he was skeptical if it was due to the liquor; and to prove this to his own satisfaction, and to conform to the stern rules of custom, he tipped the bottle over his glass and passed it on its way, gesturing widely with a hand.

"We drinks this un in silence, to the dead," he said, sniffling. Somehow the farther he went, the deader Hank seemed to get. He began to wonder vaguely if there was a minister in town. It would be so fitting to have him say a few words for the eternal rest of the hard-boiled sinner, who at that wet moment was panning for dear life. How it would please Hank, too! That person, with his funeral services already conducted, could be easy in his mind; no matter when he died, or where, he would have had the benefit of clergy. That would please Hank, and anything that would please Hank should be done, and done in style. Tears began to fill his eyes at the touching scenes his mental eye was witnessing, but they did not obscure the generous hand of Sagebrush Joe, who was spending dust like the sport he was. The bottle was passing again, and with its progress the need for a minister grew.

Jim was beginning to lean on the stalwart figure of Sagebrush Joe, who had reason to be proud of his capacity for liquor; and in this particular instance he had made doubly sure by filling his glass with steadily decreasing amounts. A doubt began to assail him. Perhaps, after all, Hank Simpson was dead, and old Jim telling the truth. Remembering what he had over-heard of the latter's conversation in the store, he turned, facing Jim, and asked a question.

"Now that yo're all alone, Jim, what you aimin' fer ter do?"

"I'm goin' back ter Nevaddy, where me'n Hank teamed up, more'n forty years ago," whimpered Jim, who seemed to be careless of his geography.

At this slip of the tongue Sagebrush glanced knowingly at the bartender.

"Ain't aimin' ter go alone, are ye, Jim? Ye oughter take a new pardner for a long trip like that. Old fellers like you an' me oughtn't run single no more. *Danged* if I don't go with ye! I was borned in Nevaddy, an' I'm goin' back! Set 'em up ag'in, Laramie, ter celebrate a new pardnership!"

Now there was no doubt at all in Jim Hankins's mind that his partner was dead. He was not only dead, but well buried.

"'Fore I jine up with ye, Joe," he blubbered, "I gotta finish with pore Hank, rest his soul. I gotta find a sky-pilot an' do this here funeral up right an' proper. Hank ain't goin' ter be planted like no heathen. Reckon I oughter git flowers, Joe?"

Joe was hit between wind and water, and swiftly reckoned up what he had spent in getting this old tumble-bug drunk. If Hank were really dead, then Jim's appearance with the two burros was entirely logical and above suspicion. There was no doubt about it: Hank was *dead*. He was deader than dead and buried, in the bargain. As he hurriedly began now gracefully to back out of his new partnership, a look from the bartender, freighted with meaning, caught him in mid stride, as it were, and made him mill in indecision. He followed the bartender's guarded glance, and his questioning gaze rested on a small heap of gold dust in a whiskey glass, which had been carefully kept apart from all other dust paid in for the drinks. The significance of this isolation came to him instantly.

"Not bein' what ye might call a religious man, I don't reckon Hank would want no parson yappin' over his distant remains," he said, earnestly, not caring to chip in to help pay for a minister. "Hank warn't one o' them critters that leads a sinful life an' then wants squarin' up fer after he's in the ground. No, sir;

Hank warn't no hypercrite. I thought a hull lot o' Hank Simpson, an' I'd shore hold out through hell an' high water fer ter do anythin' I reckoned he'd want. I don't reckon he wants no parson palaverin' over him. Come ter think of it, now, I remember plain that Hank onct said as how he didn't want no parson showin' off over *his* grave. An', by th' way, Jim: where is good old Hank buried?" Poorly disguised eagerness hung on the answer to this question.

"I'm allowin' I won't team up with no human as don't want pore old Hank fer to have Christian burial," asserted Jim, defiant through his tears. "Hank wouldn't 'a' treated you that way, Joe. Hank was plumb tender-hearted, he was. He didn't show it, but he had a heart like a little child, *he* did!" A fit of weeping seized him and he staggered to the nearest chair and collapsed.

The bartender leaned swiftly across the counter, and Joe's quick movement was in harmony.

"That ol' hypercrite's dust ain't like none I ever saw 'round these diggin's," whispered the dispenser of drinks. He glanced at Jim, reached behind him, and slid the glass containing the dust under Sagebrush's eager eyes.

Sagebrush examined it critically, and his doubts cleared on one point, at least. If Hank was alive he was panning in mighty rich gravel; if he was really dead, then his grave would be well worth a pilgrimage. He glanced hastily around the room, and frowned. Men had drifted in by ones and twos until there were a dozen sympathetic miners lined up at the bar, forgetting their drinks in honour of the dear departed in their keen interest in what was taking place between the bartender and Sagebrush Joe. The latter, realizing that the cat was getting out of the bag with a celerity famous in cats, made the best of the situation. Hank's burial place must become known. He whispered to the man next to him, and the whisper ran along the bar and out of the door and to every part of the little town; it left the town, gained strength, and leaped hills and gulches to echo and reëcho for miles around. Nerves became tense and eyes blazed with avarice.

A committee made up of every man in the saloon and every man who hurriedly entered to pack it full of wild, eager, and straining humanity, appointed unto itself the task of learning the whereabouts of Hank Simpson, alive or dead. Its method of procedure was well known from experience. Jim Hankins, after a certain number of drinks, would confess to a murder if he were guilty of it, and tell everything he knew. Jim became instantly popular and gradually loquacious. He could easily see that he was the hero of this pleasant gathering of cheerful spenders, and the more he felt like a hero the more he forgot that Hank was either alive or dead. He grew boastful, and their disbelief irritated him. He could prove it, every last word of it. Challenged by cold-eyed skeptics, he did prove it so far as words could go; and two of those words rang out and were tossed about by the echoing hills.

"Cottonwood Gulch!" yelled Sagebrush, endeavouring to vanish, but every man in the room was endeavouring to do the very same thing, at the very same time, and the door was none too wide. Old friendships, careless friendships, and potential friendships went a-glimmering in the fight to get through that inelastic doorway. Boots rose and fell, ham-like hands thrashed valiantly, voices roared, and the room became full of dust. Through a side window dived the stage-driver, his news-vending soul afire. Like Paul Revere he burned to ride and spread the news through every wayside village and farm. To be the first to carry that news would be fame enough, and the drinks he had absorbed did not in the least deter him from seizing his opportunity. It lacked only an hour before time for the coach to leave with its booked passengers, but neither passengers nor schedules were in his mind. He made a wild dash for the stables, a thrill of joy running through him as he saw the four-horse team hitched to the Concord and tied to a post. The stableman, hungry before his appointed hour, had hitched up and hastened to his dinner, intending to return in time to hand the reins up to the driver.

Past the stage office rolled the coach on two wheels, the blacksnake whip writhing through the air before it straightened to clip hair from the leaping teams. The station agent, his mouth agape, stood helplessly in the door of the office and stared, pop-eyed, at the careening Concord in its sea of dust. The street was full of running men and racing horses, plodding horses and limping horses; magically, pack mules began to appear, belaboured by shouting owners; across the street from the stage station a canvas gambling establishment was settling to the earth like a stricken animal, and being bundled, yard after yard, into the wagon which had brought it to Box Elder four years before. A lumber wagon, clattering with boards for sluices, rattled past behind four mules, its load worth real money in the new Cottonwood Gulch diggings. Vehicles new and ancient, laden with foodstuffs, kegged and bottled goods, gambling paraphernalia, and everything else that might prove to be profitable, careened through the dusty street to the chorus of cursing drivers, snapping whips, the jingle of chains, and the protesting squeak of straining harness. Over the hill like a great hedge of fog lay the dust, constantly whirling higher. The station agent, straining his ears to pick out a coherent sentence in all the uproar, suddenly heard that sentence. He wheeled, jumped back into the room, kicked shut the door of the safe, spun the combination, and in three minutes was hanging to the tailboard of a lurching wagon, half suffocated by the dust, but bearing all grimly.

Quarrels and fist fights for the right of way blocked the road here and there in the narrow stretches, but the surging traffic, taking the banks at peril of upsetting, swept around such barriers like a speeding torrent around stubborn boulders. A glance behind would have shown Box Elder shrinking building by building, great puffs of dust telling of falling walls; and all through the afternoon and night, the night made bright by bonfires and oil flares, wagonloads of shanties and shacks joined the advancing army, a belated but hopeful and determined rear-guard. Box Elder was going as it had come: on wheels, and swiftly.

CHAPTER II

COTTONWOOD

NOT far from where the Placer saloon had stood only a few hours before, a booted, rough-clad old man slept stertorously, sprawled on his back, his mouth open to the heavens, his arms flung out from his body. The crack of splitting wood under crowbar and axe, the din of heavy hammering on resounding walls, the shouts and curses, the leaping fires, and the soaring dust were all matters beyond his consciousness. Gone were his burros and the supplies he had paid for but never received; but for the moment he was oblivious of such calamities. Daylight stirred him, but only to gropingly turn face down and hide his eyes from the sunlight. Noon found him gradually awakening, blurred and chaotic impressions conflicting in his mind. The sight his aching eyes looked upon made him blink, and blink again. This persistent nightmare disturbed him and he tried to awaken, and was surprised to find that he was awake. He searched his memory for something to combat the stubborn belief that he had gone to sleep in Box Elder; he scrutinized the hills and the sloping valley floor, and became more deeply puzzled. Bare, dust-covered, rectangular blotches stood out plainly against the earth surrounding them, marking the sites of buildings which had mysteriously disappeared. The street was plain enough, and was flanked on both sides by what was left of flimsy foundations. The stage office alone stood untouched, its windows and doors seeming to gape at this base desertion.

Old Jim Hankins blinked again, believed, and became immobile while he delved into conjectures. Bit by bit it returned to him, whirling crazily in his liquor-cursed brain, a kaleidoscope of stunning calamity: His partner was dead, and buried; he had lost his burros, his money, and his supplies; Box Elder, by some trick of hell, had sneaked away and left him alone while he slept; he had been drinking, and when he drank he talked; but what had he said to cause this scandalous desertion? Slowly he searched this out, and knew; and bitterly he cursed as he scrambled to his shaking legs and weaved down the deserted street. Box Elder had moved, overnight; but he knew where to find it!

In Cottonwood Gulch, twenty-five miles southwest of Box Elder, the peace and quiet were no more disturbed by the placer operations of Hank Simpson than the placid surface of a sleeping sea would have been by the skimming dip of a gull. Hank, himself, was more disturbed than the gulch. Had old Jim kept sober until he had attended to the business that had taken him away? Had he kept sober before and after the business that had taken him away? Had he kept sober until he had put Box Elder behind him? Hank's impatience and anxiety had grown with the passing of the hours, for each hour brought that much nearer the answer to his fears.

Hank straightened his back and grudgingly blew out a thoroughly prospected chew of plug tobacco, eyeing it contritely: he might have made it last longer. There was a chill in the early morning hour that accounted for the coat he wore, and into one of its capacious side pockets he thrust a hand to explore it thoroughly. An object as small as the remainder of that plug, in a pocket so large, called for a thorough searching. The plug was not to be found. Hurriedly he searched his other pockets, of which two were intact. Panic crept upon him, and he searched again, and stiffened as a finger found and went through the hole in the bottom seam. With his other hand he grabbed the lower edge of the coat, and his face brightened as his grip closed upon a small, hard object of irregular shape. The finger in the hole of the pocket wriggled farther through it, poking and coaxing and twisting at its find. A breath of relief came from him like a blast and he drew out the modest plug, eyeing it greedily, but holding his greed in check to ponder over a matter of some moment. Should he flirt with it to make it last until night, or gamble on old Jim returning before then? At best it was only half a chew, and old Jim was due to return at any minute. Despite nearly four decades of warning experiences, he decided to gamble on his partner's promptness. Besides, he might easily lose the minute remainder.

As the early morning hours passed, his glances at the skyline followed each other at shorter intervals, for there was now added to the fear of a rush the further fear caused by failing supplies and the end of the plug.

After forty years of prospecting he had plenty of experience in starving, but he had found that there was only one cure for it, and he had not yet learned to enjoy the pangs of hunger. He asked little enough of his food; not that it tempt him by its taste, but only that it sustain him.

He picked up the battered pan, but before he bent down to go to work he glanced once more at the skyline; and with a muttered curse he let loose of the pan and scrambled to the bank, his old face glowering, his hand on his gun. A horseman was feeling his way down a steeper part of the hill, pulling stubbornly on the lead rope of a pack horse loaded down with supplies. Behind him on the rim appeared another rider, who took a longer but easier way down; and behind him popped into sight two more. Hank took a few steps forward, the gun gleaming nakedly in his half-raised hand, his face flushed with anger.

"You clear to hell an' gone outer here!" he shouted, hoping to run his bluff successfully.

The newcomers did not pay him the compliment of a reply or more than a hasty glance. Leaving their animals to wander at will for a few minutes, they jerked their pans from the huge packs and ran to the creek, burning with the gold fever. Frantic exertions were followed by simultaneous shouts of exultation as they scratched the bottom of their pans with trembling forefingers.

"By glory, she's *here!*" yelled the first of the four.

"Gregory Diggin's warn't in it with this!" shouted another, and straightway riding horses and pack horses were blotted from their minds, and their ears remained deaf to all that Hank was calling them.

Hank swore, shook his fist at them, at the hills, at the blue sky above, and then whirled to dash after his gold pan floating grandly down the creek, a creek transparent no longer.

The skyline became like the stage of a puppet show, its actors jacks-in-the-box. They popped up here, there, and yonder, by ones and twos, to stand for a moment silhouetted against the sky, and then to plunge down the slopes. Faster and faster they popped and dropped, whole groups together rising and falling, until by noon a hundred men had utterly shattered the peace and quiet of the valley. Packs lay here and there, helter-skelter; horses, mules, and burros grazed at the ends of picket ropes, or wandered over the hillside; smoke climbed heavenward in wavering columns of blue or gray, while gold-crazed men filled the creek with savage labours and turned its crystal waters to the colour of its sands. By nightfall the hundred had been multiplied by three, and sounds of hammer and axe rang through the air. The tents and canvas buildings went up first, like magically growing mushrooms; there were alien noises in Cottonwood Gulch, through which squeaked and whined the fiddles of a dance hall open for business, the alluring invitations of the proprietors of chuck-a-luck, three-card monte, and the elusive pea. Dust lay heavy in the air and danced in wavering clouds along the skyline, trees were falling under the axe to be turned into sluice lumber by the saw, and everywhere there was a great but deceptive confusion. Before noon of another day the canvas shacks had been joined by their brothers of boards; the Miners' Rest now faced the Placer squarely, and Tom Buckner's general store, still a chaos of piled merchandise, shouldered Tim Healy's Elite Dance Hall. There had been a new shuffle, but the deck remained the same; but in a few more hours the new town of Cottonwood would have an identity all its own.

It grew like a cloud on a heat-cursed horizon. The first rush had brought mostly miners, with a scattering of more or less orderly caterers to their needs, for when Box Elder had slumped two years before, the hawks and the vultures, the wolves and the coyotes had departed for better fields. True, there were even now gambling games and gamblers, and a dance hall and saloons; there was noise and an occasional fight; but somehow it was tame and anæmic, and the greater part of the population was too busy in their feverish washing and panning to take time for drinking bouts and brawls; they scarcely took time to bolt half-raw food, or left the creek until darkness forced them to. Cottonwood was too busy to be lawless, and the pity was that it had to change.

On the morning of the third day it swiftly became apparent that the stage-coach Paul Revere had sowed his news on fertile ground. The steady stream of newcomers changed in nature, for now the hawks and the vultures, the wolves and the coyotes, flew, leaped, or crept into the camp, spreading among the growing crowds like mould through bread. With the quick shifting of the stage line to its new terminus, the influx multiplied; and by the end of the fourth day a motley population delved and panned, sold and bartered, cheated and stole and killed. In Cottonwood the stage was set, like many another stage in the crimson West, for robbery and murder.

Old Jim Hankins, returning on foot and without supplies, staggered down the scored and rutted hillside, groping for his partner's camp, to salvage what he could. Wordless, looking neither to the right nor left, he found the camp and slumped down before the little tent, vaguely surprised that he should find it thus. On a box inside the sloping canvas roof were cold beans and greasy bacon and a coffee pot half filled with its cold and muddy infusion. A pan of sour-dough biscuits, burned on the outside and sticky within, gave up a unit to his clutching grasp. Time enough to inquire into miracles after his hunger had been appeased. He stuffed his mouth with beans, crowded in a strip of bacon to serve as lubricant, and rammed home the charge with half a biscuit. Gulps of bitter and astringent coffee sent it on its way past temporary jams, to the accompanying aid of throaty contortions. The beans and the bacon, having disappeared, were followed by the remaining biscuits and the last obtainable drop of coffee. Poor Hank: when he had cooked this food he did not know that he would be dead and could not eat it. Old Jim's chin quivered, but he fought back his sense of loss and his loneliness, and resolved to rest awhile before hunting for the pan and shovel. Then he became ashamed of what he had momentarily forgotten: Hank should have a minister to speak over his grave if there was one in the new camp. Upon this resolution he acted at once, and arose to search the camp. As his head rose above the top of the low lean-to he gasped and staggered back, his shaking hands upraised to fend off this apparition: Hank had returned in spirit to punish him for his broken promises, his wordy treachery. A cry of horror burst from him and he whirled, to race over the uneven ground like a jackrabbit of youth and energy. Men looked up from their placering to grin at the pursued and the pursuer, and instantly looked down again, the picture effaced from their minds.

"You damn varmint!" pantingly roared the vengeful apparition. "I'll git ye if I has ter chase ye clean ter the Gulf! Stop, dang ye! Ye might as well!"

The horrified fugitive cast a despairing look over his shoulder, tripped on a peeled log, and dived headlong to the ground.

Hank managed to stop, wheeled, and returned, and stood looking down on his prostrate partner, his grim countenance slowly softening. Bending sidewise, he saw a trickle of blood on old Jim's dirty face, and the vengeance in his heart forthwith died.

"Gosh dang it," he growled, "I'd 'a' done the same thing myself if I'd 'a' gone ter town instid o' him."

Two pistol shots sounded flatly from the main street, followed by a running fusillade. A hubbub of yells and curses swelled up swiftly, and as swiftly died. Hank pulled his belt a little more to the left as he scowled in the direction of the disturbing sounds, stood watchfully erect for a moment, and then, growling, bent down over his stirring partner, and shook him gently.

Jim opened his eyes and they instantly filled with horror; but the look slowly faded out as amazement took its place, to be followed in turn by a timid joy.

"Ain't ye dead, Hank?" he quavered, afraid to let belief take hold of him.

"Good Godfrey, *no!*" snorted Hank, in utter amazement. "Never was aliver in all my life!"

"An' there ain't no call fer ter git a minister fer ye?" persisted old Jim.

"Hell, no! What's got inter ye?"

"Gosh dang!" fervently muttered Jim, sitting up. "I heard ye was dead, Hank; an' it must 'a' druv me ter drink. If ye was dead, dead an' buried, it didn't make no difference how much I blabbered; so I jest went an' told 'em the hull shootin' match." He glanced around the valley. "Don't she look fine, Hank. Did they name her arter me?"

"She looks like hell, an' they didn't name her arter you!" roared Hank, fires of suspicion brightly burning in his spotted soul. "Who in tarnation told ye I war dead an' buried? Tell me that, dang ye! Who was a-tellin' ye of it, with you jest havin' left me alive an' well? Answer me *that*, ye lyin' old hypercrite! Answer me *that!*"

"Don't jest remember, Hank, who 'twas; but thar ain't no tellin' 'bout death," replied Jim, defensively. "You *know* it sneaks up on a feller without no warnin'! Ye might 'a' been dead by the time I got ter Box Elder, *mightn't* ye, now?"

Hank scratched his head, reluctant to admit that he might have been; but he was fair and just sometimes.

This was one of them. He grudgingly nodded his head.

"Yes, I *might* 'a' been; but I *warn't!*"

"Shore ye warn't; but that warn't no fault o' *mine*, was it?" demanded Jim, growing a little pugnacious at his partner's stupidity. "Was it, ye old fool?" he demanded, his stubble-covered, tobacco-stained jaw pushing out aggressively. "*Was* it, now?"

"No; 'twarn't!" growled Hank, wondering how it was that what he had thought to be an unassailable position of strength and righteousness should so quickly fade away and leave him culpable. This wasn't the first time that he had seen his foundations turn to sand.

"Wall, then, ye better know what yer doin' afore ye chase me the *next* time!" snorted old Jim. "Fer a fair-sized chaw o' tobaccy I'd bash ye in th' eye! Yes, fer a little *mite* o' a chaw I would!" He turned his back on his stunned and guilty partner and stalked toward the lean-to tent like a stiff-legged mastiff through a group of chows, leaving his groping friend scratching and scratching.

CHAPTER III

THE STATUS OF THE B—B

DAVE SAUNDERS rode carelessly across the bunch-grass valley which lay between Crow Range on the west and Brule Range on the east. Down its middle the valley was nearly as level as the surface of a lake, but east and west it sloped gradually to the narrow belt of the foothills of the mountain spurs, and it contained a fortune in that most nutritious of all grasses. Not a sage-brush was to be found short of the foothills, while the greasewood, infallible indicator of a soil worthless from any standpoint, could be found only nearer the spurs themselves, where an occasional small and desolate plain was cursed with black alkali. Down the middle of the valley meandered a sizable stream, never dry in the memory of man, its feeders twisting and shrinking as they neared the mountains. Here was a range capable of feeding over two hundred head to the square mile, while at present it was supporting less than a quarter of that number. The lower end of the valley, nearer the bunkhouse, cut by many streams, provided hay bottoms of an acreage enough to feed through the winter six times this herd. With its ravines, its timber, and sheer rock ridges facing southward it could not be improved upon for winter shelter. Grass-crowned ridges thrust up above the hollows and bits of level pastures, where winter winds swept off the snow and laid bare the cured grass for winter grazing. Cold as some of the winters had been, keen and cutting some of their winds, and deep their snows, there had not yet occurred a serious drift of the B—B herds.

Dave, a Texan of a stern school, at first had not taken kindly to this northern range, and still less kindly to the reason for his choosing it; but if a Texan wanted to be hard to find, then this locality hardly could be improved upon. It lay well off the main trail, was not a short-cut to any distributing or delivery point, and its isolation was all a man could wish for. No town lay nearer than forty miles, and Dave's annual beef drive into Nebraska followed a trail of his own choosing. He could see the faint traces of it lying up the slope toward a little gap in the hills, a moth-eaten, winding strip in the greenery of the bunch-grass and his only link with the outside world. As he glanced at it a frown clouded his face, for it brought to mind the reason for his emigration, and he grew hard and cold; but no man, alone on this Montana range in May, could hold to such a mood for long.

Down in Texas, Dave Saunders had been a common puncher, even though a top hand; but when he had found a good place it was only a matter of time before he would be forced to give it up, and move on, to find another. Because of his nature his trouble was not a matter that could be cured by recourse to his gun, although he had been sorely tempted to put it into that class, and cure it in the smoke of a rolling tattoo.

In his hands a forty-five performed with a grace and speed he had yet to see equalled.

Dave was long and thin, his height causing him to slouch over in the saddle; the huge hands at the ends of his long arms swung low along his thighs, and his great thumbs were peculiarly fitted for a certain kind of gun-play. A cursory examination of his Colt would have yielded nothing; but were an attempt made to cock it an interesting fact would have been disclosed. Dave's gun would not remain cocked, the hammer would not stay up; yet the trigger spring was strong, and the trigger lay in its wonted position, clearing the rear of the guard by a quarter of an inch. Another fact would have been revealed: although the gun was six-chambered, only five of them were loaded. The sixth, under the long, sharp pin of the hammer, contained an exploded shell. Here were facts to challenge careful thought, and the thought to win a certain respect. In Dave's "war-bag" under his bunk, was the twin of the weapon at his thigh. Had he chosen to end the troubles which had forced him out of Texas, no man could have ended them more swiftly.

Dave was foreman of the B—B, with five good men under him who never acutely realized his directing hand. They were friends of the Texan, bunkhouse mates, good men and true, and they had yet to clash among themselves. In some fields of human endeavour the northern winters huddle men within imprisoning walls, where sullen animosities creep, fuse-like, to the inevitable explosion; but on the B—B the winter found these riders constantly afield, looking after their cattle with the loyal solicitude of a sheep dog for his flock. Some reason for this might have been found in a carefully worked-out scale of bonuses, inversely proportionate to the percentage of winter-killed animals. The B—B was at peace with itself and with all the world.

The drive trail on the slopes awakened his memory and took him back into the years, none too many; back to the trailing of the first herd of longhorns that had entered this part of the country; back to the Long Trail, over which so many thousands of Texan cattle were to wind their leisurely way before the days of the drive were ended.

Leaving his native state, Dave had thrown in with a trail crew and had taken the place made vacant by the drowning of a man in the swollen waters of Red River. Mile after mile, day after day, week after week they had plodded steadily northward, bearing a little to the west; they had seen the broad and shallow Arkansas fall behind them, and the broader and shallower Platte loom up before them as the flat plains of Kansas gave way to those of Nebraska. They were not the pioneers of the lower part of that great cattle trail, but they could claim that distinction for its extreme western section; and yet the way had been blazed out for them, years before, along that north branch of the Platte; they had but followed the ruts of the Oregon emigration for miles until their guide had met them and led them northward from that historic trace.

The herd counted and delivered, the new owner had smilingly asked what men of the drive crew would stay and help take care of it; and of these riders but Dave remained. He had found a certain grim satisfaction in watching the others ride off in a bunch around the harried driver of the trail wagon, each of them eager to find some town where their accumulated wages could get a long-promised action. With them had gone the last connecting link with his native state, with worry and uncertainty. Not one of these men had known his true name; and it would not be long before they would forget about the lone horseman who had joined them on the muddy banks of Red River.

Dave had done well in the several years that had passed, so well that old Benjamin Marmaduke Benson, crippled by misadventure in a blizzard of two years before, had been content to return to a more salubrious climate and pleasanter surroundings, and to find satisfaction in the tally sheets and drive reports rather than in the actual cattle they dealt with. The genial owner of the B—B had several irons in the fire and was a busy man, filled with political aspirations. Dave, left in charge as foreman, with autocratic powers, was conscientious and painstaking; and the results of his stewardship only increased Benson's faith in him.

On this bright May day, as Dave looked around at the grazing cattle, a reserved smile crept across his face; it was characteristic of the man that his smile was always reserved. He passed a natural amphitheatre, formed by a sharp curve in a vertical ridge of rock, its open end barricaded by a heavy fence of poles. Brown spots here and there on its green surface, and further indicated by the circular fencing, told of where huge stacks of hay had stood to tide the cattle through the more inclement spells of the winter just past. Farther on a stand of timber revealed glimpses of other brown spots through the greenery of unfolding leaves. Around the end of a ridge there came into sight a heavy corral, with winged gates, and still more haystack remnants. A branding chute led from this enclosure on its farther side, pointing straight at a large and weatherproof bunkhouse, with a closed-in stable for the corn feeding of the winter riding stock standing just behind it. Adjoining this building was a sod and pole wagon shed, one end of which was used as a blacksmith shop. From the rear of the stable a double line of fence ran to and across the little creek, to meet on the other side; and a hundred yards up-stream from this horse corral, just above a ten-foot waterfall, was the fenced-in spring, where the water needs of the outfit were taken care of, winter and summer.

A hoarse voice raised in song preceded its owner from the storehouse and granary near the stable, and hung perilously while the puncher concentrated his mind on the rusty padlock. It soared to its former strength as the lock thumped back against the door and the singer turned to go to the bunkhouse. Then it stopped.

"Hi, Dave," greeted Billy, of the B—B, which was his only name for publication.

"'Lo, Billy," answered the foreman, cheerily. "Reckon you been waitin' for me."

Billy grinned and hummed a few words of the song, which it were better not to set down here.

"Time enough," he said. "Don't aim to leave

before daylight. If you got any letters to write, get 'em done before then." His grin grew. "Make out a list of the things you want in town, an' make it as big as you want to: I don't have to worry about that. Me an' Bid has cut the cards a'ready to see who totes 'em back; an', of course, Bid lost. *Hi-diddle-dee-dee-dum dee-dum!*"

"Serves him right for usin' cards with you," chuckled Dave. "He oughta know better." The lines at the sides of the foreman's eyes grew crowded and deep and his smile was not quite as reserved as usual. "I suppose you'll back yore card-playin' agin some gambler, an' not have nothin' to bring back but his brand on yore hide."

"I'm aimin' to bring back his brand, all right," asserted Billy; "but his hide'll be under it. Lord, but I'm hungry."

When they entered the bunkhouse they found "Bid" Carter shaving off a three-days' accumulation to a running fire of comment from his companions who were not as intent on their baiting as they would have been but for the fact that the cook's melodious voice was expected to bellow out at any moment.

Bid wiped the razor blade, stropped it, and went back to work.

"Lookit him pull that cheek," said Mark Luttrell. "He's shavin' so clost he'll shore kill the roots. 'Course there ain't nothin' but roots fer him to shave."

"Goin' turtle-dovin', Bid?" asked Joe Hawkins, grinning wider.

"Hurry up, Bid!" ordered his bosom friend Billy, feeling of his own growth.

Biddle Henderson Carter squeezed his nose to force out the lather that had plugged one nostril, and regarded his friend with supercilious disdain.

"I'm ownin' this here razor, an' aim to take my time. While yo're waitin' you might throw Joe onto the wood-pile, an' save me messin' my hands."

"Who is she *this* time?" demanded Frank Hitchcock, remembering the one outstanding feature of Bid's courtships.

"He don't know *yet*, you chump," replied Mark. "Want me to scrape yore neck, Bid?"

"Scrape is shore 'nuff right, for he keeps them neck hairs well hilled up," laughed Joe. "Y'oughta seen him the time——"

"I'll throw it away!" yelled a human fog horn, and Bid was forthwith left to finish his shave in peace.

When the outfit of the B—B was at table there was no attempt made to hide the fact, so far as silence was concerned; while conversation dragged and was reduced to a minimum, other sounds filled the room. Hitchcock shot his long arm across the table and brought back a boiled potato on the end of his fork. Potatoes were something of a luxury, and he was making sure that he would receive his full share. He glanced at the hurrying Bid and clumsily peeled off the potato skin.

"There's some of that there ointment left, if you want it, Bid," he remarked. There was no reply from Bid, and the business of eating went on for a few minutes. Then Hawkins reached for a second cup of coffee.

"Cut hisself?" he asked, appalled by the thought of horse liniment in a cut.

Another conversational silence ensued and Hitchcock reloaded his plate with beans, as Bid came to the table.

"Reckon not," he answered, and fell to again.

The cook made two trips and retired to his kitchen, where he was heard enthusiastically damning the stove.

"Then why the liniment?" persisted Hawkins, who admitted that he was never curious.

"He done used up all that hair oil he sent for, didn't he?" asked Hitchcock. "Liniment ain't got such a bad smell if you ain't particular."

"Then you oughta use some!" snapped Bid, making up for lost time. His plate had assumed the general shape of a cone and for the next few minutes his knife was very busy making conic sections of increasing area.

"Aimin' to see Bob Shea?" asked Mark, carefully ignoring the self-conscious foreman.

"Where else would I leave the hoss?" demanded Bid.

"Common cow-wrastlers let em' stand 'round 'most any place an' forget 'em," retorted Mark, still ignoring the foreman, whose interest in Bob Shea's daughter was known to be deep and serious. Alice Shea was the one woman in Box Elder who had the unqualified and unanimous respect of the B—B outfit; and the fact that her brother was of no account only deepened their regard for her. Dave knew how his men felt about her, and took their mild chaffing without animus.

"If one of this team of jackasses *don't* see Bob Shea, I'll peg his hide on the granary wall," threatened the foreman. "I ain't ridin' no pen an' ink for nothin'."

Through the laughter Mark's voice could be heard.

"Reckon we can make a job for Red?" he asked,

seriously, his squinting eyes covering the conjectures behind them. It was not necessary to explain that question in the B—B bunkhouse; every man knew what had prompted it. Red Shea's daily life was a successful attempt to avoid making a living by any honest effort. Ugly tales were built around his name, but no man had called him to a halt for the reason that Red's shiftlessness did not pertain to his vindictiveness or to the quality of his gun-play. All eyes turned expectantly to the foreman.

"This is a six-man ranch, with a six-man outfit," answered Dave, imperturbably. "It stays that way. I got a list to make out, an' a letter to write, an' if you boys want to play a few hands while I'm doin' them things, I'll set in later."

Mark Luttrell's suggestion for an attempt at the regeneration of Red Shea was thus disposed of, to the secret relief of the outfit. While they would make sacrifices toward the redemption of Alice Shea's brother, not a man of them believed that such a redemption was possible. The offer had been made to show their readiness, and had been turned down. To cover the momentary embarrassment that most rough men feel when detected in a charitable or reformative effort, a general noisy bustle pervaded the bunkhouse, and the game was soon under way.

CHAPTER IV

COTTONWOOD DISCOVERED

THE earlier the two B—B punchers left the ranch, the earlier they would reach Box Elder, which appears to be logical, and which was impressed so thoroughly on the cook's mind that this person arose half an hour before his accustomed time, and then spent most of it in arguments tending to prove why they should get up.

The sun had not yet risen over Brule Range when they turned their backs on the bunkhouse and pushed along over a faint trail leading to a pass in the range. This was an old Indian trail, but the Indians found it laid out for them and marked by those sagacious road engineers, the buffalo, after whom, indeed, the little pass had been named. They climbed steadily, passed through the gap, and descended on the far side, where the trail became gradually fainter until it was only by looking well ahead that it could be seen. Across the level pastures the trace was very faint, which was proof enough as to its origin, but it became plain again when obstructing hills drew close together. In a little clump of trees lay the ruins of an Indian fort, silent marker of some inter-tribal strife. The mouldering logs of the circular breastwork, enriching the immediate soil, were nearly covered with weeds and brush. They glanced at it, commented about it, and rode on without pause. They swept down into another little valley and went up the eastern slope at a walk. From its crest they could plainly see the western ridge of Cottonwood Gulch, along the upper end of which lay the trail. Talking sporadically, they pushed on, carelessly observant. The trail, crossing the north-and-south watershed, dipped sharply, ran for a few miles along the base of a high and rocky ridge, crossed through a steep-walled pass, and curved down into Cottonwood Gulch.

Billy was riding in the lead through the narrow chasm and had swung around in his saddle, facing forward again after speaking to his companion, when he pulled up sharply and swore in amazement and disbelief. The sight was so unexpected, so past belief, that he doubted his eyes and his mind.

"Great mavericks! What the——"

Bid pushed up alongside, standing in his stirrups and leaning forward, and the sight that burst upon his startled gaze robbed him of speech for a moment; but when speech came, it came with pent-up energy, a profane request for enlightenment and assurance.

"Lookit!" exclaimed Billy. "There's Buckner's store! An' if *that* ain't the Miners' Rest, I'll swear off even thinkin' about likker!"

"An' there goes the stage: see that pinto near-leader?" excitedly cried his companion. He rubbed a hand slowly across his forehead and reverently replaced his hat, his stare returning to the sprawled-out town below him. The growing consciousness of a slowly recognized difference budded into a flower of thought. "*This* ain't—this *ain't* Box Elder! In the first place, it's four times as big; an,' in the second place, it's in the wrong place; but there's Buckner's, an' the Miners' Rest, an' if that ain't the Placer, then I never saw it! We *both* can't be loco in the same way! Ain't felt no earthquake, have you?"

"Aw, earthquake wouldn't do *that!* If *you* wasn't seein' it, *too*," replied Billy, and paused. He pulled his sombrero tightly on his head and sent his horse on again. "Quickest way to find out about it is to *find* out. Come on, Bid: we've shore saved twenty-five miles ridin' to-day!"

Bid swaggered a little.

"'Tain't every outfit as gets the nearest town moved twenty-five miles closter to 'em," he bragged.

It was not only in size or location that this town was different from Box Elder, for the latter had been reasonably quiet and law-abiding; the town before them was humming like a telegraph wire in a high wind, a sullen overtone of sound. Its already dusty streets, blotched with the hardier grass tufts, contained a shifting, weaving population of honest men and cut-throats, in hard boots and soft boots, in flannel shirts and frock coats; but not a man of them was unbelted or unarmed.

Dust arose and eddied, saturated with the odour of frontier whiskey coming from the miserable saloons standing shoulder to shoulder along both sides of the street, shot through with strata of tainted meats and decaying vegetable refuse, with streaks of greasy smoke from sputtering frying pans. Conversation was loud, coarse, and boisterous; squeaky fiddles and rasping accordions vied desperately in drawing trade, and the heavy stamp of booted feet made a vibrant background for a mad cacophony. Maudlin disagreements broke into noisy brawls, and snatches of drunken song arose in faltering cadences, like coyote concerts in honour to the moon. Itinerant gambling layouts filled in the scant and narrow spaces between the shacks, the raucous voices of the proprietors huskily barking.

Billy leaned over and accosted a fiery-faced, whiskey-smelling bull-whacker, who had just ceased roaring because of lack of breath.

"What town is this, friend?"

The bull-whacker rocked back and partly turned on his heels, scowling into the smiling face above him.

"What town is this?" he roared, his thumb persistently missing the armhole of his vest. "This town's Cottonwood, you —— damn fool!"

Billy's tan took on a reddish tint as a sharp retort trembled on his tongue; but, seeing that the freighter was nearly blind drunk, he held back the words, jammed the other's big hat down past the flaming ears, and pushed on through the crowd. The profane bellowing grew less behind him in the general uproar, and he followed his companion in the direction of Tom Buckner's store, and pulled up quickly as Bid stopped before an alluring gambling layout.

The hawk-faced proprietor shot him a sidewise glance, and began his monotonous exhortations anew, calling attention to the rich prizes scattered on the numbered squares of the soiled oilcloth. There were "gold" watches and "silver" watches, checks calling for pearl-handled Colts, and on two of the squares were greenbacks of fifty and one hundred dollars denomination, respectively. More prominent even than the greenbacks was a stack of ten twenty-dollar gold pieces. The last three items were the sucker baits, while the pearl-handled guns had a universal appeal. The proprietor looked directly at Bid, smiled and pointed carelessly to the greenbacks and gold pieces.

"Try yer luck, friend," he invited. "Only four bits a throw. Somebody's got to win 'em, an' it might be you. See if this is your lucky day, gents," he called, slowly looking at the faces before him.

Bid hesitated, and then felt his companion's hand on his arm, and heard Billy's quiet voice behind him.

"With six dice it'll be a long time before anybody wins that stack on 36, or the hundred-dollar bill on 6, or the fifty-dollar bills on 7 an' 35, or them pearl-handled guns goin' with the checks on 34 an' 8. I don't see nothin' of no account on none of the squares between 9 an' 33. Let me shuffle the prizes around a little, an' we'll throw you till yo're black in th' face."

"Hell you will!" snapped the proprietor. "You play her as she lays, or not a-tall! If you ain't got the nerve or money to play, git outa the way of them that has. Here you are, boys! Step up an' try yore luck! I'll buy back the guns for thirty dollars apiece! Step up, gents! *Somebody's* got to win the big prizes. Here we are: six honest dice, an' only four bits a throw!"

Bid, his gaze riveted on the stacked gold-pieces, dug

down into his pocket again, and again felt his companion's hand on his arm.

"To draw down that gold you've got to throw six sixes," warned Billy in a low voice. "If I told you what th' odds against you are, you'd not believe me. If she runs true to averages, them gold pieces'll cost the winner thousands of dollars. Come on: let's move along."

Bid reluctantly obeyed, a little sullen at being balked at his chance to win some easy money, and after a moment he put his objections into words.

"But there was more'n gold pieces," he growled, looking at his friend. "There was six numbers with good prizes on 'em; I had a chance to win *one* of 'em, didn't I?"

Billy turned an inscrutable countenance to his youthful friend, thus proving that an occupation intensively carried on through years will mark a man. The subject of gambling automatically masked his face with an expression that was as near a blank as it was humanly possible for it to be. Realizing that there was no need to wear a mask before his companion, he allowed a smile to creep to his face, and his eyes twinkled.

"Yore winter wages, with mine added, wouldn't buy enough throws to win any of the six," he said. "Offhand I'd say it's over forty thousand to one against winnin' with 6 or 36, and more'n a thousand to one against takin' away any one of the six big prizes. It's been all figgered out, Bid. This town's the most amazin' thing I ever saw. Wonder how long it's been here?" His roving glance settled on an old prospector who was swinging up the slope from the creek. "There's old Jim Hankins; hey, *Jim!*"

Jim's hand fell even with his thigh as he looked in the direction of the hail, and then his wrinkled old face beamed a welcome.

"Gosh dang it!" he chuckled as the two riders reached his side. "Welcome ter Cottonwood! What ye think o' my town, anyhow?"

"Yore town?"

"You betcha! It was me as put her here." And he briefly sketched recent history, strictly from his own viewpoint. "I'm tellin' ye that I felt funny when I waked up in Box Elder an' found she'd moved. At fust I suspicioned as they'd done me a great honour. Mostly when a town like Box Elder wants ter git rid of a feller, they jest throw him out. I suspicioned as mebby they war afraid ter tackle me, an' jest up an' moved the town instid when I war asleep! *He-he-he!* Ye might call Cottonwood a monyment ter the mem'ry o' Hank Simpson; they shore put her right whar they reckoned Hank was planted. Hank fooled 'em, fer he ain't buried here a-tall! *He-he-he!*"

"Hank dead?" asked Billy.

Old Jim led them through a space between two buildings and extended his arm in line with a certain place on the creek where a grotesque figure was straightening up to rest his back.

"That's Hank, alive as he ever was," chuckled old Jim. "Prancin' 'round in his shirt tail, like a heathen, washin' gold. Scandalous, *I* tells him. That ain't no way ter act in a town like this. I told him he should oughter dry his pants farther from the fire, unless he stayed thar ter watch 'em clost, but he knowed more'n me." He grinned up into their smiling faces. "Got him jest whar I want him, picketed out on the rope o' modesty. *He-he-he!* He says ter me when I left the crick, that if I don't git back danged quick, an' rock the cradle, that he'll come up here a-kitin' an' drag me back by the scruff o' my neck. He forgot he ain't got no pants! *He-he-he!*" He hitched at his belt and faced the main street again. "Whar ye goin'?"

"Buckner's, for supplies," answered Billy. "After which we aims to see the sights."

"I gotta go ter Tom's, too, to git me four ounces worth o' grub an' sichlike that he done me outer over to Box Elder. Then I gotta hunt up our burros," said the old man; "but fust I'm goin' ter take a look in at the Elite. Thar's a red-haired gal in thar that shore can step fancy. Comin'?"

"Not yet, Jim," answered Billy. "We'll look in after while."

Tom Buckner was glad to see them. His merchandise was put in order and he was idling behind the counter when they came in.

"Well, we saved the B—B quite a ride, didn't we?" he chuckled.

"Only left us fifteen outa forty," replied Bid with a laugh. He drew out the foreman's list. "Round up this stuff for us between now an' to-morrow afternoon. Just saw old Jim Hankins, an' he said he was goin' to call on you for some stuff you owed him. Somebody stole his burros. Damn shame to do a thing like that to a man as old as him."

"*Is* it!" blazed Buckner. "*There's* his supplies, all tied up like they was in Box Elder. I packed 'em all the way for him. An' nobody stole his burros: he turned 'em lose to wander into Bob Shea's stable, an' Bob brought 'em along with the rest of his animals."

"Which reminds me," muttered Billy, his hand straying to the letter in his pocket. "Tell us how Box Elder come to move, Tom. Old Jim told us, but we hanker for the straight of it."

Half an hour later they went out laughing, stopped in the Placer for a drink and certain humorous amplifications on recent history, and then rode up to Bob Shea's livery barn and stables. The loud and angry voices of the liveryman and his son sounded from the rear of the building, and the two punchers exchanged looks as they dismounted.

"Give him one more trial, Father," said a woman's voice, tense with anxiety and fear. They had never heard Alice Shea's voice sound like that.

"Another one, is it?" answered her father in a roar. "How many chances do ye be after thinkin' he's had? Money, money, money! That's all he can say. If I asks him to help me with the hosses, he's too damn busy bummin' 'round saloon or hell-hole, playin' cards an' drinkin'! He's a low-down, sneakin' bum"—he whirled to face his scowling son—"*don't* ye look *at* me that way, ye worthless bum! Ye can scare yer equals with yer scowl an' yer six-gun; but ye try it on me an' I'll wear out a whip on yer worthless carcass! Go in

there an' clean out the stables, or I'll clean 'em *with* ye!
I like to broke me heart when yer mother died; but I'm
thankin' the good Lord she's dead!" He paused, and
in the silence low sobs could be heard. "There, there,
Alice; I didn't mean the last, 'though it was a mercy to
her. Dry yer eyes; I'm thinkin' yer cryin' from the
wrong reason. Yer tears should be for where he's
headin', with the brakes off. Mind ye now: ye'll
not give him a cent. When the stables're clean I'll
give him the price of a round of drinks, to guzzle with
the swine, an' *worse!*" He turned his head quickly at
the sound of whistling, coming nearer through the livery
barn, and his daughter fled into the living quarters.

"Hello, Bob!" came a cheery, inquiring hail from the
poorly lighted barn. "Hello, *Bob!*"

"Hello, hello!" he answered, impatiently. "Who is
it?" He stepped to the door and looked in. "Is it
Billy, of the B—B? Sure it is! Me boy, I'm glad to
see ye, an' you, too, Bid. How's everybody on the
ranch?" He craned his neck to peer past them.
"Dave with ye?"

"Not this time, Bob; but he sent this to Miss Alice.
How is she?"

Bob took the letter, gravely read the superscription,
upside down, and shook his head.

"Too full o' faith, I'm thinkin'."

The two punchers exchanged glances, which the
liveryman noticed. He placed his hand quickly on
Billy's arm, and held out the letter.

"I'm not speakin' about this, the man that wrote it,
or any man on his ranch," he earnestly assured them,

and, facing the living quarters, raised his voice. "*Alice!* When ye can't have the greater, ye must do with the less: here's a nice letter from Dave Saunders. He bids ye the top of the mornin', an' says he's got another girl. Don't ye want it?"

"I can't—come for it, Father," came the reply, a little shaky and uncertain.

"Sure, I forgot!" he called, and flung an explanation to his two callers. "'Tain't often she has a headache. Be with ye in a shake. There's chairs out front."

Bid led his companion through the dim building, shaking his head.

"It's a damn shame! Don't you reckon Dave could make a man of that cub, out on the ranch?"

Billy smiled knowingly.

"Dave's got a long head, an' he's usin' it. Muddy water don't get no clearer by stirrin' it up."

Behind them there suddenly rang out angry, high-pitched voices, those of Bob Shea and his son, who had renewed their quarrel. There came the sound of a blow and a fall. Spinning around, the two punchers raced back the way they had come, and paused in the wide door.

Red Shea, rising to one hand and knee, a cut on his cheek oozing crimson, held his right hand on the sheath at his side; but his angry stare took in the alert and poised figure of Billy, and he loosed the hold, arose slowly to his feet and went around the corner of the building. Billy relaxed and turned, walking slowly and thoughtfully toward the street door, his face a mask again. Waiting a few minutes for the liveryman, they gratefully slipped away and joined the weaving crowd.

"Judas priest!" muttered Bid, uneasily.

"Let's find old Jim," said Billy. "I can stand a little fun about now."

On their way to Healy's dance hall they kept their ears open to the conversations in the crowd, which began with gold, ran through a scale composed of liquor, gambling, dance halls, lost animals, a murder not three hours old, several thefts, high prices, scarcity of palatable beef, and gold, gold, gold. Three quarters of the population were gold mad, and the other quarter was taking advantage of it. Rough lumber for sluices was selling for one hundred and twenty-five dollars a thousand board feet, but buyers were holding off because of a rumour that four great freight wagons, loaded with this commodity, were on their way to Cottonwood. A square meal of very little variety cost five dollars. Liquor was selling for fifty cents a drink, and there wasn't a decent drink to be had.

Bid was all eyes, all ears; taking in his surroundings with avid interest, asking endless questions of his companion; and finding his companion growing slowly more reserved, more alert, with cynicism on the increase. The pleas of three-card monte men, shell-game proprietors, chuck-a-luck gamblers, found the elder puncher without interest. A drunken brawl blazing swiftly high in front of them caused a quick scattering of the crowd, and Bid felt himself hauled back to one side. The drunken victor, crimson with blood, liquor, and rage, unsteadily kicked the body of his prostrate victim without intercession from the by-standers.

Bid tore loose and leaped forward, knocking the swaying bully sprawling, and was surprised to find himself jeered instead of applauded. The crowd shifted on, leaving behind it uncomplimentary and fragmentary comment on the youth's greenness. Angry, uncertain, he looked appealingly for his companion, and saw him leaning against the corner post of a canvas gambling hell, regarding the immediate crowd through half-closed lids, his expression a blank. Bid joined him, staring curiously.

"Didn't you see it?" he demanded, his voice breaking from anger and excitement.

"This way," grunted Billy, pushing him along the side of the tent. "The other feller would 'a' done the same, if he had the chance. Seems to me that beef is goin' to be worth good money in this town. Dave'll be glad to know it, I reckon." For some reason he scowled, momentarily disturbing his mask. Not very old in years, he was old in experience. "Beef's 'way up; lives, 'way down, an' goin' lower. It's the same thing all over ag'in."

"Mebby we can sell our beef cattle right here, an' won't have to drive all them miles," remarked Bid, trying to adjust himself to his surroundings. Somehow he felt lost, and sick of the town already. They gained the main street again, and saw the crowd splitting frantically to make way for a shouting horseman, whose voice was lost in the yelling on all sides of him. The news spread like quicksilver on a billiard ball. The

stage had been held up, twelve miles out of town, and
cleaned to the last dollar.   It had gone on again, minus
fourteen-hundred-odd ounces of gold dust and the
valuables of the passengers.

A hard-faced, desperate-looking individual herded
five men before him to horses and the group galloped
out of town to run down the highwaymen, relieving all
others of the need to mount and scour the hills.
Vociferous volunteers, balked by this back-firing,
appeared reluctant to stay off the trail, but quickly
disappeared to drown their sorrow.

Bid's eyes gleamed at the celerity with which the
posse had formed and got down to business, and he
spoke with enthusiasm.

Billy glanced at him somewhat pityingly, a smile
flickering about his lips.

"Almost seems like they was waitin' to go," he
remarked.   "Don't forget their faces, if you ain't
already."

A new altercation burst upon their ears and soon they
saw the disputants.   It appeared that they had been
partners, but were now separating, and quarrelling over
the ownership of the mule between them.   Their curses
filled the air, but the matter was brought to a close by
the man on the far side shoving a revolver muzzle across
the mule's back.   His title to the chattel was now good,
and he offered to fight any man in the crowd who
doubted it.

Tim Healy's Elite Dance Hall might be described as
a thin canvas cover around an uproar.   Body odours
mingled with the earthy smell of the dust and with the

fumes of whiskey. The floor quivered and shook, per-
spiring dancers collided and scowled, while the envious
stood ready to preëmpt the first space abandoned.

Old Jim Hankins caught sight of the entering punchers
and raised his inharmonious voice above the noise. He
was entertaining a red-haired woman who was almost
plastered with cosmetics to fill in the wrinkles.

"Meet Della, you fellers. Billy an' Bid, Della,"
said Jim, waving his hand with large and generous
motion. "They're punchin' fer the B—B," he told
her. "Billy used ter preach the Gospel over ter
Virginia City when the town had hair on. He used a
deck o' cards fer it." He looked up at the two. "I war
jest tellin' how Hank loves the ladies. *Ha-ha-ha!
Ho-ho-ho!* Della says Sadie wants ter meet Hank!
Pronto, this minute, right away quick." He wiped his
eyes and held his sides, rocking back and forth on his
chair as he pictured his trouserless partner.

"Sadie bein' my sister," explained the red-head, and
looked indignantly at her spry entertainer, who was
snorting with glee.

"You git Sadie," said old Jim. "Git her now, an'
we'll all go down an' visit Hank. He'll be plumb——"
Laughter made him wordless.

Bid was about to object, vividly picturing Hank
according to old Jim's previous statements; but
Billy's elbows stopped the words.

Sadie hurriedly joined them, making eyes at each in
turn, but she gave old Jim most of her attention.
Jim's poke held plenty of dust, and that of his partner
should be as well filled.

"If Hank's as spry as you, Old Timer," she said, "he oughter come up an' dance once in a while."

Jim visualized Hank's spindle shanks undraped by trousers, and in his mind's eye he could see them twinkling down the gulch, bearing their panicky owner rapidly away from female visitors. Tears welled into his eyes.

"You'll find Hank spry as a jackrabbit," he said, and suffered a spasm as he pictured Hank's flapping shirt-tail bobbing behind him. "An' dance! *Oh, me; oh, my!* Hank'll dance fer ye, soon's we git thar. He'll dance like the spirit o' Spring, acrost the hills an' dales. *Oh, me; oh, my!*" He wiped his eyes and looked up at the two punchers, and the look of indignation on Bid's face sent him off again.

"You *loco?*" demanded Sadie. "Or drunk? Huh! I don't believe Hank can dance a-tall!"

"Can't, huh?" snorted old Jim, arising with considerable effort. "You jest wait. Hank likes ter dance so much that he'll bust right out the minute he sees us." He took Della on one arm and Sadie on the other, and led the way to the street; but when he turned down the path to the creek he found that the two punchers had become lost in the crowd. Looking in the direction of his camp he saw a familiar figure straighten up to rest its back; and quickly looked away again lest his companions follow his gaze.

"We'll go down this way, an' come up ter the camp through a little gully," he said, choking. "Hank's so cussed bashful that he scares easy. Come along."

He was right in every claim.   Hank was bashful, he scared easily, he was spry, and he danced like the spirit of Spring over hill and dale, making twelve miles an hour on the flats and much better time down hill.

CHAPTER V

THE HORSE COMES BACK

THE foreman of the B—B, with the rest of the outfit, listened in amazement to the report of Billy and Bid. In the discussion which followed there seemed to be a great deal of satisfaction at the location of a base of supplies, and a probable market for beef, so close to the ranch, but the foreman was uneasy, and glanced at Billy, on whose face was a frown. Dave had never known the life of a mining camp, but he had heard considerable about it; and he was well posted regarding certain men who had lived by their guns and died with their boots on.

According to precedent, Cottonwood was certain to become the Mecca of the worst type of badman in the West. Each gold rush was followed by the Slades, the Helms, the Plummers; to such fields came the Ollingers, the McCalls, and the Thompsons. As individuals they were bad enough, but when banded together and surrounded by their spies, they dominated whole communities, and murdered without fear of molestation. These conditions, known to Dave by hearsay, were known to Billy by experience. The two men exchanged looks freighted with meaning, and without a word Dave went to his bunk, drew his war-bag from under it, and took out the second belt and gun. It was done un-ostentatiously, almost sorrowfully; but the hard look on his face and the tightness of his lips stilled any joking comment.

Bid, his back to the foreman, did not see what was going on. He was speaking hopefully of the new market for beef cattle, so near the ranch; and of the prices that should be obtained. Dave stepped past him to a shelf and reached up, breaking open the boxes of cartridges that lay on it. Bid's eyes slowly opened, his gaze fixed on the left-hand gun. He never had suspected that the quiet Texan was a two-gunman.

"What you wearin' two for?" he asked, his face a study of conjecture. "Can you use a left-hand gun, Dave?"

Dave ignored the question and let his hand fall on the opened boxes. He looked around the little circle and spoke quietly.

"Hell's fixin' to blossom hereabouts. We're six that know how to use weapons. As long as we stick together we got a fair chance. We ain't startin' nothin'. We stay outa town as much as we can; an' when we can't, we drink no liquor there."

Bid's mouth was open and he was staring blankly at this changed foreman.

"Why, what's wrong, Dave?" he blurted.

"All creation," growled Dave, smiling a little at Bid's expression. He looked around the circle again. "It'll mebby take some time for 'em to get notions about this ranch; but when they do get notions, we got to be ready." He paused. "I been talkin' on the basis that all you boys are goin' to stay with me. Mebby there's some of you that itch for the feel of a gold pan." His eye was caught by a squirming and he smiled. "Got the fever, Mark?"

Mark Luttrell grinned self-consciously.

"Shore have, Dave; can't hardly set still." His eyes gleamed with avarice. "They'll pan twenty, thirty dollars a day."

"Some will, an' some won't," said Dave. "You might be one of the lucky ones. Anybody else feelin' the itch?"

Bid glanced at the floor, trying to hide his excitement. The fever had been working in him all the way from town, and Mark's estimate set him on fire. He looked up to find the foreman's eyes on him, and he flushed.

"All right, Bid," said Dave, kindly. "I don't blame nobody. All I want to know is how many of you boys are goin'. I can't stack up ag'in that kind of money. Best I can do is offer each of you fifteen dollars more a month; an' that ain't nothin' ag'in twenty, thirty dollars a day. However, it's net. What are prices for grub over in Cottonwood?"

Billy told him sharply, and his growl rumbled after the words.

"I got the itch," he confessed. "Allus got it, every time. This is one time I aim to stay where I am, an' scratch it, regardless." He looked at the restless Bid. "You better do the same, Bid."

Dave spoke up.

"Bid's goin' to do just what he wants. So is every man here. Them that stays, stays of their own accord.

Them that leaves, leave with my best wishes. I wouldn't blame you if you all went."

Frank Hitchcock rolled a cigarette with fingers that trembled, spilling tobacco on his knee. He glanced at Joe Hawkins and raised his brows. Joe nodded, and arose.

"Dave," he said, nervously, "I don't want to go back on you; but I got to try a whirl with the pan. Mebby we'll all come back ag'in, huh, Frank?"

Frank nodded, wondering at this madness. Only an hour before there was not a man in the outfit who would not have ridiculed such an amazing change. It is futile to try to explain the gold madness.

Dave, still smiling outwardly, shook his head.

"I got to fill yore places, boys, if I can. If they're filled when you want 'em back——"

Billy leaped to his feet, his face stern and hard.

"If you once wash a pan, you fellers, you'll never be worth a damn for anythin' else. I ain't guessin'; I *know*. Look at old Jim, an' Hank, an' Sagebrush Joe: there *you* are, years from now! Bums, livin' in everlastin' hope of strikin' it rich; an' if you do strike it, you'll go broke near as fast. Gamblin', supplies, liquor, an' frontier wimmin: they'll take it as fast as you wash it. Half yore lives'll be spent in lookin' for grub-stakes; an' the other half in usin' the stakes up. I been through it, an' I know. I'm stayin' with Dave. You better do the same thing."

Youth scorns good advice, even knowing that it is good. In Bid there worked a yeasty fever, consuming him, making him deaf to all persuasion. Twenty or thirty dollars a day, and perhaps a find that would enrich him beyond a lifetime's needs. The temptations of the town would not sway him; he would stay with his claim, save his dust, work hard, and lay up a stake to last him all his days. His face was flushed, his hands itching; and he saw the same signs in Frank and Joe. They had known each other for several years, and could trust one another. Mark and himself; Frank and Joe. He looked at Mark inquiringly, his eyes following the pacing man to and fro. Then Mark stopped and made a sharp gesture.

"Suits me, right here," he growled. "Three of us can swing this ranch durin' the summer; an' when the fall winds begin to cut, there'll be a stampede for any place feedin' three square meals a day over the winter; an' not much said about wages." He turned to the restless three. "You fellers can team up three-cornered. I'm pullin' leather, but I'm stickin' to the saddle. My old dad was a Forty-niner."

The foreman regarded him closely.

"Don't you stick out of any sympathy to me," he said. "You do just what you wants, Mark."

"I am; didn't I just say my old dad was a Forty-niner?" and with this ambiguous remark he left the bunkhouse, and went whistling toward the corral. Passing the cook shack, he wondered at its silence. At this time of the day there should have been great activity going on in the little shanty. He looked in curiously. The fire was out and dishes stood in the cold and greasy dishwater; a batch of biscuit dough stood in the mixing pan. Mark stepped inside, grinning even while he swore. The cook's bunk was in disorder, his clothing and other possessions gone. On the table was a wrinkled piece of paper held down by a soda tin. Mark picked up the scrawled message and read it.

Dear Dave.   I'll leave the hoss with Shea.
You can leave what's owing me with Buckner.
I'm a prospector now.   Yours truley,
Mr. William H. Norris.

Mark laughed.

"Yours truly, Mr. William H. Norris!" he snorted. "Mister William H. Norris.   Damned if the old fool ain't rich already, in his mind."

He built up a fire in the stove and then wandered back to the bunkhouse, the paper in his hand. There were signs of confusion inside. Three men were collecting their belongings, in readiness to leave the next day at dawn.

"Where's my other pair of socks?"   Bid was monotonously demanding as he moved in circles over the same ground.

Joe Hawkins squirmed backward from under his bunk, sneezing the dust out of his throat and nostrils. In one hand was a pocket knife, in the other an old pair of trousers.   He arose to his knees and held up the knife in triumph.

"I found my knife!" he exulted.   "Where'd you reckon it was?"

Hitchcock flashed a scornful glance at the dust-covered man.

"Out behind the stable," he replied, sarcastically.

"No, sir!" laughed Joe, triumphantly. "Right here, under my bunk!"

Mark stopped at the table, where the foreman was counting money and scowling at a well-thumbed and well-cursed account.

"Got a note for you, Dave, from Mister William H. Norris," he said, placing the paper under the foreman's nose.

Dave looked from the note to the man who had brought it, searching his memory for such a name. He shook his head and scratched it frankly.

"Never heard of him; but when a stranger's got gall enough to borry a cayuse without askin' for it, I'm shore anxious to meet up with him. What the hell's he mean by sayin' to leave his money in town? What money?"

"Stub's," answered Mark, keeping his face straight.

"Stub's?" cogitated the foreman, looking at the note. "Stub's?" he repeated. He showed signs of intense concentration. "What did Stub say about it?"

"We've lost our cook," said Mark. "The Honorable Mister William H. Norris, Esquire. Stub's him."

A profane chorus arose, wavered to flirt with laughter and, in flirting, died. Wherever Stub was at that particular moment, his ears must have burned.

"We'll find him an' make him cook for *us!*" exclaimed Joe Hawkins, one of the uncertainties thus being removed from the uncertain future. His grin slowly changed. "Mister William H. Norris, huh?" he asked, a gleam in his eye. "Stub he *was*, an' Stub he'll *stay!*"

"Damn Stub!" snorted Frank. "What I want to know is who's goin' to cook supper an' breakfast?"

"I'm cookin' supper, Frankie," said Mark with great sweetness. "*Yo*'re cookin' breakfast," and he departed hurriedly to assume his new duties. He was glad of one thing: Mr. William H. Norris had kindly mixed biscuits before he had yielded to the imperious call of wealth, and Mark gave no thought to how long the dough had stood. He shaped the biscuits one by one and placed them in the oven, thus innocently building up a reputation as a bullet-moulder that would live as long as he lived, and longer.

* * *

Cottonwood Gulch lay in the semi-darkness under a new moon, here and there lighted fitfully by the dying campfires along the creek, which glowed and winked responsively to furtive zephyrs. The gulch was wrapped in sleep except for the bibulous bawling of some musically inclined miner staggering campward from the noise and lights of a town that never slept.

On the edge of the town facing the lower reach of the gulch two men stood motionless and talked in undertones as their predatory gaze wandered over the dark gulch below them. They were sullen and disgruntled from heavy losses at faro and roulette; they were hungry and their throats demanded liquor with an insistence not to be denied. Behind them arose the alluring chants of dealer and come-on; the rhythmic pounding of feet in the dance halls, the roaring conversations of many saloons. Ribald songs and obscene shoutings here and there arose above the general turmoil. They turned as a third man joined them, a man whose apparel had little in common with their own.

This third man, new to the camp and not yet in his place of power, seemed to be the leader. He swore under his breath and asked a question of his companions. The younger of the two made answer, quoting a certain Della, and drawing on the power of his imagination for trimmings and extra touches.

"You know where to find them?" asked the leader, his mind made up. To the confident answer he made a decisive reply. "Get your horse and join us at the end of the slope, at the elbow of the second trail. We'll scatter, ride south and come into town on the stage road, innocent as preachers." He peered closely into the face of the youngest. "You got the stomach to go through with this, without blundering, or turning to water?"

The answer came in fine disdain and the trio split, melting into the night along the rear of the squalid shacks, the leader and his friend taking the east line of buildings while their youthful partner chose the west. The first two were hardened desperadoes, graduates of many affrays and hold-ups; the young man, making up in zeal what he lacked in experience, was growing into this life with the speed of some poisonous fungus in a stinking swamp. He had no horse, having lost it at cards, but such a need could soon be remedied. The animals in front of the buildings were in a busy street, and to steal them would be too much of a risk. He went on behind the shacks, hotly impatient, peering eagerly about him in the moon-leavened dark.

Behind the Cottonwood Gulch Saloon stood an old horse, wise in the ways of cattle and with strong memories of certain trails, its neatly stamped brand away from the searcher. On its back was a saddle pad, strapped tightly, but of saddle there was none. For hours it had stood thus behind this drinking dive, where its temporary master had stopped to quench a thirst which so far had proved to be quenchless. The old horse raised its dejected head at the approach of the furtive searcher, and its ears swung forward as a hand reached out and grasped the bridle. Hungry and thirsty, the old cow pony obediently obeyed its new master and stepped reluctantly into the dark, its equine thoughts on rations of corn and a windblown remnant of a haystack near its winter stable. Thus does Destiny work its way through curious agents, while Fate laughs in its sleeve.

At the elbow of the second trail three men foregathered, and rode in single file down the second slope, the darkness of the lower levels submerging them and blotting them out. They left the trail at the creek and rode down its middle, leaving it along a naked ridge of rock where no hoofmarks would greet the coming day. Wisps of cloud paraded past the baby moon, alternately masking and revealing it, and drawing brief curtains over the faintly lighted valley. The horsemen pushed slowly onward, into and along a steep-walled wash, the first two horses thinking only of their footing; the last, only of his gnawing belly and distant rations of corn, both by now an impelling obsession subordinating all else. The riders turned out of the gully, through a branch wash on their right, and shortly stopped under a clump of cottonwoods, two of the animals falling to grazing on scattered tufts of grass; but the third was thinking of corn and where it could be found. Its master, consulting in low voice, looked idly at his stolen mount as the infant moon shone down through a rift in the passing clouds. He bent over, his face close to the cow pony's side, and strained his eyes to make out the brand, aiding sight by touch. A grin passed across his face, the brand passed from his mind under the press of matters of more moment, and he slipped into the night after his companions. With his going went the stolid apathy of the cow pony, and corn became its compass, its course, and its destination. The animal walked slowly toward the pin points of light, where the town lay directly between it and a stable which was home to it, and certain equine companions whose company meant contentment.

The little lean-to with its canvas roof lay open toward the fitful fire, where softly glowing embers crackled gently and threw soft radiance for a dozen feet round-about. Camp duffle and placer tools lay scattered on the ground, and scurrying field mice abandoned the baffling tins of tempting food to seek safety in cunning shelters.

Old Hank Simpson, his head and shoulders under the lean-to, his bootless feet toward the fire, slept soundly and snored with a gargling sound; his old partner whistled at the end of every crescendo. They slept the sleep of the just and the successful, for in their pokes lay the pilfered riches of a small pocket run to its hiding place that afternoon. Six pounds of dust and minute nuggets stood to their joint account, but did not spoil their sleep; to-morrow was another day, and it was coming with the sun. That the sun would rise for one alone was beyond their knowledge.

Warned by some unnamed instinct old Jim opened his eyes in time to see the gleam of the descending knife, and heard Hank's death rattle; he wriggled frantically toward the pinned edge of the canvas roof while his groping hand seized upon and flung the pepper can without aim. Its loose top, springing from the sudden bulge of the can under Jim's spasmodic grip, released the stinging powder into eyes and mouths and nostrils, evoking enraged profanity and the whistling breath of pain. The weather-rotted tent cords parted under Jim's surging bulk and he rolled free of the lean-to as three guns blazed blindly into the darkness.

Leaping to his feet Jim jerked his own gun from its holster and emptied it behind him as he fled, thus giving three pairs of ears just what they sought, and grooving the answering shots in his direction. He staggered, fell, clambered to his feet and staggered on, burning with two bullet wounds, running blindly, urged by horror and an unreasoning terror. Had he stood his ground and kept cool he could have shot down the blinded three with as many shots; and were this scene to be acted over again, like as not he would have stood his ground, and wiped out that brutal murder. Jim was not lacking in physical courage, whatever he lacked in moral; but there are human impulses that baffle understanding. Old Jim fled on, staggering this way and that through the darkness of the brush and scattered trees, sobs punctuating his whistling breath; and he bumped squarely into a disgusted cow pony making its cautious way homeward. The animal meekly allowed the sagging fugitive to claw and scramble to the saddle pad on its back, and then seemed to sense that the rider had no chosen course to steer. The pony pricked up its ears and started once more for its distant stable and a feed of corn.

Dave awakened with a start and heard other bunks creaking. The sound came again, but was lost in the querulous inquiries of the awakened outfit. He slid from his bunk, drew on his trousers, and slung a gun belt about him. A match sputtered greenishly, filling the room with sulphur smoke, and revealed Bid's anxious face; but a puff of Billy's breath killed the flame as the foreman was about to order it put out. Sharp, metallic clickings ran around the room. Again came the sound, barely audible. It had aroused the bunkhouse not by its loudness, but by some inherent quality which rang on the nerves like a hammer on an alarm bell. There was noticeable another peculiarity: not a man awakened from deep sleep was confused or groping, not one of them but was as wide awake and clear-headed as though he had not been asleep. Dave stepped quickly toward the door, cat-like in his poise and silence. He flung open the swinging barricade of planks and writhed to one side as something shadowy pitched into the room and slumped on the floor, misshapen in the faint light of the new moon.

Swift, furtive movements centred about this object, dragged it inside and shut the door. Again a speck of greenish light sprang out in the darkness, slowly becoming yellower and reaching faintly to the walls. Its pale light fastened to a smelly wick, which sputtered, stank, and smoked as the chimney surrounded it.

Dave, on his knees beside the alien object, swore venomously under his breath, and helped Billy carry the pitiable figure to the nearest bunk, tense faces staring out of the semi-darkness like gargoyles from a fog. Someone lit the big lamp and carried it swiftly to the bunk, where eager hands were ministering almost by the sense of touch. Against the pillow an aged, wrinkled face lay like a grotesque mask bathed in blood.

"Old Jim Hankins!" muttered Mark, peering closer to make certain. He stepped back to make room for the hurrying men about him, who brought water, whiskey, clean rags, and a towel. In silence the work went on, but the silence was at last quaveringly broken by moans and broken words. The quantity of liquor administered was a shock even to that saturated carcass, and awakened a slow movement of head and hands. Old Jim Hankins opened his eyes, stirred fretfully, and blinked into the lamp-lighted ring of faces around the bunk. A look of fear and rage passed over his countenance, and slowly changed to that of recognition. His lips moved soundlessly as the fear leaped back again; and a tear trickled down his seamed and wrinkled face.

"Hank's gone!" he whispered. "Don't let 'em git me!" The effort punished him and he closed his eyes again to rest. More liquor and a spell of waiting, and the old eyes opened again. "Murdered for our little poke o' dust. I——" Again he rested, his fingers weakly picking at the coverlet. "How'd I git here?"

"That don't matter, Jim," answered the foreman, reaching behind him for his second belt. He slung it around him, pulled on a coat, took a rifle from the rack and went to the door. "Blow out them lights till I get outside." His voice was hoarse with anger and he was clipping his words as though with a chisel. The door swung a little inward in the dark of the room, and closed gently.

"Damn their souls!" came a whispered curse from the bunk. "Knifed him like——"

Billy had stepped swiftly toward the injured prospector and stopped the sentence.

"Keep yore trap shut, Jim," he said, kindly. "No talkin'. Go to sleep. You can talk later, when yo're stronger."

"But they'll foller me!" whined Jim.

"If they do they'll beat you to hell by a good start!" growled Billy. "Shut yore trap: *we*'ll handle this from here on!"

Joe Hawkins searched for his rifle, forgetting that he had stacked it with his belongings in a corner. Stumbling over it, he patted it unconsciously and then looked in the darkness toward his groping friends.

"But how'd he git here?" he marvelled. "It's more'n fifteen miles from the gulch!"

"Never mind that," said Billy, feeling for the door.

"You fellers best stay here to hold the house. I'm scoutin' till daylight."

Dawn crept over the hills and sent a ghost-like glow speeding across the valley, magically whisking reclining and feeding cattle out of oblivion. A pale streamer of light reached high into the heavens, grew rapidly and spread, reaching lower until the tops of the west range were gilt against a sullen sky. Bands of golden light swept downward into the valley itself and transformed it as the sun rose majestically over the near horizon.

In the corral beside the trail to town a man slowly arose to his hands and knees, peering through a crack between the posts. He stood the heavy rifle against the wall and briskly rubbed his legs and arms to dispel the chill. Behind him stood a gray horse, a saddle blanket cinched tightly on its back. The foreman turned slowly, saw it, and walked nearer, his gaze on the clotted blood. As he mechanically removed the pad he began to understand. This was the horse Stub had borrowed; and this must be the horse that had brought old Jim those fifteen miles through the dark from the gulch. How Jim chanced to find it was a question that could wait. A sudden sound made him drop both hands to his holsters and crouch in eager readiness. Billy's head appeared in the granary door and was gratefully followed by the rest of his body. Some people might find it pleasant to lie for two hours across the opened ends of barrels filled with corn, but it was not to his liking. The ends of the staves had branded him deeply through his clothes; but the strategic value of his peephole had warranted the torture. In Billy was the stuff that martyrs are made of.

Dave straightened up, his expression a mixture of surprise and disappointment.

"How'd you get in there without me hearin' you?" he demanded.

Billy continued to rub certain curvilinear lines pressed into his flesh, and grinned.

"Didn't you hear me? Gosh, I reckoned they could hear me clean over to Cottonwood!" He flexed an arm. "How'd he git here?"

"The cayuse Stub borrowed."

Billy's gaze followed his foreman's gesture, and he nodded.

"Well, he couldn't 'a' picked a more reliable vehicle," he said, following his companion around to the bunkhouse door.

The smoke of the greasy frying pan assailed their nostrils as they passed the cook shack, where Frank Hitchcock petulantly cursed the stove and the need which forced him to fill the gap left open by Stub's desertion. The bunkhouse door was open and they saw the rest of the outfit silently moving about, careful not to awaken old Jim. As they entered the house they stopped just inside the door and raised inquiring eyebrows, looking significantly at the occupied bunk.

"Sleepin'," whispered Joe. He came nearer. "Looks like the old boy ain't hurt so bad. Reckon it's the blood he lost."

Dave nodded and tip-toed to the bunk, looking down

on its sleeping inmate. As he was about to turn away, the eyes opened and fixed him with a steady stare. There was no terror in them now, no horror; but only a sadness, through which slowly crept a look of vindictive hatred that made the foreman's face go hard.

"I'm too damn tough to go under, Dave," said the wounded man in a low voice, and slowly. The words carried throughout the room and stopped every puncher in his tracks. "I got a quick look at one of 'em, an' think mebby I've seen him som'ers before. Time'll tell, time an' me; an' when I'm dead shore, I'll send him ter the hell he come from." The look on the old man's face changed perceptibly, and a peculiar look of wonder took its place as he regarded the quiet foreman. It seemed almost to be asking a question; a question which would find its answer in the days to come. "I nicked one of 'em, Dave," continued the old man with a little satisfaction. "I reckon the coyote saw me lookin' at him, an' figgers mebby I recognized him. I dassn't go back ter the Gulch an' placerin'. They'd kill me ter shet my mouth. Mebby you got some kind of a job fer me, peelin' potaters, watchin' o' nights out on the range, or somethin'?"

Dave smiled.

"Give you Stub's job, wrastlin' the grub," he offered.

Jim's eyes lighted and he closed them in assent. He rested a moment and then spoke again.

"They won't be easy till they find me," he said, wearily. "I can't fight back, the way I am; an' I can't leave the country. If I could leave I wouldn't,

till I do the job I gotta do. Jest don't say nothin'
ter nobody about yer new cook, Dave. I'll lay sorta
low when visitors come." Again he rested. "Of
course, I don't want you boys ter git inter no trouble
about me. If they come, an' find me, don't try ter
stop 'em. Thar's trouble enough comin' ter this ranch
afore snow flies, 'thout makin' any extry."

"Nobody takes you off this ranch, or harms you,
without mixin' up with me," said Dave, his eyes
glinting. "Yo're one of the B—B now, an' the B—B
sticks up for every man in its outfit, through hell an'
high water. Go to sleep, Jim; an' don't fret."

Billy grinned cheerfully and stepped to his foreman's
side, hitching up his gun belt.

"Dave called the turn, Old Timer," he said. "There
ain't enough murderin' skunks in the hull of th' Gulch
to pry you loose from this here ranch. If you want to
lay low when anybody comes a-callin' on us, that's
yore business; but I'm tellin' you right out loud that
you don't have to lay low a damn bit."

"They'll come fer me if they learn I'm here," warned
old Jim.

"Let 'em, then!" snapped Joe Hawkins, his face
hard as granite. He walked over to his piled belongings
and kicked the pile apart. "I ain't no damn dog,
leavin' this ranch when it needs every man. To hell
with placerin'!"

Bid Carter scowled at his own pile of possessions and
then looked around at his companions, the gold lust
struggling against an awakened loyalty and the promise
of impending warfare. He removed his sombrero to

scratch his head, and with a sudden gesture tossed the hat on his bunk.

"I'm ridin' with the B—B, Dave," he said; "an' I don't care where!"

Dave's face was radiant and he laughed low in his throat.

"A gang like this shore will take a lot of lickin'," he observed, and went out to see how Frank Hitchcock was coming along with the belated breakfast.

Old Jim chuckled contentedly, turned over, and went to sleep again.

CHAPTER VI

WELL-TO-DO OR WELL-TO-WATCH

HENRY DANGERFIELD was a prepossessing gentleman, immaculate in his apparel as the limitations of the new camp permitted. His features were well chiselled to patrician lines, his mouth thin-lipped and not too large, his nose slightly aquiline, his forehead broad and high. His black eyes revealed a glowing friendliness, with fine lines of humour crinkling from them. His thick black hair, always carefully brushed, was innocent of artificial aids to glossiness. He stood five feet eleven, was slender of waist and full of chest, and had a generous spread of shoulders. Quiet, reserved, soft of speech, and free from that overflowing profanity so common in mining camps, he nevertheless gave no one the misleading impression that he could be imposed upon. Despite the whiteness of his even teeth and other signs of refinement which marked him as apart from the motley crowd, there was an air about him that warned against undue familiarity or encroachments on his rights. He appeared to be perfectly balanced mentally and physically, self-contained, and needing the aid of no other man. The quiet richness of his attire, devoid of all jewellery except an exquisite ruby pin slanted through his full black tie, was increased in effect by the careless ease with which he carried it. One might judge that the man gave little thought to the art of dressing and thus would have been in error: no man gave more. To Henry Dangerfield his appearance was an asset of no small value, and he spent more time in putting on his clothes than any four men in the camp, not grudging an hour, if need be, to attain that careful carelessness.

Men without occupation call attention to themselves, being rated either as well-to-do or well-to-watch. To be known as well-to-do was to incur certain obligations and unreasonable expectations, to be cultivated by pan-handlers, and sought out by the honestly needy. To refuse unreasonable charity would be to create potential enemies, all the more dangerous because they were in the wrong. The other contingency was not to be considered for a moment: trouble came easily enough as one went along or was sometimes generated spontaneously; to deliberately sow it in fertile ground were madness.

The morning after his arrival in Cottonwood, Henry Dangerfield strolled along the street which ceased to be a street and became a trail on the first abrupt dip of the hillside overlooking the creek. His roving gaze followed the course of the little stream and grew gently humorous as camp after camp unfolded itself, and the teeming activity along that wandering strip of harried and discoloured water impressed itself on his mind. For an instant his gaze rested on one camp in particular, where no spiral of smoke climbed heavenward; and then he turned to retrace his steps the way he had come.

In front of Shea's livery stable the honest proprietor leaned back in his oft-mended chair, placidly observing the busy street at the corner. He turned his head as if in answer to a call, and a smile broke across his face as his daughter stepped from the building.

"Och, Alice; but yer a pitchure," he said. "I'm wonderin' how Dave Saunders can keep so busy on that ranch. If 'twas me, now——"

"Now, Father!" protested Alice, quickly.

He laughed at her confusion, and waved a finger at her.

"I don't know what's the matter with the boys these days. It's past all understandin'. Whist, now! There's a fine-lookin' man. Yonder, comin' from the edge of the hill," he whispered.

Alice turned and her eyes met the humorous but very appreciative eyes of Henry Dangerfield, and as he approached she drew back inside the stable in swift confusion, where she scored herself for her unaccountable flight, and slipped along the front wall toward the feed bins.

Her father, ignorant of her flight, continued in a low voice:

"A fine, upstandin' man, he is, with an air about him that ye don't see these days. If Dave, now," he suggested, looking up to wink at his daughter; and easily turned his words to another pair of ears. "How do ye do, sir?" he said, smiling at the calm stranger. "Fine days we be havin'."

"How do you do, sir?" replied the stranger with easy affability. "The weather could not be better." He stepped through the big door and glanced about the building, apparently not noticing the figure flattened in the poor light against the wall. He stepped out again and looked down at the proprietor, his mind instantly made up. "I like your stable, Mr. ——?"

"Shea, without the O; Bob Shea, sir."

The stranger's sudden interest was well masked, and he continued easily:

"Glad to meet you, Mr. Shea. My name's Danger-field, Henry Dangerfield. As I was saying, I like the looks of your stable; and its comparative lack of odours." He paused reflectively and made a swift gesture of disapproval. "I have a horse, sir; a rather fine animal, but the pleasure of riding is spoiled by the hole it is kept in. If you have room for it, and the time to look after it well, I shall be very glad to change its quarters. A fine animal deserves consideration. Most stables in this country are not fit for pig styes.'"

Bob Shea's face glowed with the pleasure of a compliment well deserved but too often withheld. He sprang to his feet.

"An' why they put pigs in a puddle of muck is beyond me understandin'," he replied. "If ye'll tell me where to find yer horse, I'll get it this minute, an' give yer back yer pleasure in ridin'."

"I'll not trouble you to that extent, Mr. Shea," said the other, smiling. "If you'll show me a box stall, with a window open to the sun."

"With two winders, 'though only one is facin' the sun; which is better for lettin' the air through," said the proprietor, turning with alacrity. "This way, sir."

The stall examined casually and appreciatively, the new patron of Shea's livery stables stepped through the rear door and let his glance rest on the little house behind it.

"Neat," he said, nodding. "You live here alone, sir?"

"Alone with me daughter an' the boy," answered Shea, a shadow crossing his face.

Henry Dangerfield showed a polite surprise although he felt none.

"I should have suspected a woman's presence," he replied. "Certain touches make it plain. That bow of ribbon on those crisp curtains, for instance. Is the little lady well and content?"

"Yer own eyes can answer that better than any words of mine, sir," chuckled Bob Shea, proudly. He raised his voice. "Alice!" There came no response and he frowned slightly. "Now I wonder where she went? She was out front but a moment past. I hope——" The frown disappeared at a reassuring thought. "She's around somewhere. She *never* would go ten steps past the front door."

Dangerfield nodded understandingly.

"She never would," he said, crisply, and turned back into the stable, his eyes carefully avoiding the corner where the feed bins stood as he reached the other end. "It must be a heavy responsibility to be the father of a pretty daughter in such a town as this. Honey lures the bees and butterflies; but beauty——" he ceased significantly.

Bob Shea's throaty rumble died slowly as he nodded.

"I've a shotgun in the house," he said, and changed the subject to that of fine horses and their proper care; and when the pleasant stranger had said good-bye and went sauntering up the street toward the surging, noisy tide of the town's main thoroughfare, the livery-man looked beamingly after him, and nodded in appreciation.

Following the eddying stream on the right-hand side of the main street, Henry Dangerfield slowed, and waited for a man who hurried toward him up a cross street. The newcomer was hard-bitted, belted and armed, and walked awkwardly on legs which suggested a life-time in the saddle. This was Clem Lipscomb and he was born and raised in Texas. He stopped before Dangerfield and the two held a short conversation, at its close being joined by Red Shea. Clem and Red turned into the crowd flowing northward along the main street, while Dangerfield went on his way, stepped with careless dignity into the Argonaut, and looked calmly and deliberately about him.

He saw a well-ordered gambling establishment, somewhat garish to his discriminating eye, but greatly subdued when contrasted with the other gambling houses in town. The bar was in the rear, as it should be, and partly screened, as was proper where refreshments were an adjunct rather than the main purpose. The roulette layout was of American walnut oiled to a richness that was restful; the faro tables were also of walnut, as was the face and counter of the bar. Dangerfield nodded in appreciation and sauntered to the faro table farthest from the door, where he calmly seated himself in the dealer's chair, removed his broad-brimmed hat, and gratefully relaxed, the slender white fingers of one slender white hand resting motionless on the dark wood. From a pocket he took what looked to be a new deck of cards, and deftly slipped them into the faro box, which for some reason had been left on the table.

Near the rear door, sweeping diligently, a bull-necked bouncer and man of all work lifted the last of the sand and dust over the sill. Turning, he was about to go to other duties, when the motionless stranger behind the faro table caught his eye. He swelled ominously, scowled, and started for the usurper, his expression proclaiming his intentions; but he now was about to come into contact with the sort of man he never had met before. As he took the first step, Henry Dangerfield raised the white hand and beckoned with it, a gesture graceful, natural, and without conscious imperiousness; but the bouncer's intentions faded from his mind like storm clouds drifting from sight over the horizon. The distance was twenty steps from where he stood to the faro table, but were belligerency a material substance instead of an attitude of mind, his trail would have been plainly marked with fragments of it.

"Well?" he said, as he stopped before the table, his voice proclaiming that he was strictly neutral in thought for the moment.

Dangerfield smiled and was subtly friendly in an aloof sort of way. Absently he removed the deck from the faro-box, picked it up idly and squared the edges. Then he shuffled, cut, and dealt an ace, king, queen, jack, and ten along the edge of the table. This had taken but a moment, and had been done in that unconscious detachment with which some men drum their fingers on a table. Its effect on the bouncer was ludicrous. He was neutral in thought no longer. While Dangerfield had squared, shuffled, cut, and dealt he had spoken in a pleasantly modulated voice, not an accent of it lost on the bouncer.

"I would very much like to speak to the proprietor," he said; "but there is no hurry."

The bouncer smiled, and shifted his weight back to a single leg.

"He oughta be in 'most any minute. I'll tell him soon's he comes. Can you do that ag'in?" he asked, his eyes on the cards.

Dangerfield was politely curious, letting his expression ask his question.

The bouncer waved a hand at the royal family and the attendant ten-spot, doubt hovering in his eyes.

Dangerfield glanced down at the cards, and his face expressed surprise.

"Well, well!" he gently exclaimed, and looked up to meet the other's gaze. "I hardly believe I can. That's most remarkable."

The bouncer grinned knowingly, his body slowly turning while his eyes read the mocking black ones at the table. He did not stop to think that the cards were removed from the boxes every night, but, with the average mind of the uncritical, he accepted this miracle at face value.

"*Ain't* it, now?" he asked, and abruptly departed, to speak confidentially with the second bartender, whose grouchiness was due to lack of proper sleep. He had finished with his last cuspidor when a quiet step across the door sill reached his ear, and he straightened up to face the proprietor.

"How are you, Ike?"

"Solid gold, boss." The tousled head jerked backward in the general direction of the last faro layout. "Gent over there wants to see you."

The proprietor nodded and walked to the table, smiling tentatively.

"You look at home," he said, pleasantly. He had had a really good breakfast and was feeling kindly disposed to all the world.

"I never was more so, except that I miss the splash of the paddle-wheels," replied Dangerfield as he arose, and bowed almost imperceptibly. "My name is Henry Dangerfield."

"Glad to meet you, Mr. Dangerfield. I am Colonel Hutton. What can I do for you?"

"Permit me to occupy this chair during busier hours," answered Dangerfield, smiling gently, his white hand resting on the chair back.

Colonel Hutton replied without taking his eyes from those of the cool stranger.

"Sit down, Mr. Dangerfield. This table came in yesterday, and so far I have no one especially in mind." He remembered the other's remark about the sound of the paddle-wheels. "Mississippi?"

"St. Louis to New Orleans."

"The change appears to be unfortunate," said Colonel Hutton politely, but his words asked a question.

Dangerfield nodded. "Without the facts, yes. They are strictly personal and have nothing to do with gaming."

Colonel Hutton's gesture delicately waived the question, and he turned in the chair, ordering Ike to bring cards, despite those on the table. Taking them from the bouncer's hand, he placed them on the table in front of his calm companion, and sat back expectantly. Ike was all eyes, and hovered discreetly near.

Dangerfield arranged the box and lifted his hands from it, revealing the deck in place.

"Straight, or ——" he asked, casually.

Colonel Hutton did not seem to find the question amiss. Gambling was his business, and all its terms were impersonal in such circumstances.

"The Argonaut's games are honest. I find the percentages sufficient."

Dangerfield nodded appreciatively.

"The best policy, especially in gaming." He sat squarely in the chair and his hand paused over the box. "Honesty at times needs safeguarding, for the profession is not unanimous in accepting that maxim; although I was thinking less of faro-bank than other games. If you will play against me and watch carefully, Colonel Hutton, I shall endeavour to deal both single-odd and double-odd; and bet you ten dollars against discovery. Other improvements over the accepted game will be used from time to time, as necessities arise. If you please, sir."

For an hour Colonel Hutton played the best he knew how, but steadily the game went against him. He was surprised by the remarkable number of splits which Mr. Dangerfield's dealing developed, steady losses to his side of the table. The game not only went against him, but it went overwhelmingly so, and had he been playing for stakes he would have found himself a heavy loser at the end of the play.

"Your absence will be noticed on the Mississippi, Mr. Dangerfield," he said, smiling.

"Perhaps for a time, sir. Would you care to watch a round of stud, and indicate my partner's seat?" The cards were falling deftly, no hand being powerful, but strong enough for stud-horse. A wise player regards big hands with suspicion; but on several rounds "sucker" cards proclaimed that suckers were supposed to be sitting in. Usually when the hole cards were turned, the winning hand was a pair of jacks, with queen high; or queens, with a ten high; while one hand held king, queen, ten, five, and deuce, the king being the hole card. Every known trick of shuffling, cutting, and dealing was resorted to, without detection. A pleasant half-hour was spent in this fangless game of stud, at the end of which Colonel Hutton spread his hands over the edge of the table and leaned back.

"I repeat that you look at home, Mr. Dangerfield," he said without enthusiasm. "It seems to be a question of terms. Have you been considering any figure?" he politely asked.

"Ten per cent. of the winnings," answered Dangerfield, pleasantly.

"You are willing to gamble on this table to that extent?"

"*This* table?" inquired the dealer.

"Did I misunderstand you, sir?"

"The fault is mine. I should have been more explicit. I was thinking of the house, of course, and thought you would understand me."

Colonel Hutton stiffened, his gambler's mask askew.

"The house?" he exclaimed. "But that is preposterous, sir!"

"Then you force me to the other alternative," sadly replied Mr. Dangerfield.

Colonel Hutton needed no verbal explanation as to what the words meant, and he was not pleased by the thought that this man would play against the house. "But, Mr. Dangerfield," he expostulated. "To share in the profits of an establishment it is considered equitable to provide part of the capital."

"Exactly, sir," said Mr. Dangerfield, his teeth revealed in a smile of genuine pleasure. "For my services, and ten per cent. of the profits—or losses, of course—I purpose to provide the same per centum in capital."

The proposition was not as distasteful to the Colonel as might be supposed. To have a genius playing for the house, with the interest of the house honestly at heart, was worth considerable; not to have a genius playing against the house was also worth considerable. While Henry Dangerfield watched the play, or participated in it, there was small chance of losses being incurred through cheating. The Colonel, in the last reflection, had stepped on an idea that unfolded itself swiftly in his mind. This cool stranger would be lost behind a faro table; it would be like hanging rare paintings in a cellar.

"You are not at home, after all, Mr. Dangerfield," said the Colonel, smiling expansively, "while you occupy that chair. Your attainments demand a wider field, and your value to this establishment is worth your stated conditions only if you do not confine yourself to faro-bank."

"You honour me, Colonel Hutton; and relieve me, in the same breath. I find faro deadly monotonous. The beauty of the table intrigued me into sitting behind it. Then, sir, I may consider the matter favourably acted upon?"

"And closed. Permit me to show you around."

Thus it was that Henry Dangerfield lost misleading prominence and became an accepted fixture in the life of Cottonwood, playing his natural part in the scheme of things with dignity, calmness, assurance, and a personality which most men envied without much malice. It was not long before his name was mentioned in conjunction with the phrase "square gambler," and he became a solid and well-regarded member of the community. No man had seen him drink too much, although he drank enough; no man had seen him give way to anger, or heard him raise his voice above the pleasant level of ordinary conversation. He listened to their stories, innocent or salacious, with smiling interest; and to win a flashing smile from Henry Dangerfield was to be pleasantly self-conscious for hours afterward. Seldom offering assistance, he seldom refused it; and once given, the aid was kept secret. Men told him their troubles and found comfort in his ready understanding; they told him of their growing fortune and found him glad with them. In this desert of crime he stood out like an oasis, offering comfort and security. His magnetic personality warmed and charmed; he kept his own counsels and was quietly observant; and steadily his personal following grew, recruited from all walks of life, numbering honest men and desperadoes, hard-working miners and the unfortunate flotsam of humanity that begged its food and performed menial labours for its drinks.

Crime was increasing steadily, disconnected outrages flaring here and there throughout the community, ranging from petty thefts to highway robbery, occasionally emphasized by murderous affrays on the open streets. As yet the criminals lacked the effrontery to reveal their identities, and safeguarded themselves by secrecy. They were unbanded units, each working on his own, each fearful of society, unwelded as it was. The shooting affrays grew from flaming quarrels over gaming, women, or liquor; and bore the general aspects of duels, although at times this designation could well be questioned; they still were clothed in the protecting habiliments of personal matters, in which society in general had no call to meddle, for society was unformed and was merely a collection of sovereign individuals with a status not unlike the individuals composing wolf packs or jungle life. The dead men must have read their danger, and met it as best they could; they had been victims of their own weaknesses, of an inexorable law which wills that the fittest shall survive. The hard-working miners were too busy to leave their claims and meddle in the affairs of others, and those better men in town could not afford to jeopardize their trade, and incur unnecessary enmities. So the cancer in the body politic grew steadily, spreading along the lines of least resistance and greater traction, pushing its exploring malignancy into every layer of society, and pushing secretively as yet.

CHAPTER VII

A CASUAL VISIT

DAVE SAUNDERS lounged in the bunkhouse door, a pleasant vista under his eyes, idly watching a speck which crawled along the northern skyline, where Mark Luttrell rode along the so-called line which was supposed to divide the grass lands from the brush lands. Mark was riding sign, alert for those indications which told of cattle straying from their allotted range, and ready to follow such signs and drive back the wanderers. Up to now this work largely had been ignored, for the brush lands were bounded by sheer ridges on the north, and it had mattered little whether the cattle sought the brush or kept to the open range; they would not stray far from the plentiful bunch grass, and those few that preferred the privacy of the brush to a more easily obtained sustenance would be driven out at round-up time. Mark was swearing monotonously, not at the work itself, but at the need for it.

Dave was not gifted with any miraculous sense of hearing, but he knew that Mark was swearing; were it otherwise, Mark would be the only man of the outfit, except the foreman, who was not swearing. Frank Hitchcock was going through the same ritual to the god

of profanity somewhere along the eastern benches;
between him and Mark, Joe Hawkins and Bid Carter
were scouring the brush, shedding language carelessly;
while Billy rode farther afield and made the ritual
unanimous.

Dave, in his mind's eye, saw all this activity, but he
could not be expected to see anything out of the routine
of the work. He could not be expected to see the
sudden interest that Billy was taking in the peaceful gap
through which lay the trail to Cottonwood, and through
which now rode a single horseman, the sullen, suspicious
expression on his face doubtless caused by the dingy
bandage that slanted from right temple to right ear
and covered a scar more vertical than horizontal.
Gunshot scars usually ran in the horizontal plane, being
in line with the course of the bullet; bullets were seldom
fired from the air, and there were but few upper stories
to the buildings of Cottonwood. Yet this scar ran
obliquely vertical, and suggested to a suspicious mind
the downward stroke of a knife. The sullen possessor
of the scar would not have thought of such an obvious
explanation, except for Henry Dangerfield's sympathetic observation.

Henry had met the bandaged man on the street
and Henry's keen eyes barely traced the suggestion of a
shadowy, dark red line through the masking linen.
His smile contained a suggestion of prompting and
warning.

"Knife fighters are bad propositions, Red," he said,
moving his head downward in following the direction
of the wound, as though his eyes were rigid in their

sockets. "That slanting cut might have destroyed your sight."

For a moment Red Shea had looked wonderingly at the gambler, and then nodded slowly, the ghost of a grin flickering to his face. Henry Dangerfield was an asset to any community.

Hatless in his perch on the brushy hillside, Billy, of the B—B, sat motionless in the saddle, peering through an opening in the shielding leaves. His eyes followed the lazy rider until a wooded hump of the hill hid him from sight; and then the suspicious watcher rode painstakingly along certain aisles in the brush and reached the trail below, along which he rode with corresponding laziness. Reaching the end of the gap, he pulled up beside a copse and waited until the visiting rider was well out on the open plain, pushing steadily along the trail for the bunkhouse. Having tacitly turned Red Shea over to other eyes, he withdrew into the brush and regained his former vantage point.

Dave had lounged to the corner of the house and as he turned it he let his roving glance rest on the nearing horseman, his face void of any indicative expression.

"'Lo, Dave," carelessly said the horseman as he pulled up at the foreman's side, and grinned affably.

"'Lo, Red," responded the foreman in casual friendliness. "How's things?" His glance impersonally rested on the bandage and returned to the eyes near it.

Red grinned still wider, and his hand instinctively touched the linen.

"Knife fightin' is a greaser trick," he grunted; "but some white men take to it easy. Got any beef cattle you want to sell?"

"Reckon so," answered Dave. He smiled whimsically. "Reckon I can find one or two. You buyin' beef?"

Red remembered his instructions and let his gaze wander about the premises.

"Might, if prices are right." He grinned impudently as though he believed he had something thrown and hog-tied. He was prepared to drive a hard bargain. "How much you want for good beef critters, on the hoof, at yore corrals?"

Dave became thoughtful, several factors focussing to a price mark. He could drive in his own cattle and get seven cents a pound, delivered in Cottonwood, if he held out for it. This was almost a famine price. He could, on the other hand, sell at a good profit and give Red Shea a chance to earn some honest money; and keep his own men, not only on the ranch, but also from the hell's broth simmering in the town.

"Five an' a half to you, Red," he offered, swiftly calculating. "Them I'll pick out will average twelve fifty. You can sell for seven cents, an' make more'n eighteen dollars a head. You easy oughta sell ten a week."

Red laughed derisively.

"They're bringin' 'em up th' trail, over three hundred miles, an' sellin' 'em for six."

"An' losin' weight an' quality at every step," said Dave. "I know them cattle. They're trailers from

Texas, an' they won't scale more'n a thousand pounds. There ain't fat on 'em to make tallow for a candle."

"Reckon you better keep 'em," said Red, anger glimmering in his eyes. While the main purpose for his visit was not the buying of cattle, he had, nevertheless, hoped to combine great profit with it.

"Don't aim to keep 'em, as long's there's only fifteen miles of trail between here an' Cottonwood," replied the foreman with easy good humour. "It's an open field, Red, and a beggin' market. Tell you what: I'll sell 'em to you for a cent an' a half less than you get for 'em, an' give you the field to yoreself. There won't be no gamble for you that way, an' you'll make near nineteen dollars a head for just drivin' 'em fifteen miles over a good trail. That suit you?"

Red lazily dismounted and felt in his pocket for tobacco and papers.

"I'll think it over, Dave, an' let you know right soon. Got to talk it over with my buyer. I ain't slaughterin' or retailin'. Don't know what makes me so thirsty," he said, moving toward the bunkhouse door.

"There's a bucket in the kitchen," said the foreman, innocently stepping between the caller and the door, a puzzling question in his mind. For a moment his eyes rested on the bandage.

Red masked his thoughts and went on past the half-closed door, the foreman at his side, whose thirst was as sincere as that of his caller. They both managed to empty half a dipperful, and then wandered back in front of the bunkhouse.

"I see you lost yore cook," said Red, leaning against

the wall close to the door. His fingers suddenly became clumsy and dropped the cigarette papers, which the wind wafted gently into the building; and, growling at his stupidity, he pushed open the door in swift pursuit. Politeness sent Dave with him to the floor. The papers which the foreman reached for remained motionless for his grasp; those under the reaching hands of Red seemed endowed with life and lifted from the floor under the puffing breath of their pursuer. While Red was on his hands and knees Dave glanced swiftly about the room, felt relief, and then glanced at the slanting bandage. The visitor cornered the last elusive paper between the bunks, arose grumblingly and, turning completely around, swept the room with his eyes and slouched back to the doorway. In his heart the foreman was grateful that the bunkhouse water bucket was empty, for it gave endorsement for the use of the one in the kitchen.

"How's yore father, an' Alice?" asked Dave as he seated himself on the wash-bench just outside the door, and gestured for his visitor to sit down.

"The old man's grouchy as ever, an' Alice is putting up with him like she was an angel. Reckon she'd be interested to learn when yo're ridin' in, though she ain't said so."

Dave laughed gently.

"You tell her I'm aimin' to ride in right soon. Cottonwood's so big an' noisy I sorta hate to visit it. Purty rough town, ain't it?"

"Dave, you ain't never seen the like," asserted Red, his hand rising part way to the bandage. "There's a couple o' men killed 'most every day. Remember Hank Simpson? Well, he was murdered, an' nobody ain't seen his old partner since. Some of the boys near their camp said they'd struck a pocket. It's gettin' so it's plumb dangerous to strike gold, or make a fair winnin' in the gamblin' halls."

Dave nodded understandingly.

"That's too bad about Hank," he said. "I'm plumb sorry to hear it. He wasn't of much account, but I allus liked the old cuss. An' so old Jim Hankins is missin'? Who'd they reckon done it?"

"Folks ain't got much time to reckon things like that," answered Red, carelessly. "Them that has are figgerin' it don't look none too good for Jim; but I reckon there ain't nothin' in that." He lit the cigarette and tossed the match away. "It don't stand to reason, somehow; though there ain't no tellin' what the gold fever'll do to a man." He arose. "Got any beef critters in the corral for me to look at?"

"No, seein' that I didn't expect any buyer. Has Stub got rich yet?"

"Which reminds me," quickly said the visitor, snapping his fingers in irritation at the shortness of his memory. "Stub wants you to know that somebody rustled that hoss he borrowed of you. He says you can take it outa the wages that are due him, an' will you send the balance in by me? He ain't hardly drawed a sober breath since he struck town, an' I reckon he needs money bad."

Dave chuckled and lazily arose.

"The cayuse showed up bright an' early the very

next mornin', so Stub don't owe us nothin'. I'm plumb outa cash, but I'll give you a writin' to Tom Buckner, tellin' him to give Stub the money an' charge it against our account."

Red followed the foreman into the bunkhouse, frankly open to him now, and let his gaze roam around the room while the labour of writing was performed.

"Funny where old Jim went," he observed, not discovering an article that he could associate with the old prospector.

Dave grinned and waved the paper to dry the ink.

"Reckon he's prospectin' 'round in the hills som'ers, if he's alive. He'll show up when his thirst gets too strong. Here you are, Red. Give it to Buckner an' tell Stub about it. Let me know as soon's you make up yore mind about them beef critters, an' be shore to tell Alice that I'll be in right soon. Want another drink before you go?"

"Had about all the water I want," answered the visitor, grinning provocatively, his eyes resting on a bottle on a shelf.

Dave arose and took down the bottle, handing it to his caller while his eyes searched the room for a glass or cup.

"N'mind no cup, Dave," chuckled Red, and tilted the bottle to his lips. He handed it back, its level well lowered, smacked his lips and drew a sleeve across them. "There ain't no likker like that in Cottonwood." He stepped to the door. "Well, so-long. I'll give you a quick answer about the beef cattle." He went around to his horse, Dave following slowly, mounted, and waved his hand. "So-long, Dave."

"So-long, Red," called the foreman, and leaned against the wall to watch the rider as long as he was in sight. Proportionate to the increasing distance between the two men, a frown appeared and grew on the foreman's face; and with a muttered curse he pushed suddenly from the wall and walked quickly to the granary, fumbling in his pocket for the key to the padlock.

"That you, Dave?" asked a querulous voice from within. "Where the hell you been all this time?"

Dave opened the door and let the sunlight stream in. He looked reproachfully at the old man lying on the blankets on the floor, and nodded in answer to an unspoken question.

"Yo're gettin' so ornery I reckon yo're near well," he observed. "Red Shea just came out to borry a drink of water an' talk beef cattle that he ain't aimin' to buy. Somebody's slashed him from temple to ear with a knife. He tells me Hank's dead an' yo're missin'. An' Stub was awful anxious to know if the cayuse come back. I know Stub: when he's drunk he don't remember nothin', hosses least of all." He plunged a hand into a trouser pocket and there came the musical clinking of gold pieces. He grinned. "Bein' short of cash, I gave Red a writin' to Tom Buckner so Stub could draw his wages. Stub'll mebby need that thirty dollars mighty bad. How you feelin', you old pole-cat?"

"Middlin', Dave; middlin'," answered old Jim.

"Ain't mindin' that, not near as much as I am about that there claim o' Hank's an' mine. I'm bettin' you six dollars some skunk has shore jumped it; an' I'm bettin' you six dollars more that if it *is* jumped, there'll be some lively jumpin' o' another kind, soon's I can make out ter slip inter the gulch some dark night. Nothin's safe in this damn country!"

"Nothin's safe," echoed Dave, moving back toward the bunkhouse.

CHAPTER VIII

FATE SNICKERS

ALICE SHEA fretted and daily grew more restless. Dave's note, delivered by Billy, was plain enough; but she was reluctant to believe that even the spring round-up warranted his continued absence. When she had lived at Box Elder he had ridden in at least once a week, except during certain intervals of the winter when blizzard weather made the round-trip of eighty miles out of the question. Now the round-trip had been cut to thirty, and the weather was ideal. She had not seen Dave Saunders for two weeks. True, the letter had explained it; but she was not looking for explanations. What she failed to consider was the fact that as long as Dave took wages for looking after the ranch, his sense of honour made the ranch his first consideration when consideration was needed. While Dave was not superstitious, he believed in shadows, the shadows of impending events.

Alice's frame of mind was the result of several disturbing forces. The breach between her father and her brother grew steadily wider, and they seldom exchanged words. When her father knocked Red down she felt that it had been saved from becoming something infinitely worse only by the opportune appearance of Billy and Bid. Since that episode Red scarcely used his bed at night, and wandered in at all hours. He no longer ate his meals at home, except, perhaps, his breakfast; and to eat in town meant an opulence long a stranger to him. His new soft leather boots had not cost a cent under thirty dollars, his heavy sombrero had cost as much, and she could not estimate the cost of his horse, or of his new saddle, which was decorated with silver. He had become grouchy and unusually secretive, and she could see that he was worrying greatly. At times he eyed her speculatively, and on several occasions was on the verge of speaking something of his thoughts; but each time he had scowled and kept silent. The last time the thought had flashed across her mind that it had something to do with her, but she pushed the idea into the background as being ridiculous.

She was cooped up in the little shack, virtually a prisoner. In Box Elder she had gone and come as she pleased, finding a pleasure in her marketing. She had ridden abroad whenever her work permitted, and she laid out her work herself. In Cottonwood she was forbidden to leave the premises, and rides were clearly out of the question. Her father would not even permit her to go to a store with himself as escort, saying that what wasn't known wasn't wanted. Nothing had been added to compensate for what had been taken away, and now she found Dave's absence hard to bear. There had been no avowal of love between them, but what woman needs an avowal to establish a fact of this nature? Dave understood that she would not leave her father.

Guarded as she was, she could sense the spirit of lawlessness in the town, which not only increased steadily, but was becoming more audacious. Men had been shot down without warning, in daylight on the main street, and no one had dared to intercept the slayers. Robberies were becoming more numerous, and growing into deadly affairs. On the stage road and the trails no man was safe, and the stage-coach had become a very dangerous vehicle. Dead men were found close to the trails and the road, killed to take advantage of the maxim that dead men tell no tales. There had been but one murder in the gulch proper, that of Hank Simpson, for since then the miners had taken to grouping their camps.

The law-abiding were not organized; but there was some reason to believe that the law-breakers were. Interference with any of them brought swift retribution, although they could quarrel and kill among themselves. To be favoured by fortune was to be placed in jeopardy: if the fortunate winner of pan or table attempted to leave the vicinity he faced robbery and death; if he stuck to the town he was no better off.

Bitter thoughts were in Alice Shea's mind this bright May morning, and she was so lonely that she ached. Her father had gone to Tom Buckner's for supplies, Red had not been seen by either of them since the evening before, and her work was finished. She could think of nothing more to do to occupy her time, and when a housekeeper reaches that unbelievable point it speaks volumes.   She stood in the door, frowning at the little yard, and raised her eyes at a sudden movement in a stable window.   A jet-black horse had jerked its head from the north window with a suddenness that meant only one thing: Henry Dangerfield was coming through the building.

Her eyes sparkled and her face lost its frown.   She hardly dared to admit to herself how much she thought of Dave Saunders; she had been afraid to have him speak what she knew was in him for fear that she could not resist him and would desert her father.   The relations between this father and daughter were built up on a loving, mutual dependence and reached almost to adoration.   It was a relationship rare and beautiful, and Alice Shea would deny herself to the utmost to keep the bond and companionship unchanged.   But Dave Saunders had sent her explanations which now began to pique her; evidently Dave took too much for granted.   Very well: he was due for a shaking up.

The black horse pawed restlessly and whinnied, and a whistle of five liquid and rising notes replied to it.   Alice smiled with pleasure.   Such an affectionate companionship between horse and rider spoke well for both.   She knew that Dangerfield had a very soft spot in his heart for the black, because not a day passed that he did not drop in to talk to it, pet it, and surrender a little sugar to its eagerly searching muzzle.   Sometimes he dropped in twice a day, and on every other day could be counted on to go for a canter over the hills. This was a dangerous pleasure these days and Bob Shea had remonstrated with him, but Dangerfield had laughed off the warning by saying that forbidden fruits were the sweetest, and that as long as riding had become dangerous, no man who thought anything of himself could afford to refrain from such an excellent exercise. As his visits to the stable had increased in frequency they also had increased in length, and so naturally as not to be noticeable.

His calm voice came from across the stable, followed by a low chuckle.

"And egotistical humans arrogate to themselves an immortal soul, and deny it to you. They make me laugh, Blackie; and laugh, and laugh, and laugh. If their souls have anything in common with their natures I'll take my chance with you."

The speaker moved nearer to the door and bent his head back from the following muzzle, and in turning, caught sight of the woman in the door of the living quarters. Never had he espied her deliberately; it always was incidental to something he was doing, and somehow it never failed to pique her a little, and to turn her thoughts to him at odd moments during the day. She had even given thought to revenge for this, but was waiting until she found a method which would not be linked to the offence. Alice preferred her punishments to be edged by thought and retrospection long after their administering; if the motive were hidden there would be more of a scramble and one of wider range to pin it down and properly connect it. How a guilty conscience hates this shotgun shooting!

Dangerfield smiled and bowed and his hand carelessly

groped for and found the black muzzle, and stroked it gently.

"Miss Alice," he said, "I wonder if Blackie would look for me as eagerly if I neglected to bring him his sugar."

"I'm sure he would.   He'd be disappointed, but he'd look for you just as eagerly."

He considered this a moment.

"Yes; I suppose so," he slowly answered, and a shadow passed across his face. "And he would look for me as eagerly if he understood how I make a living. Animals look deeper than surface indications when they give their affections."

She remembered his casual discoveries of herself, always incidental to something else.   Here was a good opportunity impersonally to shake him out of his self-complacency.

"You think so?" she asked, smiling sweetly.   "Then why is it that the most worthless human beings have the most loyal dogs?"

She caught her breath at the malignancy which blazed up in his eyes and was gone so swiftly as almost to make her doubt that she had seen it.   She little dreamed of how many bull's-eyes that load of verbal buckshot had struck; but she sensed that it had hit more than air, and she became unaccountably afraid.   He had kept the muscles of his face unchanged; his smile did not waver; but he could not control certain reflexes connected with the vascular system, and the blood returned to his face with a rush.

Fearful of what she unwittingly had done, she tried to smooth it over, and made it worse.

"In this country, where I've been brought up, a square gambler's not much looked down upon," she said. "Anybody looking under the surface wouldn't be stopped by that alone from thinking well of a square gambler."

To an ordinary man the words would have held out a large measure of hope; and to Henry Dangerfield they held out a large measure of hope, but a measure so large that he doubted any part of it. Either it was a promise so unqualified as to be unbelievable, or it was a warning so sinister as to constitute a living, flaming menace. What did she mean? And how he silently cursed the tell-tale burning of his cheeks!

"That only proves my point, Miss Alice," he replied, studying her intently. "The dog—or the horse—looks under the surface indications, far under, and sees some nugget that the wisest men overlook. He is not concerned with what the world has set its arbitrary seal upon. He cares nothing for failure, shiftlessness, weak will, giving in to the insatiable cravings of under-mining habits. He sees some inherent characteristic that is gold; and he will find it through whatever intervenes, as the needle of the compass will find the pole."

She could do one of two things. She could change the subject, or she could follow the flood and attempt to ride it out. Where it would lead her she did not know; and Bob Shea's daughter little cared.

"Then it seems to depend on what a dog thinks is gold," she replied, seating herself on the step. Sub-consciously urged to take the sting out of this argument she had so blindly started, she almost unconsciously invited him, by a gesture, to share the step with her; and that gesture greatly reassured him. It appeared that she was arguing purely for the sake of the argument; but only thought and time would set the seal of confidence on that probability. Alice was speaking while she gestured. "It's said a dog can't reason. His nugget might be valuable to him, but really only a mouldy bone."

Dangerfield was regarding her with a new respect, the sudden, astonished respect that a master swordsman might feel in crossing blades with a country bumpkin, only to discover an adversary worthy of his skill. He had refrained from ever deliberately discovering her in an effort to pique her, to get her thoughts to turn to him, for she figured largely in his plans for the future; but now it was a case of the engineer being hoisted by his own petard; Henry Dangerfield was to find thoughts of her popping into his mind during the tensest play; to wake up in the night thinking about her, and not altogether pleasant thoughts; to argue her pro and con, now for her and now against her, and to spend many hours in devising leads more fully to expose her thoughts. To find so great a potential danger in a vessel regarded as powerless to harm him was not pleasant. He was further perturbed by the fact that she was the sister of Red Shea.

He threw up his hands, tossed back his head and laughed, his face crinkling and his eyes twinkling.

"You win! You broke the bank! If this devastating logic of yours is inherited, I'll take care to step softly

around your father." He leaned forward a little.
"This is a beautiful day for a ride. What do you say:
will you chance it?"

He was looking eagerly into her face; and she,
flushing, was smiling at him, her eyes bright from her
victory. She had just raised an admonishing finger
in his face when there broke into their careless hearing
the sounds of steps; and both looked without much
interest toward the sounds, both expecting the return of
Bob Shea.

"You shouldn't ask me that," she chided, smiling;
and then felt something she could not name. Hurriedly
turning her head, she saw Dave Saunders standing in
the barn door, and her cheeks flushed crimson.

"How are you?" asked Dave, drawling serenely to
master the situation and himself. Man-like, Dave had
thought that his honest explanations had explained, and
thus was hopelessly out of touch with the present moment. His first look had been at Alice, but his gaze
had passed on and come to rest on Dangerfield.

"Dave Saunders!" exclaimed Alice, waving him to
her. "Come here. Want you to meet Mr. Dangerfield.
This is Dave Saunders, Mr. Dangerfield. Dave, I've
just been invited to go for a ride!"

Dave and Henry gravely shook hands with no
hypocritical crunching of bones, and limply let them
fall. Two pleasantly curious poker faces dumbly
examined each other, and found nothing enlightening,
each hiding his animosity. Dave was the taller of the
two, and his shoulders, slightly rounded, did not look
any broader than those of the gambler; his waist,

without a coat, looked more slender; his neck was brown and corded, and his hands were broad, calloused, and covered with dust.

Dave broke the locked gaze first, at which Dangerfield smiled inwardly.

"Pleased to meet you," said Dave, casually, as his eyes turned to Alice. "Don't you let me stop you from takin' no ride, Alice. I'll hunt up yore dad an' get him in a cribbage game. It's been 'most a month since we had a session. Where is he?"

Alice's eyes snapped, but she controlled her voice. "Doing his housewifely duties at Tom Buckner's. I don't see how you've been able to get along without your game for so long a time."

Dave laughed gently.

"Cards never bothered me none," he said. "Barrin' the dust, it's a fine day for ridin'." He looked at Dangerfield. "That yore black in there?"

Dangerfield nodded with a note of regret in his voice.

"It is; but Miss Shea believes it to be too dangerous for riding in the hills. We are not going."

Alice flushed at this high-handed disposal of the matter, which she believed should have come from her, and she was about to assert herself when Dave's drawl saved her from rashness, and preserved her face.

"Reckon you got the wrong idear, Mr. Dangerfield. Reckon mebby her dad asked her not to. Alice sets a heap on her dad."

Dangerfield nodded, his grave eyes on the speaker, pleasantly aware of how favourably he stood in contrast to the carelessly dressed, carelessly speaking cow-man.

His slow gaze took in every detail of the other's dress, and he smiled enigmatically as he looked into his eyes.

"At first guess I'd say you are a cow-hand, Mr. Saunders."

The gray eyes of Dave rested for an instant on the white, slender, and well-kept hands of the gambler, moved slowly upward over the latest fashion in vests, past the soft black tie and blood-red ruby, and gazed into the black orbs of Dangerfield as calmly and deliberately as a mule beginning to balk. Both men were smiling with their faces, but only Dave's included his eyes; far back in the gambler's, pale little lights glinted, like the flash of steel saddle ornaments picked out by the flickering light of a campfire. Dave took plenty of time in his scrutiny, and then politely asked a question.

"Travellin' man, Mr. Dangerfield?"

Dangerfield's smile grew wider.

"Well, hardly; although I've done a lot of travelling. Travelling is a great education, or rather a polishing influence on an education already acquired."

"Reckon so," agreed Dave. "Some folks find it plumb onhealthy to settle in one spot very long. It sorta agrees with me, though; but one man's pleasure is another man's hurt, as the Injun said when he lifted the scalp." At a low whinny behind him he turned to see a shapely black head thrust through the north window of a box stall. "You've shore got a plumb fine cayuse for travelling, Mr. Dangerfield. Reckon she's right fast."

"It takes a Southerner to appreciate a fine horse," replied Dangerfield, not forgetting the word "cayuse."

"He's vastly different from the scrubs they raise down in Texas."

"They don't raise scrubs in Texas," answered Dave. "The scrubs raise themselves. I'll have to tell Billy what you said; he'll climb up on his hind laigs," and the speaker calmly settled himself at Alice's feet to spend a p easant day.

Out in the street leading to the stable Fate was staging one of her plays. Two men were riding down it, one a little in advance of the other, but both bound for the same place. One was Clem Lipscomb, with whom Dangerfield had talked on the morning when he had arranged with Bob Shea for stabling his horse. The other rider was Billy of the B—B. Never before had their paths crossed. The second rider, familiar with the layout of Bob Shea's buildings and well known to the Shea family, dismounted in front of the livery barn and strode carelessly through it; the first, following terse directions, turned from the street and rode along the side of the building. Both men were careless, neither dreaming of the tableau about to be presented. They came to the little yard in front of the Sheas' living quarters at the same time, and both stopped short. Across the face of each surged a look of strong disbelief, and each strove to readjust himself to this totally unexpected sight.

Billy tensed, one hand moving upward to remove his hat while the other lifted slightly until its curling fingers were just below the walnut handles of his Colt; Clem Lipscomb let his breath loose in a low whistle, and a sinister grin crept across his countenance. They flashed a look at each other, and then back at the objects which had surprised them, their lines of vision crossing, each gaze challenging an answering one, and remaining fixed.

The surprise on Dave Saunders's face was shot through with a sullen rage and in his eyes danger flared up in one high, licking flame, to die out and yield place to a look of dogged determination. Dangerfield felt the heat of returning blood in his cheeks. His face was hard and the grisly visage of murder peered out from between his half-lidded eyes. For a space the two pairs of men exchanged looks in silence, and then Clem Lipscomb laughed gently, exultation ringing in his voice.

"Hello, Dave!" he said. "You've come a long way from Texas! How'd you cover yore trail so good?"

"What devil's trick brought *you* up here?" snapped Dave.

"I was plumb lonesome fer you, Dave," chuckled Clem, throwing a leg over the pommel of his saddle. "You shouldn't 'a' run away like that." His ringing laugh seemed to be deliberately provocative, but he gave no heed to any thought of defence. It appeared that he was baiting a bear which he knew had no claws. "You an' me are goin' to have a nice little pow-wow, Davie; I'm fair itch'n' to swap idears with you," and again his laughter rang out, spontaneous and unaffected.

Dave was on his feet now, growling in his throat, and he glanced quickly about to catch the expressions on the faces of the others; and he froze, Clem for the moment forgotten. The attitude of the second pair took his full attention.

Billy and Dangerfield had not said a word, but if looks meant anything, here was giant powder with a short fuse. Billy, a deadly sneer on his face, was poised like a spider about to spring. His curling fingers now touched the walnut, his body leaned slightly forward, balanced on the balls of his feet. Not for an instant had his gaze flickered from the malignancy of Henry Dangerfield's dark countenance. He hardly seemed to breathe. Dangerfield was rigid, first from a paralysing surprise, and as it died away the rigidity had been maintained by hatred and the urgent need for watchfulness. So they stood, freezing the others into silent immobility.

Clem was the first to break it. His exulting gaze left the foreman and settled on the bow-legged puncher poised in the barn door. Clem seemed to be considering, to be weighing something of vital importance. A nod from Dangerfield would have sent him into explosive action, trusting in Billy's hypnotic interest to give him an instant's start; but Dangerfield did not nod. Out of the corner of his eye he saw the foreman watching him, the two guns below the narrow waist, and read in the cold eyes the unhesitant loyalty of the B—B outfit, and something more.

Neither of these clashing pairs knew the motives actuating the other; but each man sensed that death hung poised, waiting for a sign. Clem knew that Dave would not draw against him, but for Dangerfield there was no such assurance; and Clem knew that Dave's safety was in Billy's capable keeping. Billy, seeing that his foreman was closely watching Dangerfield, shifted his gaze to the man in the saddle, and Clem's opportunity for mischief shifted with it.

"Git!" said Billy, shuffling forward. His movements were like those of a grizzly, gracefully awkward, concealing dynamic power and deadliness.

"Git!" said Dave to Dangerfield. "Keep on travellin'. It's an eddication. Keep yore hands from under yore coat, an' *travel!*"

Clem hazarded a light laugh, a nervous and doubtful laugh. He took his eyes from the alert Billy and glanced at the foreman.

"See you later, Davie," he said, and, wheeling, rode along the side of the barn, back the way he had come, with Billy shuffling after.

Dangerfield turned to bow to Alice Shea, and found her place vacant. She was not in sight. He looked calmly at the grim foreman and bowed ironically.

"The pleasure has all been yours, Mr. Saunders," he said.

"I'm aimin' to keep it that way," retorted Dave, grimly. "Jest now I'm waitin'."

Dangerfield turned on his heel and strode with dignified slowness into the barn, and through it, Dave politely walking behind him. Silently mourning the disadvantages of a shoulder holster, the gambler emerged into the street and walked up it to where Clem Lipscomb gracefully sat in his saddle, waiting. The two moved on into the crowd of the main street and were lost to sight. A grunted curse came from the front of the barn and Billy shuffled up to the open door and stopped at his foreman's side.

"Which I says was worth the ride to town," he remarked, his fingers uncurling and dropping from under the handle of the Colt. "Who *is* this here old friend of yourn, Dave?"

"Clem Lipscomb, damn him!" snapped the foreman, his face suddenly becoming weighted with care and dulled by helplessness.

"How-come you let him ride you, Dave? 'Twasn't like you, a-tall."

"He's been ridin' me near all my life, Billy. I reckoned I'd got clear of him. Aw, what the hell's the use!"

Billy, serenely confident of the courage of his foreman, was considering thoughtfully, and guessing mighty close.

"Um!" he said. "Reckon he better be damn careful pickin' his saddle cayuses: I ain't never been rid *yet*. What you think o' *my* little pet?"

"Who is he?" asked Dave, breathing with sudden relief. Clem Lipscomb might ride him, but he was exultantly certain that Henry Dangerfield could not, or any other man living. Then his face fell: what a sorry figure he had cut before Alice Shea, allowing any man to treat him as Clem had done.

"Tell you all about him, Dave, on the way up to the ranch," answered Billy. "Go back an' see Miss Alice. I'll wait for you right here, inside the door, where the view's so pretty! You might lead our cayuses out back while yo're about it: we're ridin' home another way."

Dave looked at him in surprise.

"How come?"

Billy removed his sombrero and looked carefully into it.

"I'm tired o' ridin' home the same way all the time. Tell you all about it later. Travellin' reckless is plumb dangerous these days, with Cottonwood boilin' up like a little piece of hell." He did not mention the fact that he had cheerfully enough ridden through the town on his way to the stable; but, instead, he turned the hat over as if he suspected what he was looking for had filtered through the felt and might be found clinging to the outside of the sombrero. "G'wan back an' talk to her. She looked sorta bothered. It was shore a hell of a thing to spring in front of a lady."

Dave stepped into the street, took hold of the reins hanging down in front of the two saddle horses, and slowly reëntered the building, Billy remaining near the door; but when the foreman had stepped from the stable, Billy slipped to the back door and chose a more sheltered and advantageous position. He was still frowning at the careless way the foreman had stepped into the open when he brought the horses into the building. Billy had no illusions, and he was shamelessly suspicious. A mess of shacks like Cottonwood provided a richness of cover for ambitious sharpshooters.

CHAPTER IX

CROSS PURPOSES

DAVE climbed the three steps before the door of the little house as though he were very tired, and knocked. After a moment's silence a low, hesitant voice bade him enter, and he stepped into the combined living and dining room, closing the door carefully behind him. With his entry Alice had arisen from a rocker and stood against the dining table, her face pale and her heart palpitant. She could not understand the happenings of the last few minutes. Her effort at coquetry had been engulfed in a deluge of great forces, as though she had unwittingly pried loose the key timber of a log jam. Startled and frightened by such a reaction, she groped helplessly for understanding.

"What—what's it all about, Dave?" she asked, staring into the dull gray eyes of the foreman. "What does it all mean? You and the man on the horse; Billy and Mr. Dangerfield? What started it? Where's it going to end?"

Dave placed his sombrero on the back of a chair and regarded her apathetically, slowly shaking his head. The misery in his eyes held her, and through the chaos in her mind she sensed his hopelessness. He looked like a beaten man, and she pushed aside the tumult of her conjectures to rally to his aid. Never before had she allowed herself to admit frankly that she loved him; but this man was not the confident, dominating Dave Saunders that she had known. For a moment she needed the support of the table and then, as a flush crept into her cheeks, she motioned for him to be seated and sank into the rocker.

"I don't know," he answered. "The whole thing was a devil brew. I know my part of it, an' Clem's; but that was plumb swallered up by Billy an' Danger-field." He passed a hand across his forehead. "Billy's aimin' to tell me; but he ain't told me yet." He sighed heavily. "It shore was hair-trigger for a little while."

"But what about you an' Clem?" she asked, study-ing him closely. "Why can he act like he did, an' you stand there helpless, an' not raise a hand to stop him? That wasn't my idea of Dave Saunders!"

"He's the only man alive that can do it," he growled. "The only man on earth."

"But that's one man too many," she retorted. "What made him so sure of himself?"

Dave squirmed. The remark held unpleasant im-plications and made him waver; but he doggedly ignored it, and looked at her calmly.

"Practice, I reckon; he's an old hand at ridin' me."

"Dave Saunders!" she exclaimed, doubting her ears, and not knowing just how to reply to this amazing admission. She went at it round-about, "He didn't ride Billy. Billy looked him right in the eye and told him to get out."

"An' he wouldn't 'a' rid me, neither, if his name

wasn't Clem Lipscomb," retorted Dave, his eyes sparking. "You didn't see yore friend Dangerfield doin'
no ridin', did you?" He chuckled. "He's twice as
dangerous as Clem."

"It might be that Mr. Dangerfield remembered that
there was a woman present," rejoined Alice with spirit.

"Reckon mebby he was glad of that; as glad of it as
I was sorry. If there's any trouble from Dangerfield
I'll take Billy's job off his hands. He'll find he ain't
travelled enough."

Alice noted this sign of jealousy, but pushed it aside
for future development.

"We'll leave Mr. Dangerfield and Billy out of it,"
she replied. "What I want to know is why you didn't
walk over and pull that sneering rider out of his saddle."

"That's a question I ain't aimin' to answer yet,"
replied Dave, his hand reaching toward his hat. "It
don't amount to much, no-how." He flashed her a
quick glance, appraising, searching, and then launched
a body blow. He would soon find out how strong
Dangerfield stood with the daughter of this house.
"I'm figgerin' on pullin' outa the country. Billy can
run the ranch." He laughed ironically. "Dangerfield
ain't the only man hereabouts that has travelled."

"Dave Saunders!" she snapped, standing erect and
doubting her ears. "Do you mean to tell me that
you're goin' to let that Clem Lipscomb chase you out
of the country?" Her hands clenched. "If I were a
man I'd kill anybody that tried to run me off!"

Dave found his hat to be something of absorbing
interest while he made a quick choice of one of the two

roads open to him. If Alice could not trust him under these circumstances he wanted to know it; and there was a sullen stubbornness working in him. He ignored the right road, and chose the left.

"Come to think of it," he said, "I reckon I won't let myself get run off. That'd shore suit some folks too well. Seein' as how Dangerfield seems to aim to stay on this range, I'll stay here, myself. I'll send for a new suit of clothes, a nice black tie, a red pin, an' trim the horn off'n my hands. I'll get me a shoulder holster, an' practise bendin' my back graceful. No, ma'am; I don't reckon I'll pull out a-tall."

"Dave Saunders! I don't know what's got into you! Loco weed?"

Alice was angry, and showed it plainly, but before she could get her thoughts straightened out for the guidance of further remarks, a quick step sounded outside, and the door flew open to reveal her brother's angry countenance in the opening. Seeing Dave with his sister made no difference with Red Shea; Dave was like one of the family.

"I want you to get shet of Dangerfield!" blurted the newcomer, glaring at his angry sister. "I just heard he was here ag'in. You quit yore fool nonsense, an' have nothin' a-tall to do with him! Hear me?"

If Alice was angry before, she fairly seethed now; but her anger was so great that it swept over and beyond the usual indications, and her voice almost purred when she answered:

"And why should I do that, Reddie, dear?"

"Because I tell you to!"

"You told me, only last week, what a fine man Mr. Dangerfield was, in spite of being a gambler. You remember saying that, don't you, when I told you I thought you were hanging out too much with him? Don't you, Reddie, dear?"

"I'm a man, an' a man can do things that a woman can't!" he snapped.

"Oh, you're a man, are you?" she inquired, sweetly. "Thank you for telling me; though I might have known it, from those expensive new boots, that beautiful new sombrero, those silver ornaments on your new saddle, and that fine horse you're riding. Henry Dangerfield didn't let you win all those things, did he?"

Red's face lived up to his nickname.

"No, he didn't let me win 'em!" he shouted. "*I* ain't no baby. What wou'd he do that for?"

"That's what I'm trying to find out, brother. Now, you mind your own business, Reddie, and I'll mind mine. You don't set a very good example for your little sister, sticking so close to Mr. Dangerfield." She laughed gayly, but a close observer might have detected something of hysteria in it. "I have my brother's O. K. on Mr. Dangerfield, and no sister could ask more."

"That so?" yelled Red, his face working. "You keep away from him! I won't stand for him hanging 'round here so much!"

"Because he's a square gambler?"

"Because he's the ——" Red choked on the words, suddenly helpless and frightened. "Never mind *why*: you just stop seein' him, an' that's all," he finished, lamely.

"Not quite all, Reddie, because I shall tell him that my brother says he's got to keep away from here."

Red flinched, and glanced appealingly at the foreman.

"Don't tell him that!" he blurted. "Don't tell him *nothin'*. Just act sorta cold, like you was huffed about somethin'."

Alice turned her back on her brother and smiled at Dave.

"No family is complete without having a brother to run things," she said; "but it'd be a lot better off if he could run himself."

Dave exchanged looks with her, and then glanced at the sullen youth.

"Made up yore mind, Red, about drivin' our beef steers to town?"

Red scowled, wondering what he had blundered into, and what each of these individuals knew and meant.

"Ain't had time to figger it yet," he answered, and flushed at his sister's unkind snort. "I ain't forgot it, Dave. By the way: you get a cook yet?"

Dave grinned, his own misery partly forgotten.

"Stub's job is waitin' for him any time he wants to come back. How's he makin' out prospectin'?'"

"He ain't started yet," answered Red, uneasily.

"That money I sent word to Buckner to pay him shore ain't lasted all this time, has it?"

Red moved backward toward the door, subtly conveying the idea that he was afraid to turn his back to his sister and the smiling Dave.

"He's quit drinkin'," he said. "He's shore lucky at gamblin', too". Here his gaze rested for an instant on the face of his sister with a touch of malignant satisfaction. "Near as lucky as I am, though he ain't bought no expensive boots an' such."

The door slammed shut behind him and they heard his quick steps crossing the yard and become lost in the barn. Naturally they could not see him stiffen and his hand leap to his gun as an indistinct figure, crouching in a dim corner of the building, caught his attention; and they could not hear his low challenge, or see Billy stand erect, or hear Billy's answer.

"Oh!" said Red in a low and relieved voice. "What you doin' here?"

"Keepin' in out of the sun," growled Billy. "You keep yore mouth shet tight, an' clear outa here!"

Red cogitated while his glance roved swiftly around. Billy was located where he could see the whole of Blackie's box stall, where any one going through the barn would pass him before they would discover him; and at this illuminating discovery Red's breath whistled.

"Great land of gold!" he exclaimed, and hurried on about his business, his head in a whirl.

In the house Dave was answering questions.

"Why," he said, "I told Red that I'd sell him beef cattle for Cottonwood's trade a cent an' a half less a pound than he sold them for in town. That'd earn him near nineteen dollars a head, just for drivin' 'em a matter of fifteen miles. He oughta be able to sell ten a week in a place like this. It strikes me that it's a purty good thing for a man that ain't puttin' up a cent."

Alice nodded.

"It was mighty good of you, Dave," she replied,

and hesitated a moment. "He's been too thick with Clem Lipscomb to——" she broke off abruptly at the look that leaped to Dave's face at the mention of that name, and became angry at him that he should think she was trying to bring up that subject again.

"Reckon Red ain't figgerin' to take up my offer," Dave said, with a finality that made her wonder. "What's a hundred an' ninety dollars a week to a smart young man like him?" He turned toward the door. "Which reminds me that I can't go back to the ranch none too quick, or leave it again for quite a spell. Tell yore dad that I'm sorry I missed him. I was aimin' to look him up on my way outa town, but Billy hankers to go back a new way, that ain't so well known. I'll be in again the first chance I get."

"Why do you think Red won't take up your offer?" Alice asked him, watching him closely. "That's a big profit, Dave."

"Shore is," replied the foreman, turning. He was not particularly anxious that she should read his eyes when he spoke again. "Why, Red's mebby too lucky gamblin' to go to work. Don't forget to tell yore dad that I'm sorry I didn't see him."

She waited for one more sentence, no matter what it might be so long as it was personal and kind; and waiting, saw the door slowly and gently close behind him, and heard his boots clamp down the three little steps outside. She moved impulsively after him, but caught herself and flushed at her tottering pride; and while she pampered pride there came the sound of horses leaving the yard, and then there was silence, a silence that hurt her.

CHAPTER X

THE INNOCENTS

OLD Jim Hankins was proof of the theory of the survival of the fittest. No one knew how old he was, but from careless admissions and references he was certainly old enough and shrewd enough to take care of himself. His one great handicap had been an unwise fondness for strong drink. Sober for weeks on end, he would, without warning, attempt to surround all the liquor in his vicinity; and when he was full of liquor he talked incessantly to the point where vocal paralysis choked off the words.

Those most intimate with him had heard from his own lips certain tales and names that coupled him with an era now past. He told stories wherein he linked his name with those of Jim Bridger, Robert Campbell, Thomas Fitzpatrick, and others famous in the fur and emigration days of the West. There was scarcely a part of the mountain country that he did not know; there was hardly an Indian tribe west of the Mississippi River that he did not curse because of indignities suffered at its hands. Young men had been eager to buy him liquor in the necessary quantities for the sake of listening to his tales.

When Dave Saunders had given him the sanctuary

of the B—B he had unwittingly done one of the wisest acts of his life. There are many men who never forget a kindness; but among that old breed the valuation placed on kindness, loyalty, and timely aid had no limit.

Jim's first act, when strong enough to make the attempt, had been to slip into the gulch after dark and worm his silent way to the fateful camp where Hank Simpson had lost his life. As he came in view of it he muttered with anger at sight of the small fire burning before the tent; and from then on his progress would have done credit to a Crow horse-thief. Heavy breathing from the tent told of a tired man sleeping with his mouth open; but this claim jumper's mouth opened wider and his eyes popped as he awakened to find a knife pressing at his throat.

"Who is it?" he asked in a whisper of terror.

"Hell!" snorted Jim, restraining his voice. "Sagebrush! You talk above a whisper an' I'll slit yore gizzard. What you doin' here?"

Sagebrush Joe was alive at that moment because he had early acquired the habit of quick thinking; and it now stood him in good stead.

"You come after yore share?" he asked, slowly and cautiously pushing the knife away. "I'm sayin' you got plenty o' gall, hidin' out like you has, an' leavin' me ter do all the work!"

Jim was staring at this calm interloper, his mind filled with rioting but vague memories. He ran back in his mind to that day in Box Elder, but the more he culled his memory the more uncertain he grew. This evidently was a situation that needed to be handled with gloves, until he was sure of his footing. Therefore he sparred.

"I had ter hide out!" he retorted with spirit. "I couldn't do nothin' else!"

"But you don't have ter come crawlin' 'round here with a knife in yore hand, like a bloody Injun, all set fer ter murder yer own pardner!"

Partner! His partner? He must have been unusually drunk that day in Box Elder! Coming to think about it, he had been unusually drunk. He never had been drunker in all his long, hard life.

"'Course, with Hank's passin', I ain't been hardly able ter think," admitted Jim, lugubriously. "What with dodgin' around the hills an' tryin' ter keep grub inter me, I've had a terrible time, Joe. You ain't got no idear what a terrible time." He sighed from his boots and shook his head mournfully. "It's a terrible thing fer ter be hunted like *I* been, Joe. A terrible thing!"

Joe sighed in sympathy, and pushed the knife a little farther away.

"Then no wonder I couldn't make out fer ter find ye!" he exclaimed in low tones. "Night arter night I snuk away an' tromped the hills till near daylight, a-scared somebody'd see me an' find out what I was up ter. Night arter night, Jim, till I couldn't hardly drag one achin' foot arter the other. I suspicioned they was arter ye, an' arter ye hard!"

He drew his feet up and touched them with great tenderness, shaking his head at the thought of his hopeless and unremitting task. He sighed deeply.

"I was a-scared they'd git ye, Jim; a-scared nigh ter death; but I split on the pannin', an' kept yourn fer ye. When I'm pardners with a man I'm *pardners*, through thick an' thin." He sighed again and heroically fought down a sniffle. "Jim, ye ain't got *no* idear how glad I am ter see ye!" He sat up suddenly, a fierce scowl on his face. "But I swore as I'd git them as got ye, Jim; an' give a double-barrel funeral fer you an' Hank, God rest him."

There were grave doubts in Jim's mind as to which of the two was the better liar, although he was beginning to envy the polished finish of his companion. Three thoughts presented themselves to him: Where he had believed himself to be a pauper, he was now half-owner in the earnings of a good claim; instead of the claim being lost to him because of his temporary self-banishment, it was being worked and worked hard, if he knew anything about Sagebrush Joe; and when the time came, Hank Simpson would have a first-class funeral at the joint expense of Sagebrush and himself. Things could easily be a great deal worse.

"Sagebrush," he said in touching gratitude as he slipped the knife out of sight down a bootleg, "I shore has been plumb lucky in pickin' my pardners. An' I shore won't allus have ter hide out, Joe. An' when I kin come back ag'in an' help you work the crick, we'll give old Hank a proper an' fittin funeral, won't we, Lord rest him?"

Joe's sniffle was getting the better of him, and he felt too full to do more than nod sorrowfully. It took some effort to keep his exultation from showing, and to make certain that it did not show he bent his head as if in sorrowful meditation. He sneaked one fist up and quickly dug at an eye. In all his years of prospecting Sagebrush Joe had never shared in so rich a find. He felt of his feet again, and let loose a tremulous sigh.

"Pore Hank!"

"Better pull on yer boots," said Jim in touching solicitude. "Stronger men nor you has caught their death from leavin' off their boots; an' I shore don't want ter lose another pardner." His roving glance about the little tent settled on Sagebrush and became a stare. "You got my poke right smart handy, Joe?"

Marshalling his fortitude, Sagebrush nodded. It was lucky that he had used two sacks instead of one; but he really had never expected that he would have to surrender that second poke. That was the worst of being awakened by a knife at one's throat: one leaps farther than there is any need to. He could just as easily have explained how his faithful and persistent searching at night among the hills had left him no time to pan and sluice. He had been a fool; but fool or not, he now had to go through with the play.

"How I've slaved, Jim," he said, mournfully. "Tired out by trampin' night arter night, I dassn't rest much durin' the day fer fear somebody'd smell somethin' out. There I was in the bilin' sun, workin' the crick when I couldn't hardly stand on my achin' feet, ner keep my tired eyes open. It war plumb awful."

"But it warn't too much for my pardner ter do fer me," said Jim, proudly, wondering how much Sagebrush would hold out, wondering how many caches he had made. "I'm right obliged ter ye, Joe; an' I'll never fergit it, neither." He leaned forward slightly. "Where'd ye cache it, Joe?"

Joe sighed, and picked up a short-handled shovel. "Foller me, on yer belly," he said, crawling out of the tent, and feeling uncomfortable because his grateful and affectionate partner was crowding against his feet. Into the brush they wriggled, and stopped at the base of a tender sapling, both silent and listening for sounds of spies. After a long wait, Sagebrush reluctantly became busy with the shovel, and in a few moments slowly handed to his watchful partner the sack which felt the lighter.

Jim weighed it in his eager hand and smacked his lips; but he was sorry there was not light enough for him to see how many more sacks lay in the cache. He had to admit, though, that for a man who had been exhausted by and who had spent so much time in searching the hills nights, the weight of the poke was a miracle.

"Find a pocket, Joe?" he whispered.

Sagebrush Joe was now as thoroughly awake as his new partner and was too sly a fox to be easily caught.

"*Two* of 'em, Jim," he answered in restrained glee. "Good thing, too, it was, me bein' so total exhausted. Only the hope o' findin' another kept me goin'; but I reckon *that's* too much ter hope fer." He reached out a solicitous hand in the darkness and let it rest on his partner's knee. "Reckon ye better tote that there poke away with ye, Jim? Thar's disprit robbers hangin' 'round the gulch nights. You ain't got no idear *how* disprit they be!"

"Let 'em be disprit!" replied Jim with defiance. "I took two packs o' fur through the Blackfoot country more'n forty year ago, alone by myself; let 'em hang 'round, an' be damned ter 'em!" He weighed the poke again, hefting it carefully. "Dividin' the dust in three parts, Joe?"

"What fer?" demanded Joe, uneasily.

"I reckoned mebby ye might be keepin' Hank's fer his kin-folks."

"Hank got ary kin-folks as ye know about?"

"No; but I reckoned mebby ye sorta figgered he had."

"No, I didn't think nothin' about no kin-folks o' hissn a-tall," said Joe, feeling that one truth would not mar his night's record.

"An' ye done right," said Jim. "We never could find 'em, not never."

"Now, ye know I don't want ter hurry ye, Jim," said Sagebrush, apologetically. "But ye know ye shouldn't oughter stay here too long. They're keepin' their eyes an' ears on this here camp."

"I sorta forgot," said Jim, arising. "Reckon I have stayed long enough fer to-night: but I'll come back ag'in soon. Joe, I jest had ter come an' find out about things, fer I 'spicioned ye'd mebby be here: an' huntin' nights fer me, like ye did. So-long, pardner; so-long."

"So-long, pardner," echoed Sagebrush. "Now I kin rest my pore old feet ag'in."

Jim disappeared, and after a moment Sagebrush

turned to the cache and refilled it as best he could with sand, intending to slip back again at dawn and efface all marks of this most regrettable visit. On second thought he determined that it would be far wiser to remove the remaining sack and cache it somewhere else; Jim Hankins was a canny old man and could find his way about in the dark.

"'Dividin' the dust in three parts, Joe?'" he mimicked, savagely, as he regained the tent and crawled into the blankets. "Glad *I* ain't as 'spicious as that old liar!"

Moving silently along the edge of the gulch and bearing steadily toward town, old Jim Hankins scratched his head and growled.

"If he snuk away from that ther camp o' nights, a-trompin' the hills fer sight o' me, he done it in his sleep!" He felt his heavy pocket, and chuckled, restored to placid good humour. "Betcha his back's a danged sight sorer than his feet, the lyin' old hypercrite." He came to the bottom of the hill, the yellow lights of Cottonwood above him. "Wisht I could remember jest what was said in Box Elder that day," he grumbled; "but I do remember that somethin' was said about pardners atween me an' him," and then he put all such matters from his mind, for he had before him a task in spying that would tax to the utmost even his trained expertness. It was true that the shacks had thin walls, and many of them had their floors raised off the ground, which was a condition that a clever and careful man would find very useful; but the people of Cottonwood were a lively lot, and moved about a great deal. Many a fool has blundered on to that which a smart man could never find; and to be seen and recognized in Cottonwood was not the wish of old Jim Hankins. He was making his first sortie into the stronghold of the enemy, wherein dwelt the murderers of old Hank Simpson.

CHAPTER XI

SHADOWS CAST BEFORE

A DEAD man was found near the old trail leading to and through the defunct town of Box Elder, and the next day another was discovered close to the stage road not more than fifteen miles south of Cottonwood. Both had been killed and robbed; one by a gun shot, the other by a clubbed weapon. Two days later the stage, filled with passengers, and with six thousand dollars in dust under the boot, was held up at the ford of Alder Fork, the dust taken, the passengers stripped of valuables, the shotgun messenger mortally wounded, and two passengers cruelly abused.

Cottonwood seethed when this outrage was reported, and the excitement quickly spread through the adjacent gulch. The news took a deeper hold than reports of previous outrages because of cumulative effect. Four masked men had been engaged in it, and their general descriptions varied so and were so vague that no clue was afforded. There was talk of calling a miners' meeting in the gulch to consider ways and means of putting an end to the robbery and murder rampant in the vicinity. Of what good was it to pan gold if the metal could not be transported without the almost certainty of robbery, and the murder of those carrying it?

Old Lem Cartwright, a miner of many camps, went from tent to tent urging such a meeting, speaking from his own knowledge of the benefits to arise from concerted and determined action; but, strange to say, he found the majority of the miners apathetic, or too busy placering to give any valuable time to the service of the community. These men had not been robbed: the gulch, itself, was safe; and a certain egotism led them to believe that when their time came to leave the camp they would be too smart for the outlaws. The acquisitive frenzy was still hot in their blood, and they gave slight heed to old Lem's arguments; and none of these men was certain that he could trust the others. To start an organization of this kind, which might easily prove to be abortive, was to gain deadly enemies and to become a marked man.

Cottonwood quickly heard of the suggestion for the meeting and became jealous of its place in the sun. A meeting was called and held in the Argonaut, Henry Dangerfield presiding, and the outcome of it was the appointment of four heavily armed guards to accompany the treasure coach on each Monday and Thursday. These two days were set apart for the transportation of treasure, and word of the proceedings was sent to the gulch. This quick action removed the need for a miners' meeting and strengthened the position of the dissenting dwellers of the gulch.

Old Lem argued in vain and sullenly gave up the attempt to enlist the miners for their own protection. On the following Monday the coach, with three days' accumulation of gold and with more passengers than it

had been designed to transport, rolled out of Cottonwood under its armed escort and made the run without
incident. The success of this trip brought relief to the
gulch, and many miners, now assured of the safe transportation of treasure, began to unearth their caches of
precious metal. The more timid, or far-sighted, believing that the semi-weekly treasure run only concentrated the value of each shipment, and offered three
times the inducement for robbery, looked for more
desperate efforts on the part of the robbers. Old Lem
preached this gospel to any one who would listen to him,
but made no progress. The more he talked, the less he
was listened to, and the more emphatic he became; and
the more attention his name received among a certain
class of citizens of Cottonwood.

There came a day when the state of Lem's larder
warned him to replenish it, and in mid-afternoon he
made his way up the sloping trail into town. He had
been abstemious all week, and he stopped in the first
saloon to celebrate quietly his quarter holiday. Acquaintances were met and drunk with, and as one drink
followed another Lem grew steadily more garrulous.
Under the mounting influence of the liquor his words
became more in keeping with his dominant thought,
and before he knew it he was in the centre of a small
crowd, haranguing on his pet subject. He mentioned
former gold camps, in all of which much the same
conditions had existed until the miners banded together
and made their weight count. He waxed enthusiastic
and mentioned names, more or less infamous, and
asserted that there were faces in Cottonwood entirely

too well known to him for his peace of mind and for the peace of the community. So far as the semi-weekly trips of the guarded stage were concerned, he shouted that he was too wise to add the contents of his cache to the temptation under the boot. He was cheered and jeered for half an hour, and then hauled to the bar to bathe his hard-worked throat.

From the saloon old Lem drifted around to a gambling shack and got into a game of stud poker. As the game progressed the cheating became steadily more apparent, until even the whiskey-dulled brain of the old prospector became aware of it; and in a great rage he fumbled for his gun as he shouted his accusations. His words were those generally accepted as provocation for shooting, and his clumsy draw made the matter clearly a case of self-defense. No censure attached to the man who then and there killed him, and before noon of the following day a new mound of earth on the slope of the hill added one more grave to the respectable number already in the local Boot Hill.

Old Lem had been pugnacious and cantankerous and had but few real friends. There was no mystery as to why he had died and, in fact, the killing had been done under provocation and justification much higher than the ordinary run. For a few days there was a little uneasiness in the gulch among those few miners who thought they saw something more than justifiable homicide in the killing; but this feeling slowly wore off. It was noticeable, however, that there was a great deal less talk about miners' meetings, no man caring to be the prime mover toward such an end.

Cottonwood breathed easier, except those honest men to whom law and order would have been a blessing, for Cottonwood saw in this talk of miners' meetings the sprouting of a force which had never failed to dominate any section where the miners organized. In the history of many gold camps was found the fact that when the law-abiding element forgot its differences and its diffidence, and solidly organized in a common cause against banditry and lawlessness in general, it had won out in the bitter contest. Such an organization must be stopped at all cost, and Cottonwood stirred up dissensions in the miners' ranks and inflamed personal quarrels to the point where outsiders were drawn in and sides taken; it revived and nursed the old bitterness between the North and the South, and it was not long before the gulch was split into several factions, each alertly watching the other. Rough-and-tumble fights became common and only by great efforts were kept from turning into something worse. Thus matters rested for a few weeks.

The lawlessness and turmoil of the town and the gulch seemed to be delicately felt on the B—B ranch, where a close observer would have detected faint reactions. The cattle were kept from straggling into the brush of the surrounding hills, the riders holding them to the open ground, which was peculiarly devoid of shelter for stalkers. Dave Saunders and his close friend Billy were frequently in consultation and both wore stern and anxious expressions. The rest of the outfit seemed keyed to a tension and their eyes constantly searched over the hillsides. The horse pasture contained three mounts to a man, all sleek, corn-fed animals of speed and bottom.

Old Jim Hankins kept out of sight as much as possible, and when his duties in the cook shack were over, lost no time in seeking the seclusion of the granary, one end of which had been fitted up for his use. Because of his confinement, and his plea for exercise, he had been given the use of the old cow-pony that Stub had borrowed, and on it he took long rides at night. Jim was taciturn these days, and scorned liquor. There was a strange gravity in his expression, and to his eyes came an occasional look that aroused quiet comment among his ranch mates.

One morning Bid stood just within the corral gate, lazily swinging his rope, the twitch of his hand and wrist cunningly keeping the loop open. He was looking steadily at a horse he did not want, hoping to fool the animal he did want, and to get it to work out to the edge of the cavvy. The horse he was so frankly looking at was the one now assigned to Jim Hankins, and the one horse in the bunch that paid no attention whatever to the slowly circling rope. Jim called it Claybank, and Claybank never bothered himself about any puncher looking for a remount. He took it for granted that his tour of duty was over and that he would not be called upon for a double shift; but after supper every night Claybank became a very alert and interested quadruped, which increased as darkness came on.

Bid grinned at the old pony. Then his rope shot out and dropped over the head of a very indignant roan, whose indignation became passive when the rope tightened; perhaps it would be better to say that its indignation was masked against the time when the perfidious puncher, comfortably seated in the saddle, might become too trusting. Bid led the animal outside the corral and threw the saddle on it, cinching up automatically, his eyes and thoughts on the old cow-pony in the enclosure.

"Foxy old son-of-a-gun," said Bid, grinning widely. "Even if old Jim was as bright as a new dollar every mornin', an' wide awake all day long, he couldn't fool me about his night-ridin' as long as you stand 'round an' offer yoreself a fair target to every roper. What's the old fox up to, Claybank? Where's he go nights?"

There was a wicked gleam in the eyes of the saddled roan, who knew that Bid's mind was not on the job of saddling. The roan looked big and fat around the barrel, noticeable even among the well-fed animals on the B—B; but the conjectures in Bid's mind made him oblivious to this outstanding phenomenon. He slipped on the bridle, tossed the reins on the roan's neck and stepped quickly in the stirrup. As his weight fleetingly bore down on the stirrup leather, the horse arched its back and went up into the air, all four feet leaving the ground. Perhaps Bid's weight, suddenly thrown on the stirrup, would have done the trick without other aid; but the downward pull on the stirrup leather was greatly increased by the pitch of the horse. There was a flurry, a small cloud of dust, and a string of expletives. Bid picked himself up and spread his legs as he gazed wonderingly at the saddle hanging under the belly of the cavorting roan, who was so busy in trying to kick the saddle loose that it gave no thought to flight. Bid mentally reviewed the amount of muscular energy he had put on the cinch, found it to be satisfactory according to precedent, and scratched his head in perplexity. A solution to his problem suggested itself, but Bid shook his head: the roan did not know that trick. Wandering toward the pitching horse but carefully looking elsewhere, he began the sometimes tricky operation of recovering a mount. After a little manœuvring and great dissembling, his hand grasped the reins, and he loosened the cinch, righted the saddle and, putting a knee against the side of the animal, pulled the strap as tightly as he could draw it. Then he stepped back, and regarded the horse with frank suspicion.

"Damned if you ain't!" he growled. "All swelled up like a poisoned pup, huh? Where'd you learn that trick so sudden? All right: here's where you learn another trick," and Bid, grasping the end of the cinch and putting a foot against the blown-up animal's side, surged mightily, and abruptly gained three holes in the strap. The roan, shrinking back to normal, looked dejected and ashamed. Grinning, Bid mounted and rode toward the grazing cattle, leaving the bunkhouse deserted. When near the cattle he met the foreman, who was bound in, exchanged a few words with him, and rode on again, whistling cheerily.

There were two riders making for the bunkhouse, one from the open range, the other from the hills on the north where he had been keeping watch over the valley. The foreman rode as straight as a plumb line for the buildings; on the other side, keeping the buildings between him and the foreman, the second horseman loped steadily on, a sardonic grin on his face. Evidently he was looking forward with pleasure to this meeting. He pulled up at the side of the house and waited.

Dave Saunders dismounted in front of the bunkhouse and whirled as he heard the steps of the visitor. As the sounds struck his ear his first thought was of Red Shea, but the questionable smile of welcome on his face died even as it was born. Instinctively his hand dropped to a gun, and hung there as though powerless. Anger burned through the tan on his face, and his eyes narrowed.

"What you want here?" he demanded, angrily; but the question did not carry conviction, for it sounded as though he knew the answer to it.

Clem Lipscomb's gaze shifted from that dropped hand and he ignored the motion with calm disdain. The impudent grin on his face widened and he leaned against the wall, radiating a confident assurance that was not affected.

"Give you one guess, an' bet you three to one you guess right." He motioned easily to the bench. "Set down, Dave; might as well take it easy as you can."

"Suits me standin'. What you want?"

"Same old thing, Dave. Beef's 'way up around Cottonwood. Never had such a good market before, with such a short an' easy drive. Looks like it was plumb made to order. I oughta be able to handle ten, twelve cows a week. Not havin' to pay nothin' for 'em, that'll be worth while."

"You can have all the beef cattle you want at a cent an' a half under what they sell for in Cottonwood," replied Dave. "That's the same offer I made to Red Shea. He ain't done nothin' about it. You can take it or leave it, an' you can answer quick."

Clem chuckled and dropped to the bench.

"I'm not takin' it, an' that's shore. I'm leavin' it, Dave, leavin' it flat. Red Shea won't take it, neither, when he finds out how I can undersell him. I won't ask you to round-up or cut out for me, for I ain't forgot how it's done, an' I'll mebby have plenty of help. I'll even go so far as to let you tell me what part of the range to take em' from. I don't want to make you no trouble with yore outfit or yore boss. Let's see: how 'bout Saturday night? You can let the gang go in to town for a good time. You've held 'em too close to the ranch, anyhow. A man's entitled to a reg'lar Saturday night spree. That gives him a chance to run it over inter Sunday. Where'll I start?"

Dave's face was like a thundercloud, and pin points of light danced in his eyes. He was facing his visitor squarely, his feet spread, his body relaxed, and anger prodded him into making one of the longest speeches of his life.

"You can start from here, right now!" he snapped. "All my life I've been tempted to kill you. You've come awful close to death more'n once! You've allus had the best of things, allus been pampered, takin' what you wanted, in spite of hell an' high water. You've drove me from one good job to another, till I don't give a damn what happens. You drove me from the Rio

Grande country to the Blanco; from the Blanco to the Neuces; from the Neuces to the Antonio. Allus north, farther an' farther away. I was foreman, on the Concho, makin' good money, an' you chased me away from there; an' a year later, after I got a good job on the Double Mountain Fork of the Brazos, damned if you didn't find me, an' make me leave under suspicion. I was lucky to get away. Then I jumped clean up here, off the known trails, an' worked hard till I got to be foreman of this ranch. By some trick of hell you've blundered onto me ag'in. I'm not leavin' this ranch. We'll have the showdown the first time you show yore hand. It don't make much difference to me, no more, which of us gets killed, just as long as one of us does. That's flat an' final. You get off this ranch, an' stay off. This outfit has its orders. They're right plain an' simple. We'll all of us shoot to kill if we catch anybody rustlin' our cattle. There ain't no exceptions, a-tall. You've got ears, an' you've been usin' 'em; you've got laigs, an' yo're damn quick goin' to use 'em. Climb on yore cayuse, an' get the hell outa here!"

Clem laughed nastily and re-crossed his legs.

"If it was pitch dark an' I didn't know yore voice, or even that you was outa Texas, I'd shore know it was you talkin', Dave," he sneered. "I know that there piece by heart. You allus speak it; an' then you clear out on the sly an' make me hunt for you all over ag'in. This is one time you ain't goin' to clear out. Yo're goin' to stay right here on this ranch an' keep one section clean of yore men on Saturday nights. Every trail's closed to you, you'll be watched from the hills, an' if you try to get away you'll be stopped an' turned back. If you don't turn back somethin' nasty will happen to you. Now, then: where'll I bring my boys this comin' Saturday night?"

"That's where you've got to gamble," retorted the foreman. "You can bring 'em any damn place you want; but they want to have eyes in the back of their heads, an' their hands on their guns. I mean what I say: we shoot without warnin', an' we keep on shootin' as long as we can pull trigger. I'm all through talkin' to you, Clem." The foreman turned swiftly toward the bunkhouse door, but Clem leaped before it to bar the way, his eyes blazing.

"You ain't told me what section, Dave!" he snapped.

Dave stiffened and again his hand dropped to a gun.

"The whole ranch is yore section, you cow thief, if you've got the nerve to come!" he retorted. "If you *do* come, you come a-shootin'."

"This corner up here gives us a shorter drive, an' an easier one," said Clem, sneering at the other's gun-hand. "We'll use it. You keep yore men off'n it Saturday night." His sneer rode on a chuckle. "That's twice you've touched walnut: lemme see you pull that gun, an' use it!"

"You hound of hell!" grated Dave, his face as livid as the tan would permit. "You rotten hound of hell!"

Clem grinned with pleasure, and cocked his head on one side.

"Can't do it, can you?" he demanded, and laughed

at the foreman's expression. "You allus get that far, an' then stop, don't you? Human nature's a funny thing, Dave: here you are, able to beat me on the draw an' outshoot me, even with yore left hand—you allus was a howlin' wonder with a gun, Dave—an' prodded past the point where you'd shore as hell shoot anybody else: but you can't shoot me. Jest can't do it, can you, Dave? Somethin' inside of you holds you back, 'though you'd give yore chance of heaven to plant one slug in me." He reached out an arm to rest his hand on the foreman's shoulder, but was whirled almost off his balance by the swinging thrust of the foreman's arm. Recovering himself, Clem rocked back on his heels and chuckled. "I don't like to be pawed, myself; no wild animal does, an' I'm shore wild, Dave. Now suppose you name that section, an' we'll get it all over with, here and now."

"Yo're right, Clem; I can't kill you," admitted the foreman, his pose slumping dejectedly. "I can't kill you; but there's five good men on this ranch that ain't held back a-tall. I'm namin' no section, for yo're shore goin' to gamble with that, an' with them. An' I hope to God you gamble wrong!"

He straightened again with a snap and his hands shot out and gripped the sneering visitor. With convulsive strength the foreman swept the other from in front of him, and sent him stumbling into a sprawl, his face and chest plowing up the dust; and then the foreman slouched into that deadly relaxation of the gunman as the fallen man scrambled to his feet, spitting dust and grit.

For an instant Clem's hand poised over his gun; but he did not attempt to draw it. He felt, somehow, in a sudden, rushing warning, that this would be to press assurance too far. A gunman of Dave's calibre made some motions without thinking; and the instinctive, reflex action of a trained gun-hand was not a thing to set in motion. Besides, he had never seen Dave aroused to the pitch he was now in.

"Damn you!" gritted Clem, crouched and alert, his face pale and working with anger. "You try that ag'in an' I'll kill you!"

"Try it now," whispered Dave, his words a prayer.

"Don't you ever lay hands on me ag'in!" snapped Clem, letting the invitation pass.

"That's *one* thing I can do, Clem!" retorted Dave. "I've been a fool for not thinkin' of it before. Mebby I can't kill you; but I shore can beat you up to within an inch of yore filthy life! *That's* my play hereafter; you let me catch you foolin' 'round this ranch an' I'll turn you into pulp as soft as a paw-paw's! If my boys catch you, they'll shoot, an' shoot to kill. I'll give 'em their orders over ag'in to-night, to make shore." He whirled on his heels and went into the house, the heavy door slamming shut behind him with a force that made the dust spurt out from around the casing.

Clem glared at the planks while one might count ten, and then, going through the motions of dusting himself, slouched around the corner of the building, his curses keeping time with his steps and the swing of his body. Vaulting into the saddle, he swung the horse toward the pass on the trail to Cottonwood, and as his spurs sunk deep into the tender sides of the animal it was instantly turned into a maddened streak.

Silence followed the last note of the drumming hoof-beats, and remained unbroken; but in the silence there was movement. Caught in the cook shack and unable to reach the granary, old Jim Hankins had squeezed himself behind a faded and soiled curtain hanging down in front of one corner of the room. Now he slipped forth again, listening and watching. Cautiously peering around the edge of the window opening, and believing the coast to be clear, he crept noiselessly and alertly to the door, followed the rear wall of the bunk-house almost to the corner, and then darted across the intervening space between it and the granary. Inside the little building he breathed deeply from relief, and softly closed the door behind him. Until he came to the B—B that door had always squeaked on its hinges; but he had taken care of that as his first task.

Old Jim slowly let himself down on a box, his expression a composite of many emotions. Awed wonder might have been found there; dazed surprise loomed prominently; a fleeting suggestion of pride touched the highlights; but the dominating note was savagery, a savagery toned by cunning. There was a wicked gleam in the old eyes, and one might almost visualize the licking of the lips, the hungry licking, like that of a wolf on a hot game scent. His hands opened and shut and his gaze played with equal impartiality between the ancient cap-and-ball revolver hanging on its peg in the wall and the heavy, double-edged knife born from a hoof-file. The gaze finally settled on the ram's horn haft, and knowledge of the weapon let his imagination see those two razor-keen edges, ground and honed, and honed anew. The wrinkled face convulsed, and a cold, stark grin threatened from its centre. Then he cocked his head to listen, and gently snored.

"Jim!" came the impatient, low call. "Jim!"

From within the building there came a sound like the scraping of a box, followed by leather shuffling over sanded boards. The door opened cautiously and old Jim's face squeezed into the narrow opening. He blinked in the strong light, and bent his head to shield his eyes.

"Shore reckoned I heard a call," he said. "What you want, Dave?"

"Wake you up?" asked the foreman, concealing his suspicions.

Jim yawned gently, slowly let his old frame stiffen, and then relax ecstatically.

"It don't matter, no-how. What time is it?"

Dave glanced at his big silver watch.

"Half-past eleven: time to start dinner."

"Half—past—'leven?" inquired Jim, incredulously. "Great land o' Goshen, how time flies! Figgered on takin' forty winks, an' shore went an' let it slip inter more'n an hour. All right: be with you in a shake."

That afternoon, had an eavesdropper put a perfectly good ear to a crack in the granary wall, he might have heard a gentle, whisking sigh, repeated at intervals of a second; and while wondering what it might be, if luck was with him an occasional gentle ringing, as of fine steel, beautifully thin, might have reached his eager ear and given him the answer. This weapon was no trade-goods butcher knife, made to satisfy the ignorant Indians; but a weapon which in every way fully satisfied old Jim Hankins, who was very particular about his steel. The sound finally stopped, after certain tests on wetted thumbnail and thin gray hairs put their seal of approval on each edge in turn. If the listener were the spirit of old Hank Simpson, it would have been greatly pleased.

CHAPTER XII

ADJUSTMENTS

DAVE gulped his noon meal and rode back to the range, where he ordered the rest of the outfit to go in and get their dinner. They lost no time about it, and when they were with the cattle again Dave called them together and ordered them to search out and drive in all stragglers from the outer fringes of the open range.

"There's bound to be a raid on our cattle," he said. "Cottonwood's growin' fast an' has got a lot of mouths to fill. Fresh beef will bring good prices, an' there's plenty of men in town that'll take a chance rustlin'. Comin' right down to cases, I've heard a few things that don't set well. We've got to round-up, loose herd durin' the day, an' close herd nights. The only law up here is the law we make for ourselves: takin' prisoners ain't on our statutes. Shoot, shoot first, an' shoot to kill."

He smiled at the low growls that answered him.

"For a couple of days we can comb out the brush an' hollows without much risk; after that we want to keep away from all cover that'll hide a sharpshooter. From what's been goin' on 'round Cottonwood we know what kind of coyotes we'll mebby have to face. When we once get the stragglers out here under herd we'll stay away from the edges of this range. There's only six of us, so don't take no long chances; play safe an' shoot first. Mark an' Frank will have to ride herd days, an' the rest of us will watch 'em nights. The round-up not bein' over so long, there won't be very many cattle that have worked far back from the open ground. We'll comb the north an' northeast sections to-day an' to-morrow, an' then the east an' southeast sections. Bid, you stay here with these cows, an' keep as many of 'em from water as you can. If we can keep 'em a little thirsty durin' the day, an' fill their bellies with water just before dark, I reckon mebby they'll be easier to night herd. Come on: we ain't got none too much time."

During the afternoon small bunches of cattle, gleaned from the brush lands of the north and northeast, drifted slowly toward the big herd in the middle of the valley like soft iron toward a magnet. The fact that cattle are gregarious by nature was worth an extra dozen riders; and the quality of the grazing was such that there was slight temptation to stray from the herd. Bid put in the afternoon riding well beyond the spread-out cattle, loose-herding from a distance and not giving the animals a chance to feel under restraint. They were docile and contented, barring a few natural trouble-makers, and these were slowly weeded out and kept from mixing with the rest. When evening fell they would find themselves driven up to the corral and impounded.

At the close of the second day the great aggregation of placid cattle made a pleasing sight, and when night

fell they were compacted into a mass that was capable
of being controlled by four men, unless trouble arose.
To keep trouble at long range the riders left the herd
as soon as it had bedded down, and rode their rounds
well away from it, with ready rifles across the pommels
of their saddles.   For the last few days the weather had
been slightly threatening, but now cleared up and gave
promise of a long spell of good weather, greatly reducing
the chance of stampedes.   Well fed, well watered late
in the day, treated cunningly, the cattle bedded down
without protest or nervousness, and behaved during the
nights like so many four-footed angels.

Thursday morning saw Red Shea ride up to the
bunkhouse and stare at the closed door, trying to
convince himself that he heard snores coming from
behind it.   Among friends in that country etiquette did
not demand that a friend knock at a closed door when
he went visiting; but Red was a little doubtful as to his
rating.   He began to whistle loudly, dismounted, and
walked slowly toward the bench against the wall; and
suddenly found himself looking into the face of the
sleepy foreman.

Dave looked his relief.

"What you want, Red?   Yo're shore an early bird."

"Just had a run-in with Dangerfield, an' reckoned
Cottonwood was bad for my health," answered Red,
grinning.   "Need an extra hand?"

"I never figgered you'd let a man like Dangerfield run
you outa town," reproved Dave, now not nearly as
sleepy as he looked.

"No man can run me outa town," retorted Red,

bridling a little. He acted impatient and restless, as though he itched to be riding on again.

"But you just said Dangerfield had," replied Dave, puzzled.

"Didn't say that a-tall. I said I had a run-in with Dangerfield, an' figgered Cottonwood wasn't healthy for me."

"Shore; I heard you. Where's there any difference?"

"There's a lot of difference," answered Red. "Town ain't no place for any man that runs foul of Dangerfield."

Dave blinked, and scratched his head. Then he grinned.

"Then, accordin' to that, I better keep clear of town; is that what you come down to tell me?"

"Listen, Dave: I didn't tell you nothin' a-tall," said Red, uneasily. He scowled and shuffled a foot, his eyes on the pattern it was making in the dust. "Wish he'd keep his damn hoss som'ers else," he grumbled. "He's hangin' 'round the stables a lot too much."

Dave gripped a foolish idea that leaped, meteor-like, across the firmament of his mind.

"There's worse folks than square gamblers to be found hangin' 'round places," he said. "An' anyhow, a girl's got the right to pick for herself." He was watching his visitor closely.

Red's face paled, and then flushed. His jaw tightened, he quivered, and his eyes grew cold. About to retort to this statement, he swiftly changed his mind, and asked a question, instead.

"That the way you feel about it?" he demanded,

a certain measure of scorn reflecting itself on his countenance. "I didn't reckon you'd back down so easy." There was a sneer in his voice. "Well, Alice might do worse, at that." Again he seemed to be impatient, and a little anxious, but still he made no move to leave.

Dave was smiling thinly.

"Then you've changed yore mind about her, Red?" he asked. "I figgered you gave her good advice; that you *shore knowed* just what you was talkin' about, there in the house!"

"What you mean?" snapped Red, trying to read the calm eyes of the foreman, and betraying some anxiety lest he fail in it.

"Why, hangin' 'round town, like you do, you'd shore learn a lot about a man," answered Dave, easily. "Mebby you found out that he wasn't allus a square gambler."

A look of relief flashed across Red's face and he sighed gently.

"Far's I know, he plays square; but I just don't like him, that's all."

"How come you had a run-in with him?"

"I said I figgered mebby he wasn't payin' as much attention to his job as he oughta, seein' he spends so much time around the box-stall. We sorta had an argument about it, an' hard words was said. I got a feelin' that Cottonwood ain't right healthy for me." He hesitated a moment. "That's why I reckoned mebby you might have a job that wasn't filled."

To refuse Red a job would not be tactful; but

Dave had no intention of putting Red Shea with the cattle.

"To use yore own words, Red," he said, calmly, "I didn't reckon you'd back down so easy." He paused to let the words sink in, and then said: "Who's goin' to be on hand, in case Alice needs somebody to help her, sudden an' hard?"

"The old man's there, ain't he?"

"He ain't had the right kind of trainin', Red. It would be like puttin' a sheep on guard ag'in a pack of wolves. You know their ways, an' you got a slick gun-hand." He shook his head emphatically. "Red, if I needed a dozen men, an' needed 'em bad, I wouldn't take you away from them stables."

"Huh!" cogitated Red, shuffling the other foot in the dust. He slowly nodded, and pulled out a new gold watch. "Half-past eight," he muttered, and then grinned proudly to hide the real reason why he looked at the timepiece. "Lookit my new watch, Dave," he said, offering it to the foreman. "Won it by throwing six aces," he lied. "Don't reckon that'll ever happen to me ag'in."

"It shore is a mighty fine watch," admitted Dave, frankly admiring it. "An' I reckon you won't throw six aces ag'in in six years. I'll have to get Billy to figure out the chances ag'in it: he's handy with figgers." He reached into his pocket for his own silver timepiece. "While I got the chance I'll borrow the right time." He bent his head, and missed the black scowl that flashed across his visitor's face. "Great mavericks!" exclaimed the foreman. "Why, my old ticker says seven o'clock! Why, it just don't seem reasonable, Red! It ain't reasonable, neither. You made a big mistake when you set yore watch."

"That's the right time," retorted Red, reaching for his ornate timepiece. He was indignant, and showed it plainly, but his indignation was really caused by the thought that his scheme was beginning to look like a failure. "That old silver coffee-pot of yourn's got spring halt or somethin'."

"Just the same, it's tellin' the time we use here on the B—B long as I'm foreman," replied Dave. "Mebby there's a couple of wheels missin' in yourn, or some other little thing."

A voice sounded from within the building, and was remarkably like that of Billy.

"Half-past eight is shore right; don't you let him string you, Red."

Red laughed triumphantly, but there was something wrong with his triumph; and while he laughed, Dave Saunders looked toward the south, where the shadow of a post touched the corner of the corral. His interest in the time question was beginning to become more than casual, although at this moment he did not know why. He was quite certain that the sun had lost no wheels, and could be relied upon to tell time truthfully.

"Yore watch may be right, Red," he said, carelessly; "but this old silver coffee-pot of mine is the official time on the B—B."

The conversation did not seem to please Red. As a general thing no man likes to have his watch questioned, for most men have a foolish pride in the reputed infallibility of their timepieces. This watch was a beautiful English lever affair, easily worth two hundred dollars in that part of the country; and its authority had been questioned by a cheap silver watch of no standing. There had been entirely too much talk about the time of day, entirely too much. Red had hoped to mention, in passing and without arousing any particular interest in the question of time, that the hour was half-past eight; hoping only to make a slight dent in Dave's memory and establish an alibi for himself in case anything went wrong with a planned stage-coach hold-up. Instead of leaving a casual and unchallenged statement behind him, he would now leave an argument. The fact that Billy had called out an endorsement of the hour erroneously stated did not soothe his temper or add to his assurance. He had never been quite certain that he liked Billy; but there was no question about that now. Billy would bear watching. He took the gold watch from the foreman's hand, snapped it on the chain and slid it into a pocket. Inwardly he was raging, and some of the symptoms were apparent on the surface, and correctly read by Dave, although the cause of them was unknown.

"All right, Dave; mebby yo're right about me stickin' closer to home. I'm goin' there now, Dangerfield or no Dangerfield." His impatience was now plain to be seen, and Dave laid it to a laudable brotherly interest in the welfare of Alice Shea.

Red made his words good, truthfully anxious to get back to town; but he was cursing under his breath. Dangerfield was a smart man, but his plans were too stiff, too set; they did not possess that elasticity which would have let them allow for the unexpected. One little thing going wrong anywhere in them threw the whole action out of step. Because of this, Red had had his ride for nothing, and because Dave Saunders, like a fool, had to have a yearning for the true time. And what had made Billy stick in his oar, and why had he lied so eagerly? He would bear a lot of watching, that Billy of the B—B.

Red drew the rowels along the side of his horse and shot into Buffalo Pass; and when he emerged from it he drew rein to look sorrowfully and with grave perplexity along a faint path leading into the southeast, at the end of which he had been given an assignment. He cursed anew, with fervid sincerity. He dared not take that alluring path, no matter what Henry Dangerfield would have to say about it; and if Dangerfield was not a fool he would say nothing. Damn this stubborn, senseless loyalty to watches! What difference did it make in the cow country whether a watch was a few minutes fast or slow? Most men glanced at the sun and were satisfied. This thought electrified him: that would be the natural thing to do when a man checked up such a discrepancy in time, and he was sure that Dave was natural. Why was it that he could only see his mistakes after they had been made? All right: he told Dave that he was going back to town—and that was just what he was going to do, and the faster he went the better he would like it. But he wasn't looking ahead with any degree of pleasure to meeting Dangerfield, no matter how things turned out on the stage road. Suddenly a thought came to him and he looked quickly at his watch, allowing for that hour and a half. He could do it, and he would do it, and thereby have an excuse for Dangerfield.

Racing the horse along the Cottonwood trail, he entered and left the last gap opening to the east, dismounted at the edge of a steep-walled ravine, backed the horse to the very edge and then, shouting suddenly in the animal's ear, brought the quirt down with savage strength across the sensitive muzzle. The terrorized, pain-racked animal backed convulsively, scrambled at the passing edge and rolled and fell down the rocky wall. Red scrambled after, and when halfway down, drew his gun, aimed it carefully and fired. Then he climbed to the trail and ran along it toward town, racing on foot against time.

Back at the ranch the foreman had watched his caller fade into a speck, and then looked down at the old silver timepiece still lying on his palm. Then he sought corroboration from the shadow touching the corner of the corral. Still unsatisfied, and strangely worrying over such a small matter, he stepped from the door and backed off from the house, until he could see the sun over the roof. You could not fool Dave Saunders any hour and a half while the sun could be seen. Red had made a comical blunder when he had set the new watch; and then the foreman stopped in his tracks and looked inquiringly through the open door, on fire with a growing suspicion.

"Hey, Billy!" he called. "What's the matter with that locoed ticker of yourn? Come out here an' take a look at the sun!"

"Nothin's the matter with it!" roared Billy, who also had his suspicions, and a strong sense of loyalty, "an' I don't want no look at no sun." He snorted. "Shucks! Them new watches ain't allus worth anythin'. I claim a new watch has got to git saddle-broke."

"Some of 'em oughta get broke before they ever see a saddle!" growled Dave, leaning against the door-jamb and intently watching the careless Billy; but that worthy was innocently humming a tune and hunting for his brand-new plug of tobacco. He found the plug hidden under Joe's pillow, bit into it, and turned toward the door, wearing his poker face.

"Did you see where I found this plug?" he demanded, hoping to change the subject.

His foreman was looking steadily into his eyes, suspiciously, inquiringly, his thoughts far from the filching of plug tobacco; and he found that the eyes were as barren of information as was the hopelessly unintelligent poker face of his puncher.

"I'm wonderin' if there's any chance of forgettin' to wind this here watch to-night," said the foreman, very slowly and very plainly. He was thinking of Alice Shea, and how he might save her from pain.

"Now if that don't beat hell!" exclaimed Billy, thankful that he could let his expression express something. It now expressed a great and awed surprise. "That's what comes of two fools livin' so close together for so many years. I was thinkin' the very self-same thing!"

"I'm awful forgetful at times," said Dave, with a trace of sorrow and humility.

Billy sadly shook his head, and sighed.

"No more'n I am, Dave," he said. "Last time I looked at my watch it was half-past eight." He said it stubbornly, with emphasis.

Dave moved the hands of his own watch around until they registered the time last mentioned; and then, deliberately knocking his elbow against the door jamb, swore at his clumsiness. The watch dropped from his hand, and in his swift grab at it he managed to knock it with great force across the room and against the wall. Simulating rage because of this stupid clumsiness, he jumped on it with his heels and ground it into a hopeless wreck.

"If you ain't th' clumsiest jackass I ever saw!" marvelled Billy, restraining his admiration for such sacrifice. "It wouldn't look nowhere right if I had the same accident," he muttered. "Betcha I plumb forget to wind mine."

Dave smiled at him, enigmatically but knowingly.

"Billy, I'm scared you won't come to no good end."

"'Fraid yo're right, Dave," replied Billy, chuckling; "but there's one thing to be thankful for: shore as hell you'll be there with me." He craned his neck to see through the doorway. "Here comes them no-account wranglers. It's a hell of a ranch when it takes two men to wrangle in a little hoss herd like that."

In the kitchen, old Jim Hankins, so sleepy that he did not dare to trust to long-range vision, was also suspicious, and he plodded out to take a closer look at something near the granary; and the next morning, when that shadow had nearly reached the same position, he led Joe Hawkins aside to ask him confidentially the time of day.   Jim knew it from the shadow; but in case he had to testify under oath, he wanted acceptable corroboration.

CHAPTER XIII

MENDING FENCES

I N COTTONWOOD, Henry Dangerfield was standing outside the north window of a box-stall of
Shea's livery barn, rubbing the head of his horse
and paying no particular attention to the little house
in the rear; but he was keyed to anything that might
take place in it. Under the surface he was perturbed
by what Alice had said during their fencing of a few days
before, and he was very anxious to talk to her again.
In regard to Alice Shea he had a definite plan of action
which would end in possession of her, and he was so sure
of himself that the question of time did not enter to any
degree; but whatever affection there might be in him
for Alice was subordinated to the possible threat of
danger which he feared had lurked in her words.
While he waited for her to show herself, he heard
running steps in the barn, and he moved back to look
in through the door. Silhouetted against the light of
the street door was a hurrying, stumbling man; and a
surge of rage went through the gambler. He stepped
quickly into the building so as to stop the newcomer
inside it and out of sight of the little house.

"What do you mean?" he snapped, grasping Red's
arm and whirling its possessor into the dim light at one

side of the building. "Why are you *here?* Why aren't you on duty?"

"Hoss broke its leg an' I had to shoot it, an' then hoof it all the way back!" panted Red, who was very much out of breath. There was no pretense about that, no acting. The blood pounded in his temples and his breath rasped in his throat. He was trembling with fatigue.

Dangerfield silently admitted the truth of the symptoms, but was skeptical about the truth of their cause.

"I shouldn't have expected much more from a blundering fool like you!" he snapped, his eyes sending little shivers along Red's back. "You had a part to play. On it largely depended the safety of the others. Your stupid blundering may cost many lives. Where did all this happen, and when?"

Red told him between gulps for breath, adding that he had been so desperate to get back to town that he had left his trappings on the dead horse, intending to get a mount and return for them.

"What were you doing in that part of the country?" demanded Dangerfield, dangerously. "Didn't you remember what you were to do?"

Red nodded, setting himself to face any movement.

"Shore; but you told me to ask Dave Saunders for a job, didn't you?"

"I did; but I did not tell you to ask him *to-day!* *Why* did you ask him to-day?"

"Well, I wanted to leave a trail from the B—B straight to the ford," he lied. "It'd mebby take a little attention from us fellers in town."

"You damn fool!" snorted Dangerfield, holding down his rage. "You poor damn fool! All those B—B men are herding close together, and not one of them could leave the ranch without the others knowing of it. And knowing that not one of them had left the ranch this morning, they would mighty quickly explain that track to the ford as having been made by a visitor. You were the only visitor. You stupid damn fool!" He shoved his face to within a few inches of the other's. "Now, I want the truth: Why did you go to the B—B this morning?"

"I wanted to have an alibi," confessed Red, not revealing that it was his fear of Dangerfield framing him that had made him so eager to have proof of his innocence in this morning's work which so bothered them both. For Dangerfield knew how he opposed these visits to his sister; and when anybody blocked Dangerfield's road, accidents were due to happen. In a general way he was very near the truth, but he did not take into consideration Henry Dangerfield's more subtle and valuable methods. To have Red Shea caught in something that could be made grounds for a hanging was all right; but to use it for a hanging, directly and without squeezing out the last drop of possibility, would be to work and plan without a definite end, to waste energy and thought: Henry Dangerfield was far too efficient for that.

"You wanted to have an alibi!" sneered the gambler. "*You* wanted an alibi! What about the lives of the others, and the success of the play? What about the danger to all of us if the hold-up goes wrong? Suppose one of them is caught, and made to talk? What then? *Answer* me, you idiot!"

Red could not answer him. This very contingency had tortured him all the way to town. His throat was too dry, too constricted, to let him speak.

"Well," snapped Dangerfield, "that's something I shall have to take care of. If one of them is caught ——" He paused, and did not finish the thought. "I'll have more to say to you after I look out for this new danger. You stupid idiot! You senseless, stupid idiot!"

Stung to sudden anger, Red flared.

"I ain't no idiot, an' no man's goin' to call me one!"

Dangerfield's left hand rested on Red's right, while his own right hand had slipped under his long black coat.

"You *are* an idiot; and *I* say so!" he retorted. "Don't get any dangerous notions in your empty head, or you'll find yourself full of lead. *You* wanted to make an alibi! You do any more thinking for yourself, and I'll make something for you: a rough pine box!"

"Sh-h-h!" whispered Red, looking fearfully toward the rear door.

Dangerfield glanced out of the corner of his eye as he slightly turned his head, and the hand on Red's arm moved gently up and down, patting it.

"Too bad, Red; that was a good horse," he said, sympathetically. "You'd better take another and go after your saddle and other trappings before someone gets there ahead of you." As if suddenly aware of a third person, he turned and bowed slightly. "How do you do this bright morning, Miss Alice?"

"Very well, thank you; but what's the trouble?" Her eyes were on her brother. "What's the matter, Red?"

"Oh, nothin' much," answered Red, gloomily. "Lost my hoss, an' had to hoof it to town."

"How'd that happen?"

Red explained the accident graphically, adding a touch to increase the realism.

"Don't know how I ever got outa the saddle in time; might 'a' been killed."

Dangerfield nodded, bowed again to Alice, excused himself, and hastened away, eager to be ready to mend any break in his fences. Red watched him go, not knowing whether to be relieved or fearful. His hand rested a moment against his watch pocket, and the movement seemed to give him relief in one direction: his alibi on the B—B having been made useless, and really dangerous, he had stopped at Tom Buckner's store to ask the time, alleging that his new watch was grievously fast. Buckner had given him the right time, compared watches with him, and made a foolish joke about high-toned timepieces.

"What was Dangerfield doin' here, Alice?" he asked, looking closely at her.

"Minding his own business, Reddie," she retorted, and then relented. "He was petting his horse, as usual," she explained.

"I hope to God he don't switch from the hoss," he growled, and pushed past her toward the rear of the barn.

Alice followed him closely, her lips pressed tightly

together, but she did not speak until they had entered
the house and her brother reached up for a bottle on a
shelf. She watched him down a great swallow of
liquor and then spoke.

"Why are you so desperately worried about Henry
Dangerfield and myself?" she demanded, sharply.

"Because he's a gambler; that's why!" retorted
Red, putting back the bottle and facing her defiantly.

"I don't know what to make of you, you change
front so quickly," she replied, studying him.

"Dave Saunders might say the same thing about
another member of the Shea family," he retorted, with
apparent satisfaction.

She withheld her own retort, the name of Dave
Saunders unfolding a promising line of thought. She
was too worried about her brother's connections in
town to let her own injuries dominate her.

"Why don't you ask Dave for a job on the ranch,
and get out of Cottonwood?" she asked him, her eyes
lighting strangely.

Red laughed, a little bitterly.

"If I hadn't rode down to ask him for a job this
mornin' I wouldn't 'a' lost a good hoss. He won't
give me no job." A malicious grin wreathed his face.
"He said he wouldn't take yore brother away from yore
side while Dangerfield was pettin' his hoss twice a day."

Alice stamped her foot.

"Did Dave Saunders say that?" she demanded,
wrathfully.

"Not just them words; not nothin' about Dangerfield," admitted Red, still grinning. "He's worryin'

some, I reckon, about the town bein' so tough. He said somebody oughta stay near you that could take care of anythin' that busted loose. Dave thinks a heap about you, Al." He shook his head, the grin swiftly fading. "More than's good for him, I reckon, the way things seem to be goin'. You ain't got no sense, a-tall." He gripped her arm with cruel but thoughtless strength. "Lemme tell you somethin', Al: if you don't stop Dangerfield hangin' 'round here, *I* will, even if I have to shoot him. Put that under yore piller to dream on!" He strode quickly to and through the door without heeding her call, and hurried through the barn, eager to be found in Tom Buckner's store when the storm broke. His new saddle and riding equipment could wait, its possible loss being easily the lesser of two evils.

Alice leaned against the table, her voice dying in her throat, her hands pressed against her breast, her knees threatening to buckle. Where reason failed her, intuition came to her aid; a nameless, amorphous warning impelled her to take hold of herself and to act, to follow a blind impulse, to turn to the one man she was absolutely certain of. For a moment she had yielded to a sudden terror caused by the feel of impending danger to herself and to those whom she loved; but now she turned to action, and ran from the house.

Her horse welcomed her and pranced gently while she hurriedly threw on and fastened bridle and saddle; and once her weight settled on its back, the animal shot out through the big door, past the little stable, around back of the house, and skimmed across the face of the slope with hot eagerness and exulting strength. Alice was ignoring her father's oft-repeated warnings and inhibitions, careless of what danger might be afoot, urged to her purpose by her woman's intuition, and speeding on her mission like an arrow toward the gold.

Old Jim Hankins, listening closely, scurried from the kitchen and started for his granary, found that he could not make it without being seen, and scurried back again like a frightened rat for what cover the kitchen might afford. Behind his useful curtain he breathed with relief as the swiftly growing sounds reached and passed the bunkhouse and grew steadily lower toward the south. He ventured forth from his hiding place and peered from the window, seeing Alice Shea masterfully riding a mettled horse that had keenly missed its regular exercise and that showed little signs of the fifteen miles it had covered. Beyond the woman was the distant, grazing herd, with its slowly moving riders, and of these two shot toward the house, one steadily forging into the lead. The woman had slowed and gradually stopped, and old Jim cocked an eye at the kitchen door.

"I might stay behind the curtain an' fill my ears full," he muttered, "though I can hear purty good from the granary." He considered for a moment, and came to a decision. "They'll mebby come up here to ladidaw each other, an' go snoopin' 'round for a bite to eat," and once more he scurried for the granary, this time making it successfully.

He was right, for Alice and Dave met, exchanged

words, and side by side rode for the bunkhouse. Dave helped her from the saddle, led her into the kitchen for a drink of water and to satisfy her curiosity about ranch cooking, and then went with her around to the bench near the bunkhouse door.

She looked up from the bench at the grave man standing before her.

"Dave, did Red ask you for a job?"

"Shore did, Alice; asked for it at half-past eight this mornin'."

She stared at him unbelievingly.

"What time did you say?"

"Half-past eight; why?" asked Dave.

"David Saunders, at half-past eight this morning he was talking to me in the barn," she retorted, for a moment shunted off on a siding leading from the main line of her thought.

Dave smiled and shook his head. Half-past eight was the hour he intended to stick to, unless he found it safe and necessary to change it; and then he could lay it on his faithless and late-lamented watch. He felt that he would be doing her a great kindness to stick to that fictitious hour.

"Then Red's some boy for travellin'," he reflected with a vast respect. "I'd say, off-hand, that fifteen miles in nothin', flat, is shore movin' right along. Anyhow, it is for *this* country." He grinned masterfully. "How you come to figger you was talkin' to Red at half-past eight this mornin'?"

"Because I wanted to do some baking for dinner, and had so much work ahead of me that I tried to figure how

I could lay it out. How'd *you* know it was half-past eight when he was *here?*"

"He had a new watch that he was proud of, an' we sorta compared, which was a lot in *his* favour."

"Then he'd better get a new one, and so had you," she retorted, her eyes carelessly regarding the watch chain which dangled from a buttonhole of his vest. She pointed at it curiously, and Dave glanced down, and stifled a curse. There it hung for all the world to see, as though he did not have enough trouble on his hands without its increment. "Lose yours?" she asked.

"Busted it," answered Dave. "Dropped it, like a fool; an' then, like two fools, went an' stepped on it. You was askin' about Red askin' me for a job," he hurriedly said, driven back to a subject he had hoped to avoid. He nonchalantly tucked the loose end of the chain in a pocket.

"Dave, I'm going to ask a big favour of you," she hazarded, and then hesitated.

"You get that favour idear right outa yore head," said Dave, deciding that there was plenty of room for two on a bench which often held six. "Anythin' I can do for you ain't no favour; it's a—a favour to *me*. It's done already: what is it?"

"Give Red a job on this ranch, and keep him away from that town!"

Dave was game. He didn't hesitate.

"All right, Alice; though I shore hate to take him away from yore dad."

Alice smiled inscrutably.

"I want you to take him away from Henry Dangerfield, Dave."

Dave placed both hands on his knees, squirmed sidewise on the bench, and stared at her.

"Meanin'?" he inquired as casually as he could.

"Just that."

"Oh," he muttered, envisioning Henry Dangerfield's perfect attire and polished ways. "Reckon mebby Red is sorta nuisance, sometimes."

Alice arose to her full height of five feet three, and shed dignity like a cottonwood sheds seeds. Her eyes flashed and her face crimsoned, and then became curiously streaked with white. Dave was thoroughly familiar with certain storm signals, and blundered to his feet, wondering how he could change them to indicate pleasant weather. Before he could open his mouth, Alice was in the saddle, and her impatient horse had started for home, seemingly anxious to break all speed records for fifteen miles.

The foreman, feet spread, hands on hips, stared after her until it was too late to hope to overtake her; and with the start *that* horse had obtained, he knew that such an attempt would be hopeless. Besides, it was carrying sixty-five pounds less than his own.

He slammed his prized hat on the ground and swore. Of all the fools in Montana he was the prize fool. In less than five minutes he had complicated matters concerning a certain half-past eight; he had taken on a cow-hand whom he had determined should not, under any circumstances, be taken on; he had rendered null and void, by this promise, all old Jim's attempts remain hidden; he had offended Alice Shea; he had —— He swore with renewed vigour.

There was no echo to his words, the plain being flat and the hills too far away; but had there been an echo it would not have sounded before a frowsy old head cautiously appeared in the crack of the granary door. One swift glance around gave old Jim a vision of a hard-running horse bound for Cottonwood, already very small against the hills of the north. One hand under a sagging coat, Jim slipped from the granary to scout out the reason for the swearing, his arm tensed for a knife throw that had taken him out of trouble on more than one occasion. His other hand was behind his back, where an ancient cap-and-ball Remington lay across a shoulder-blade. Jim was hoping for peace, but fully prepared for war. He peered around the corner of the house and a puzzled expression slid to his face. Dave Saunders, foreman of the B—B, was staring in the direction of Cottonwood, and still swearing. Jim made certain that there was no one else in sight, and then wandered along the wall and sat down on the bench patiently waiting the course of events. There now being no need for masked batteries, he rested his gnarled hands on his knees, the knife in one of them and the cap-and-ball in the other. A grin spread over his face, and he started to whistle.

Dave whirled, and glared at him.

"Where'n hell did you come from, an' what'n hell you reckon yo're doin'?" he demanded, and his eyes remained fixed on the two most prominent things in the old prospector's make-up.

"Ca'm down, Dave; ca'm down," counselled the man on the bench. "Lookit where ye throwed yer hat; an' where's yer watch?"

Words failed, utterly and hopelessly failed. The foreman yanked the silver-plated chain from a swiftly torn buttonhole and threw it as far as he could. Kicking the sombrero in the opposite direction, he stamped over to the bench and dropped down on it.

"Red Shea's goin' to work for us," he blurted, passing a hand across his brow.

Old Jim spat copiously, shifted something over to the other cheek, and absent-mindedly touched the edge of the bowie knife against the nail of the other thumb.

"Things are pickin' up," he observed with great complacency, and the loud smack of his lips startled Dave.

"Pickin' up?" snapped the foreman, incredulously. "Goin' to smash, I'd say!" He glared at the old man, and his eyes took in the weapons so openly displayed. "Good Lord! You goin' *to*, or comin' *from*, a massacre?"

"You shouldn't 'a' swore like you did," reproved old Jim, moving his hands. They came out from under his coat, weaponless.

Dave gazed at the old man and his eyes softened. A smile crept to his face.

"Much obliged, Jim; but what you figger on doin', now that you can't hide yoreself no longer here on the ranch? Red'll spot you in the first hour."

"I'm goin' ter come right out in the open, with all my rattles buzzin'," grunted Jim, placidly. "Anybody steppin' on me will shore as hell get a hide full of somethin' he won't want." He scratched his nose thoughtfully. "Wonder what's the matter with them miners?" he muttered.

"What miners?" asked Dave, his thoughts elsewhere.

"*What* miners?" snorted Jim. "Why, them down in Cottonwood Gulch, a course. I can't get 'em started nohow. Reckon mebby you'll have ter do it yer ownself. An' what did ye do with yer watch, Dave?"

"Busted it," grunted the foreman.

"Total loss, *warn't* it?" inquired the old man, his face a mask.

Dave was jolted out of his absent-mindedness, and looked quickly at his companion.

"Plumb total an' complete," he admitted.

"An' to-tal *on*necessary," supplemented old Jim, arising and starting toward the kitchen, chuckling deep down in his throat.

"An' total unnecess——" Dave caught himself and looked curiously after the shuffling prospector, whose cracked voice was at that moment trying to sing a song intended to soothe the savage breast. The foreman abruptly arose, looking at the distant herd as he paused to recover his hat. Somehow he felt he would be safer, and much easier in spirit, if he was with the cows.

CHAPTER XIV

THE DEAL GOES ON

THE distant hilltop with its cluster of trees and patch of underbrush was not occupied. No keen-visioned sentry peered from the lacery of twigs and leaves. From it and below the twisting stage road lay like some tawny rope, thrown carelessly by a giant hand. Here it passed over the crest of a ridge, there it became lost in cut-bank passage or dry-wash; and at one place it dipped under the placid waters of Alder Fork, whose gravelly bottom and gentle depth made a pleasant ford.

Along the road came a dusty Concord, rocking gently on its comfort-making through-braces, and drawn by six horses whose waning energy now increased as the stage station came into sight. The stock-tender emerged from the rough stable with a relay team of six fine animals, and stopped it before the building. The stage rolled up and came to a stand, the guards hanging back to retain their freedom of action. The team un-hitched and the fresh one in its place, the stock-tender asked for a chew of tobacco as he reached up to place the reins in the driver's hands.

In a moment the stalwart vehicle rolled on again, the guards pressing it closely to escape the soaring dust, which reached the level of the faces a few yards behind them. Comfort, for them, rode either close to the stage or too far back from it. On the box sat the veteran driver, graduate master of his profession, caring little for any other occupation than this. Gold rushes meant little to him, for he loved the feel of the reins far more than that of the hickory of pick or ash of shovel. At his side was the messenger, custodian of the treasure, his person barren of keys to the pouches or to the sheet-iron treasure chest lying in the boot under his feet. Day and night he was to remain alert, snatching naps where experience told him that it was safe to sleep. To sleep on the box of a lurching coach reeling off its six and one half miles an hour, stops included, was an art he had acquired. Across his knees lay a shotgun; at his hand, strapped to the coach, was a rifle; while the weight of two Colts sagged their brass- and lead-studded belts. On rolled the Concord in its cloud of dust, with slap of leather and jingle of chains, its honest body gently squeaking as the strains shifted. Behind it came the four-man guard, armed like pirates.

A pile of rock swept into view, charged along at the side of the road, and raced rearward, shrinking rapidly. With its hurtling progress there came a subtle change. On the box the driver took a fresh grip and spread his stiffened legs as though to withstand a sudden shock; at his side the stolid messenger glanced at the rifle straps, felt each pendent holster, and slightly shifted the buck-shot weapon across his knees.

Within the coach nine passengers moved tell-tale hands instinctively over supposedly innocent portions of their clothing, and kept their fellows within the angle of their vision. On the top of the coach three serious passengers again regretted that they were not inside, giving more weight and importance to the sides of the coach than the thin wood warranted. The challenging prominence of their elevated positions rebuked their lack of modesty in seeking the limelight. They seemed to shrink from public scrutiny, although at Cottonwood they frankly had enjoyed it. Behind them, the guard was slowly shifting, spreading out in search of elbow room and for a safety not to be found in a compact mass. There came a sharp curve, and as the stage dropped back to all four wheels and the writhing blacksnake straightened and cracked, the pleasing glint of sun-kissed water lay across the road. Muscles tensed, lips tightened, eyes narrowed and became cold; the legs of the driver stiffened a little more and the line across his shoulder blades gently arched as though to find room for a sudden play of strength.

The pace remained unbroken as the stream came near; there sounded a sudden splashing, the curious noise of spokes and felloes sloshing through a foot of water, with the grating of gravel against iron tires vibrating through the coach. Myriads of drops of water separated the sunlight into its component colours, flashing iridescently as they curved through the air. Driver, messenger, passengers, and guards seemed couchant, set with hair-triggers; and then the stream and its sloping southern bank were past. Held breaths puffed softly or noisily, according to the nature of the man; lines grew fainter in relaxing faces, but still the attitudes were strained, the general atmosphere somewhat hushed. One of the more placid passengers, idly glancing at his watch, found the hour to be half-past eight. Back and yet back slipped the ford of ill-repute; ahead lay a dry-wash, curving through a swelling rise of ground. Into this ran the road, and from this wash the ford could be seen for the last time, intervening hills hiding it thereafter.

Knowing that at least one of their number should look forward to scan the tops of the high banks of the wash, every man in the guard itched to look behind him at that place of potential danger past, impelled not only by the prompting of his mind, but by some actual, although unnamed, physical sensation. All set to find danger at the ford, the threat of danger was thus localized and made subconsciously dominant. As the high banks passed rapidly behind them, more and more shutting off the view of the stream, the guards came to an unconsciously memorized place from where they could obtain their last sight of the ford; and as though they had been drilled, all four turned in their saddles as one man, and looked searchingly behind.

The study of books is a valuable thing; but the study of men, from living men, is more valuable. Whoever was the moving spirit of the outlawry besieging Cottonwood and its vicinity had studied men, and studied them well and understandingly, over a wide range of individuals. Before the guard, finding relief in a dangerless rear and relaxing from their tenseness, could turn forward again, a sharp command from the banks above sent their hands convulsively skyward; and they jerked around in their saddles to see six masked faces behind as many gun muzzles covering them and the coach, while down the bank on either side slid another masked man, hands outstretched toward the bridles of the leading horses. The brakes screamed, grinding sand; the coach rocked, shook back and forth slightly, and became motionless.

The messenger, his shotgun now off one knee, was like a leopard about to spring; but his startled gaze was focused on the top of the bank, where a black gun muzzle threatened death. He nodded, dully, and let the shotgun droop. Then it slid down his braced legs and stopped against his boots. Slowly, defiantly, and insultingly deliberate, his hands moved up past his belt, higher and yet higher, until they met and locked fingers on the top of his hat. The three passengers behind him seemed turned to stone, poignant anguish frozen on their countenances. The driver scowled, his whole attention on the team, his weight still resting on the brake although the need had ceased. Within the coach there came a sudden scrambling, querulous mutterings, and one hearty, man-like oath.

Down the banks slid masked men, two on each side. They worked with the precision of practice, and in less than a minute their victims were weaponless. The guards, afoot now, were lined up against the coach and from the open door issued a string of despondents to keep them company. The three prominent personages on the roof climbed slowly down and joined the victims on the ground.

The collection of personal treasures was disappoint-

ingly meagre, but the leader of the masked men seemed
to find mirth in this poverty. He passed slowly along
the line-up, his cunning fingers seemingly possessed of
the scent of a hound; miracles of materialization were
performed with graceful, modest nonchalance. His
hat filled, he placed it on the ground, caught a hat tossed
to him by one of his fellows, and filled that before he
reached the end of the line-up.

The treasure chest in the boot was being removed while
the passengers were yielding up dividends to daring.
The horses of the guards were led aside, one of them
being transformed into a pack animal for the bearing of
the chest, and then, taking the surrendered weapons
with them and driving the guards' horses before them,
the outlaws mounted and one by one scrambled
diagonally up the right-hand bank until all were up.
There came a sudden drumming of hoofs, and seven
masked men raced toward the maze of hills and ravines
to the west; the eighth sat alertly in his saddle, watching
the coach and the scurrying going on around it. Men
popped in one door and out of the other, to pop back
again, elbowing and colliding like tightly wound mech-
anisms lacking governors.

The driver glanced sympathetically at his messenger
companion, who had climbed apathetically back to his
seat and slumped down in it; and then, slightly chang-
ing his grip on the lines to ease his fingers, the driver
leaned over the end of the seat and looked back.
He spat with a frank and vast contempt.

"Like a lot o' cockroaches on a hot stove," he
grunted, and then let his blacksnake flick behind him.

As a frightened and agonized passenger right-about-faced in the air, the grinning wielder of the whip motioned with his thumb toward the open door of the coach.

"Git in thar, damn ye!" he bellowed. "*All* of ye! Reckon I want ter stay here all night?" He failed in the results he had hoped for, and tried another plan. "They'll be comin' back ag'in right soon: want to be here to answer questions?" He faced foward again, the coach shaking violently; when the shaking ceased he released the brake and sent his rested team on its way again without looking back to see if all were aboard.

The sullen, dejected coach-guard stood in a bunch at the bottom of the left-hand bank, watching the masked horseman on the bank across from them. This person waved gently, whirled his horse, and streaked along the bank parallel with the road; but he waved too soon. His eagerness to get away was his undoing, or perhaps the perforated handkerchief slipped and momentarily obscured his sight; but whatever the cause might be, his horse stepped into a narrow, deep and grass-covered gully and shot out from the bank, turning over completely before it struck the road. The rider, hurled from the saddle, struck the bank and rolled down it, to lie inertly at the bottom. He was pounced upon in savage eagerness, disarmed, unmasked, and shaken and cuffed to his feet, and started on his way to the relay station between the ford and the town.

Blundering had been allowed for; for Red Shea had been given the duty of watching the hold-up from the distant hill-top, to be ready to ride at top speed and carry the alarm if anything went wrong. He was not at his post. Two miles back on the road a group of armed and masked horsemen waited in the brush, received no warning from Red by the time set, and separated, each man to make his way back to town. Half an hour after they had departed, five men on foot plodded along the dusty road, one of them limping painfully. The road was open and they passed along it without challenge.

Cottonwood seethed at their approach and surged forth to meet them, shouting the identity of the prisoner whose face was well known to many. As it chanced, there were fully a score of miners in town, all armed and determined. From among them a leader arose, whose shouted words coalesced their score of individual chains of thought into one plan of action.

"To the gulch with him!" rang high the command. "This town's lousy with his friends!"

The miners swept forward, guns drawn, and surrounded the plodding five. They compacted, shoulder to shoulder, and clove through the uncertain crowd at a tangent which would lead them around the town, united into a force of unwavering strength; grim, determined, and exultant, a chip on each flannel-shirted shoulder, a glint in each cold eye. Here was organization, the organization of fighting men rendered desperate by a long chain of wrongs; here was death for him who asked for it. The crowd fell back, clamouring for a rope, for a rescue, for a trial, each demand lost in the general uproar.

A red-faced gambler leaped before the advancing phalanx, his putty-like hands aloft.

"Lynch him, here an' now!" he yelled, in his voice more fear than fierceness, for he had good reason to want that tongue stilled. He placed his hands protestingly on the leader of the guarding squad; and found himself spinning sidewise, a cold gun muzzle following his erratic progress.

"He'll get a trial in a miners' court, an' swing at daylight," shouted the leader. "That'll give him plenty of time to talk. Close up, boys, an' keep a-comin'!"

"Aye, give him time to talk!" came an exultant cry from the massed squad.

"He'll pan out amazin' rich!" came another, drowned by a gust of sardonic laughter. A bewhiskered giant, who put his trust unqualifiedly in the double-barrelled shotgun in his ham-like hands, loosed a bellow of laughter that caromed from the hills.

"An' he shore *will* talk; we've got our little ways!"

Cottonwood partisans, the morbidly curious, and the friends of the limping prisoner raggedly flanked the steadily tramping cohort, vociferously making known their thoughts; and in return received cold and threatening silence. Down the hill marched the crowd, leaving the town behind them; and then spread out a little to pass over a rough and rocky patch. For an instant the prisoner's head arose above those of his guards as he stepped on the top of a small boulder which lay squarely in his path. From behind came the spiteful, dry crack of a rifle; a spreading puff of gray-

white smoke swirled upward, torn by whispering air
currents, to weave up the side of a ramshackle building
on the edge of the town.   From the top of the boulder
the prisoner stepped far—into eternity, taking his
valuable knowledge with him.

For a moment, silence; then a roar of rage, and the
cohort convulsed, whirled, and charged back up the
slope, straight for that ramshackle shack.   There came
hot scurrying, like terriers hunting rats; but the rats
were hidden and all men were dumb.   Ominous silence!
Ominous prophecy of far-reaching power and inflexible
purpose!   Ominous warning to all the rats, that bun-
gling and capture meant death inflicted by the pack.
Dead men tell no tales; an axiom as true as it is old.
The message of the bodies along the road and the trails
was here emphasized beyond the doubts of men.
Dead men tell no tales.   Uneasy whispers filled the
town, uneasy ears listened, and believed.   And then
came a voice, ringing high above the noises of the dusty
street.   The whispers ceased and the crowd gave
curious ear to what this shouting voice might say, to
what Colonel Hutton, proprietor of the Argonaut and
a heavy loser by the despoliation of the treasure, would
make known.

"Gentlemen!" shouted the Colonel from his wide
doorway, his arms aloft toward heaven.   "Gentlemen!
Will you hear what I have to say?"

Ripples of movement ran through the crowd, and
voice after voice became silent as speech gave way to
hearing.   The miners had long since lost their grim
formation, each unit of it hurrying to partner or friends

in the gulch to tell the news, leaving the town to the townsmen.

"Gentlemen!" shouted the Colonel, his hands still upraised, and not conscious of the irony in that word. "It is time we sought protection against these thieves and murderers! It is time we took means to combat them as effectually as we know how! We want no miners' courts, no rule of terror; we want no Vigilantes, and the working out of private grudges in the name of mob law! We want no masked justice! But we must have justice and protection. If we fail to cope with this danger, if we do not do something here and now, then we shall have miners' courts, and Vigilantes! This county is unorganized, attached to courts too far away; but in this county the will of the majority is sovereign; its mandates, law! Let us then appoint officers of law, a trustworthy and capable sheriff, armed with our consent and backing as his authority. Will someone nominate a man for this office, here and now?"

The crowd cheered, and numerous names were shouted; but one name was shouted by many voices drowning out all others.

The Colonel smiled with pleasure.

"I take it that this town nominates Henry Dangerfield, by acclamation, to act as sheriff. All in favour of Henry Dangerfield, raise their right hands!" He paused while he counted. "All opposed, by the same sign. Ah! Mr. Dangerfield is elected." He turned and called into the room behind him.

Henry Dangerfield stepped to the door, smiling a little, and bowed to the crowd.

"I don't know just what authority I may have under these rather irregular proceedings," he said; "but I will accept the office. We have no court, and a court is very essential. We are so far from an organized county that it is a hardship to try our cases in any court having legal jurisdiction. What we need, if I gather the sense of this meeting, is a swift justice that will satisfy *us*, that will remove the cancer that threatens Cottonwood and the immediate region; prompt and heroic measures for our own protection against a situation which daily is growing more intolerable. No man's life is safe from one moment to the next. To make it safe, we are taking matters into our own hands, pending a petition to the Government to provide us with legal relief. These, I understand, are your wishes?"

The crowd roared that its wishes had been thoroughly understood and ably presented.

"Then," shouted Dangerfield, "I will nominate a man for judge who appears to have unusual qualifications. No doubt he is not familiar with court procedure and all the gilding of lilies usually found in legally established courts; he may not observe the niceties of legal red tape, or be able to pass with hidebound legal knowledge on the admissibility of evidence; but, gentlemen," he shouted, "he will know the value of the evidence submitted, the real, common-sense value of it; he will be ruled by common sense and a spirit of justice because he knows nothing to befog either common sense or justice! He is a man of wide knowledge, practical knowledge of men and conditions; his years and his success guarantee that. Therefore, I

take pleasure in nominating, as judge of Cottonwood
and the surrounding territory, to serve until proper
courts can be established—I take pleasure in nominating *your* friend and *my* friend: *Colonel Hutton!*"

Again the election was carried overwhelmingly,
cheers given with hearty good will, and the excited
crowd broke up to drink to the success of its appointees.
No incongruity seemed to be sensed in the appointing
of professional gamblers to these two offices. Both
were known as "square" men and believed to be
fearless: qualifications enough to satisfy this crowd.

While the celebration raged in the town, down in the
gulch ran whispering undercurrents of dissatisfaction,
an uneasy murmur among uneasy men. They had,
however, no reason to doubt the calibre of the new
judge and sheriff; and it appeared that their murmurs
and whispers and uneasiness were actuated by jealousy,
caused by Cottonwood's quick and successful move to
keep on top and to dominate the situation. Again
robbed of real and strongly actuating motives by this
quick back-firing, the miners' court again was post-
poned and was no more than a figment of hope in a few
uneasy minds.

Mindful that a prosecuting attorney, by some
oversight, had not been selected, the gulch quickly
remedied this by electing that valuable official from
among its own inhabitants; and the community waited
with eager interest for the new machinery of law and
order to get under way.

It prepared for its functioning with reassuring swiftness. Judge Hutton looked after the details of his

court, while Henry Dangerfield appointed six deputies, four of whom were named for him by an assembled crowd, a rough, boisterous, tumultuous crowd that roughly treated any man whose nominee did not suit the general mass. Such a man were lucky if he were only howled down and his hopeful voice drowned in the quick chorus of disapproval. The other two deputies, named by the sheriff, were George Tenner and Clem Lipscomb, names that greatly pleased the crowd. It gave its exuberant endorsement to the personnel of the sheriff's office, and forthwith disbanded to get hilariously drunk. The gulch swallowed the six names with a distinct effort, and seemed to find in them an astringent quality and bitter flavour; but the gulch, outnumbered, grumblingly subsided to await events, its long keen claws peacefully sheathed in their velvety pads; but its tail twitched a little, twitched nervously and spasmodically.

The dead robber's identity being known, there was great clamour for the rounding up of his associates; but when the facts were squarely faced it was found that he was a man who had kept to himself. He was known by name and sight to many, but his associates appeared to be casual acquaintances, casually met and casually ignored, as the mood had suited him, in the various saloons and gambling halls of the town. What his secret connections had been were known only to those who, naturally enough, would not speak.

The new sheriff and his deputies pushed their inquiries diligently, and diligently examined the scene of the last stage hold-up. They spent three days in unremitting search, rode a surprising number of miles, and returned downcast and disheartened. The stage-driver, being quizzed as to his observations, graphically described the hold-up, and dwelt with naïve humour on the actions of the passengers; he thought there were at least a dozen men, but when pressed to recall them to memory and to describe their horses, attire, voices, and characteristic gestures, he frankly admitted that he had been too frightened to keep the dozen separate and apart; he had observed them in the mass, and he finished his examination by carelessly remarking that he "reckoned he didn't see nothin' that nobody wanted to hear about." He did not confess that he knew he drove over the worst stage road in the country, that he wished to continue driving over it, and did not intend to make enemies by talking more than was good for him. It was not necessary for him to confess it, since every reasoning man knew it without being told.

In the next two days there were two shooting affrays in which the victor was apprehended, and the interest in how the new court would function pushed all other matters into the background. Its functioning, in re-sults, was a disappointment to many people, especially those residing in the gulch; but they had no real grounds for complaint, since the evidence, in both cases, conclusively showed that the prisoners had acted in self-defense. The jury had so found without leaving its box.

Then came a wanton murder, and the capture and trial of the murderer, who was a stranger to Cottonwood. The evidence was squarely in line with the popular demand, and the verdict of the jury was the same. He was found guilty at noon, and hanged the following morning. But even this show of prompt justice failed to quell the low growling in the gulch, where, it was rumoured, the statement was freely made that the prisoner, being a stranger and having no friends, had been too eagerly convicted. Thus matters stood, the miners waiting but quietly girding their loins. And as day followed day the robberies and murders continued throughout the countryside.

CHAPTER XV

TO-DAY: NOT YESTERDAY

WHEN the news of the stage hold-up came to Cottonwood, it found Red Shea in Buckner's store, where he took angry, but cautious, part in the excited discussion. As soon as he thought it wise to do so, he left the store and joined the crowds in the street, stopping in front of the Argonaut until the sheriff and judge had been appointed, and then he made his way to his father's stables. His father was not to be seen, which was not strange, considering the stirring events going on in the town. Passing down the aisle between the stalls, he chanced to see his sister's saddle where she had left it. It should have been resting on its part of the saddle rail. He picked it up and carried it where it belonged, noticing a darkening along the edges of the cinch, where usage had changed the colour of the brown-tanned leather. Turning from the rail, he looked in the little box-stall and scrutinized his sister's horse; and with a gentle oath he started for the dwelling in the rear.

Alice was finishing her housework, but ceased when the door opened, and looked curiously at her brother.

"What did Dad tell you about ridin'?" demanded Red with ill-concealed anxiety.

"What did he tell you about hanging around the saloons and gambling hells?" countered Alice swiftly.

"That's different; I'm a man," retorted Red, going back to his old defense. "Where'd you go?"

"I went to get you the job you couldn't get, and I got it," answered his sister. "You better pack up and start punching cattle with *honest* men."

Red stared at her.

"What you mean; *honest* men! You been down to see Dave with all this hell-raisin' goin' on?"

"You know what I mean," she retorted. "And how else could I get you the job?" She was watching him closely. "Tell me something, Red: why did Dave Saunders lie to me about the hour that you were down there?"

"What you mean?" snapped Red, flushing. "What you talkin' about?"

"Dave told me that you were talking to him at half-past eight this morning. At that hour you were right here, talking to me and Henry Dangerfield. Was Dave trying to cover you, to protect you against something?"

Red writhed. *He* had a sister, while Job only had boils.

"How do I know what Dave was doin'?" he growled. "Mebby his watch was wrong."

Alice nodded.

"Perhaps. Anyhow, he broke it. Funny that two watches would be wrong and yet both exactly an hour and a half fast. He told me he compared his with yours." She was clever enough to go no further, and perhaps follow the wrong lead, or expose her ignorance as to all else that might have happened. As it was she had hazarded a guess in going as far as she had.

"Look here, Al; I reckon we can let Dave alone. Dave's square, an' any play he makes is all right. He's plumb square."

"Square as a square gambler?" asked Alice.

"What's the matter with you? You loco? I'm tellin' you Dave's square all the way through!"

"I know it, and that's why I went down and got that job for you," retorted Alice, smiling. "It's about time you hung out with somebody that's honest, and had an honest job."

"I can't take it," growled Red, uneasily, looking at the floor. Job was lucky.

"You can't take it!" snapped his sister, her eyes sparking. "Why can't you take it? What's the reason you can't take it?" She waited a moment, but as he did not reply she went on again, with a rush: "*Why* can't you take it? Why didn't you take up his offer of driving beef steers to town? Why *didn't* you? Why is it that you hate to do anything that's honest and open? You told me more than once that you wanted a job with Dave. Look here: what was going to happen at half-past eight this morning?"

"How'd you expect me to know what's goin' to happen at half-past eight, mornin's?"

"I said *this* morning! What was it, Red?"

There came a voice from the stables, exultantly singing an Irish song, and brother and sister remained silent as their father crossed the little yard and stamped up the steps of the house. The door swung open, and Bob Shea, a look of joyous satisfaction on his honest face, let them have the latest news with a roar.

"The town's findin' itself at last!" he cried, swinging his hat over his head. "We've got a court, an' a sheriff, praise be to God! Murder an' robbery will come to an end! When the news came of the stage robbery this mornin' it broke the camel's back. When the hullabaloo quieted down, honest men took things in their own hands. Colonel Hutton will make a good judge, an' our friend Dangerfield will clean up this cursed country like a new broom." He corrected himself quickly. "Not that I have in mind the old sayin' about new brooms."

"Was the stage robbed again?" asked Alice in a voice strangely tense, her eyes on her brother.

"To the queen's taste, Al; but they got one of them." And the liveryman went on to tell of that phase of the morning's activities with great gusto, painfully in detail, and not realizing that he was talking to unheeding ears. Finishing, he waited expectantly for some sign of intelligent listening and enthusiasm, and his face fell slowly as it did not come. From disappointment he progressed to vexation, and was about to leave the house with a show of temper when his daughter's voice stopped him.

"At what time was the stage robbed, Dad?"

"Time?" he snapped. "Time! What has time to do with it? That's the woman of it! I tell her about a stage robbery an' the capture of one of the robbers an' his death; I tell her about the election, the turnin' point in the history of the town she lives in: an' damned if she don't want to know the hour!"

"Please, Dad: I have good reasons for asking. At what time was the stage robbed?" Her strained posture, her look of anxiety pacified him enough to make him heed her request, although he still regarded her with suspicion.

"What time was it? I didn't look at my watch when it happened, not knowin' it was goin' to happen, or when it did happen," he growled; "but it ain't hard to figger it out. If the stage was on time, it reached Alder Fork right clost to half-past eight; an' the dry-wash is just beyant the ford. There: now you know the time: an' much good I'm hopin' it does you!" The door slammed behind him and he stamped to the stables, muttering at every step.

Alice was looking at her brother, hardly knowing that her father had gone. Fear, scorn, contempt fought savagely within her and were mirrored on her face. Red stood rigid, staring at the floor, the colour on his face matching that of his hair.

Alice, too full of surging and clashing thoughts to give utterance to any one of them, seated herself and looked up.

"Well?" she asked, calmly, believing her brother to be a robber.

She would never know what her silence had accomplished, what her forebearance had worked. Red, caught in a rush of gratitude for being spared, was swept into something else; into something that no amount of arguments or persuasion could have accomplished.

He sighed, and leaned against the wall.

"Al, I can't work for Dave," he said, simply.

She sat erect and her eyes snapped.

"I'm glad you said it for yourself. Did Dave know?"

"Not nothin' that had a name; but he shore reckoned there was a stink somewhere. Reckon it was because I was yore brother. His watch said seven o'clock. He told you half-past eight?"

"He did; an' he stuck to it when he knew that I knew it was a lie." Her lips trembled a little. "Dave! Dave! What a man you are!"

"I'm glad yo're comin' to yore senses!" snapped her brother, leaning forward in his intensity.

"Oh, Red, I never lost them; never, not for one minute; but a woman——"

Red broke the punishing silence.

"An' Dangerfield made sheriff! God A'mighty!"

"You might choose other words for your swearing," chided Alice. She looked fearfully into her brother's eyes. "What *is* Dangerfield, Red? Tell me about him, *all* about him!"

"Dangerfield's a gambler; now he's sheriff, but *still gamblin'*. The quicker you marry Dave Saunders the better it'll be for all of us. Marry him to-morrow, Al!"

"A woman doesn't marry until she's asked."

"You'll be asked. I'm goin' down to see Dave."

She was on her feet like a flash, and for two minutes she held the floor, Red dazed by the wordy avalanche he unwittingly had brought down upon himself. He pacified her by giving his earnest assurance that he would not even remotely permit himself to play at match-making, and he meant every word that he said. To make certain that the storm would not turn back over its track, he steered the conversation into a channel which he felt would take care of that.

"Wonder why Dave let Clem Lipscomb ride him like he did, out in front here? Clem was tellin' me about it, an' laughin' fit to bust." His frown increased. "Clem's shore goin' to make trouble for Dave one of these days. There's somethin' cussed funny about them two."

Alice did not reply. She dropped to the chair again, and sat quietly regarding the wall. After a moment Red continued.

"Dave's sorta easy-goin'," he said, somewhat reluctantly. "Clem's due to prod him a lot. With the gulch simmerin', things in town goin' like they are, an' Dave stayin' quiet on the ranch, I reckon hell's fixin' to bust loose right soon." He glanced at her appraisingly. "Why don't you pack up, an' go down to visit Aunt Jennie? I'm near sick worryin' about you, Al." He paused a moment. "I can't leave town while yo're here."

"You want me to run away, so that you can run away?" she asked. "Huh! Seems to me you should save your worrying for yourself. Looks to me like you're sitting over a pretty hot fire."

Red gestured hopelessly, but said nothing.

"When are you going to raid the B—B, brother?" Alice asked with sugary sweetness.

Red jumped, and frowned.

"What you mean?" he snapped, angrily; but there was a suggestion of fear in his voice.

"Just that." Alice laughed bitterly. "I'm beginning to put things together. When are you and that Clem going to raid the ranch?"

"I ain't goin' to raid it a-tall! Think I'm a fool?"

"I sure do. What made you change your mind?"

"You better mind yore own business!"

"I believe I am. Rather hard to steal from a man who was getting ready to swear that you were with him on his ranch at half-past eight, isn't it? *Isn't* it, Red?"

"I got a notion to go to work for Dave," replied her brother, a sudden resolution pushing up a plan from the boiling mess of Fate's cauldron. The thought seemed to lead to tremendous possibilities; but it turned his face a shade paler. Whatever way he turned he could see only desperate hazard, the grisly face of Death.

Alice was staring at him in amazement, anger deepening her colour. Her brother a thief, a desperado, to go to work for Dave?

"You got a—notion—to work for Dave Saunders?" she demanded, incredulously. On her feet now, she moved slowly toward him, holding his startled gaze. "You got a notion—to work for—Dave Saunders?" she repeated almost in a whisper. Unutterable scorn and contempt blazed in her eyes. "After I asked Dave to give you a job, and got his consent against his better judgment! After I—oh, you traitor! You *traitor!*" She raised clenched fists to his face, quivering with rage, her own face livid now and working with fury.

Red grasped her wrists and held her at arms' length,

amazed by this sudden transition. He licked his lips, and gulped, searching for words, thrown totally off his mental balance, his budding scheme for the helping of Dave Saunders rendered chaotic and eluding the words which would have explained it.

"When you ask him for that job," panted Alice, wrestling to get free, "you tell him that I said not to give it to you! *Do you hear?* You tell him that *I* said not to give it to you! That I said he is free from his promise! *Traitor! Traitor! Traitor!* Let loose of me, and get out! I never want to see you again! Never! *Never!*"

"Listen, Al; *listen*, will you? I ain't goin'to ——"

"Get out! *Get out!* Don't talk to me, don't ever talk to me again! Get out! *Ge' out!*" She tore loose from his grasp, and in a fury of rage hammered him blindly, wherever her drumming fists could find a mark.

No man, least of all Red Shea, could stand up under that Berserker cyclone, and he fell back, guarding his face, and stumbled to the door, through it; and, whirling on the steps, leaped across the yard in three bounds, his ears ringing with the screamed maledictions hurtling after him. To his relief, he found that his father had left the stables, and had not heard this tempest. As Red stepped through the wide front door he bumped into Henry Dangerfield, bounced aside and crouched, hand on gun.

"What the hell you doin' *here?*" he snapped, showing his teeth like a mad wolf.

Dangerfield looked at him curiously, and found a new

lesson in human nature. The sheriff smiled gently, shook his head as he glanced down at the poised hand over the gun butt, and ignored the question.

"Red, I'm giving you just one more chance," he said, evenly. "The next time you blunder will be your last. Go find Clem: he wants to see you."

"I'm makin' my next blunder here an' now!" grated Red, every nerve tingling. "Clem can go to hell, an' you can go with him! Cram *that* down yore throat!"

Dangerfield smiled inscrutably, and hummed something in a low, rich voice. It was Chopin's Funeral March, but entirely lost on Red, whose knowledge of music was limited to the ballads sung in the dance halls. The sheriff, knowing that he stood face to face with death and that he could not hope to draw the coat-tail weapon his hand touched, or the heavier gun in the shoulder holster before Red's open holster would unleash its deadly tenant, fell back on his knowledge of men. He bowed slightly, turned on his heel, and sauntered down the street, humming louder, and then set his course at an angle that would carry him to and around the corner of the last shack on the other side of the street.

Red, quivering, still crouched, his hand still above the grips of his gun, his feet seemingly glued to the earth, slowly turned his body from the knees upward and stared after the debonair gambler. One more word, the turning of the sheriff into the stable, the slightest hint of opposition, would have sent Henry Dangerfield to join those silent ones lying in Boot Hill. The delicate push needed to made Red shoot had not been given; to shoot a man in the back was something to give most men pause. Red watched the sheriff until the latter bore off at that slight angle; and then sprang to action with desperate speed. Let Henry Dangerfield get out of his sight, or in the sight of some creature who would read and act on a subtle signal, and Boot Hill would be enriched by a member of the Shea family. Leaping into the stable, Red raced to a box-stall, urged the horse from it to the saddle rack, and saddled up with a speed he never before had attained. Vaulting into the saddle he shot from the rear door and in a moment was racing along the side of the hill, the horse following its own tracks of but a few hours before.

Alice hurried to a rear window and peered out, catching her breath at sight of her brother sitting her saddle and riding her horse at its top speed. As she looked she saw a puff of dust spring up behind the straining animal; another spurted at the left, and still another in front. The reports of a rifle came to her, and she pressed both hands against her breast, and then slid slowly to the floor.

Horsemen thundered down the main street and dashed through the outskirts of the town, heading like living arrows for a rectangular notch against the western sky, through which the trail to the B—B crossed the towering granite ridge. On that trail, rapidly growing smaller, a single horseman now bucked the slope leading up to the notch; behind him the pursuers were dropping down the opposite grassy slope at reckless speed; while from the edge of the hill overlooking this drama in horseflesh a spiteful rifle cracked in vain. Its besetting sin, while the range had been a practical one, had been over-eagerness.

Dave Saunders and Billy, of the B—B, rode side by side along a narrowing of the trail leading northeastward from the valley, where the steep rock walls crowded them together until their knees almost touched. They rode in silence, each busy with his thoughts concerning the strategic value of this narrow defile, each studying it hopefully. These two understood one another remarkably well for men who were so reticent in each other's company. It seemed almost as if they could read each other's thoughts.

Dave came to a conclusion, and gently shook his head: this defile was worthless as a defensive position unless he had several times his present number of men. A moment later Billy, also coming to a conclusion, gently shook his head, and then simultaneously both sat a little more erect in their saddles as the distant sound of a rifle was heard.

Ahead of them the narrow pass widened half its present width, where a short space gave room for three horses to move abreast. Without a word both riders pushed on rapidly, and each pulled over to his own side of the trail, where each was somewhat sheltered by a rocky shoulder of the steep wall. A muffled drumming grew louder on the trail before them, the clipping, metallic sounds of shod hoofs taking on a constantly growing ringing tone. Billy glanced sidewise at his foreman, and copied his foreman's gentle movement. It might be a bad time to have a Colt stick ever so slightly in a holster.

Over a rise of the trail a hat pushed into sight, then the face of the wearer and the head of a horse, growing in size and detail with great swiftness. Again a rifle cracked, much louder now, and the slobbering scream of the glancing bullet high over their heads made their eyes squint a trifle through narrowed lids. On the face of the racing horseman there came a look of relief and swiftly growing hope. He leaned far forward in the saddle, and raised a hand palm out, although he did not need to. They nodded to him and he shot between them, fought to check the racing horse which pain and terror still urged onward.

Over the rise in the trail two more hats, faces, and horses pushed up in sight, the riders knee to knee. Swiftly they sought to stop, amazement on their eager, vindictive faces at sight of those threatening horsemen, also knee to knee, who completely filled the narrow way and held rifles halfway to their shoulders. Billy, of the B—B, had been blessed with a hard reputation; Dave Saunders fooled few men by his easy-going ways. It was as though the walls had bulged out and blocked the trail, for granite barred the way.

Thirty steps from the B—B men the two pursuers stopped and for a moment there was a silent measuring of strength. Clem Lipscomb spoke first, his sneer trembling on quivering lips like the sneer of a jackal.

"Well?" he snarled, venomously, and pushed slightly in the lead.

"Far 'nuff!" snapped Dave, not intending that cover

should thus be afforded Clem's companion for the masking of a draw.

"It is?" sneered Clem, still moving.

"Stop!" snapped Billy.

Clem smiled, but he stopped.

"Some high-handed, blockin' trails, ain't you?" he asked.

"No trail's blocked that can be opened," countered Dave, paying strict attention to one man while he answered the other. "Some trails are blocked easy." He heard Billy's throaty growl, and laughed with genuine pleasure. "Since when are coyotes crowdin' the ridges?"

Clem laughed sneeringly.

"Meanin' that you are a pair o' loboes?"

"Meanin' mebby we hanker for coyote pelts," said Billy, generous with his information. "We been expectin' you for quite some time now. Looked for you 'most every night. Ain't lost yore guts, have you?"

"You reckon I could find any up here?" asked Clem, looking insolently at the foreman.

"Reckon mebby there'll be some to find," countered Dave. "Billy," he said out of the corner of his mouth, "keep 'em covered. Up with yore paws, Clem; an' *you*, too!"

Two pairs of hands slowly went upward, grudging each fraction of an inch. Dave dismounted, placed his rifle against the wall, and with his right hand resting on a Colt, walked slowly forward. He disarmed Clem and then showed the same courtesy to his companion. Carrying the captured weapons toward Billy, he picked up his own rifle and, stopping a few yards behind his ranch-mate, added it and his own Colts to the little pile.

Clem was watching curiously, with some disquietude, and showed his teeth as the foreman turned and started toward him.

"I told you I'd beat you within an inch of yore life every time I met you," said Dave, shedding his coat and vest. "Get off'n yore cayuse."

Clem obeyed with alacrity, anxious to be on his feet and facing forward before the foreman got too close. He laughed mirthlessly.

"This is shore funny, you fightin' for *that* yaller dog!"

"There's worse things than yaller dogs," replied Dave, starting on the second sleeve. "Red ain't yaller, he ain't no dog, an' he ain't in this a-tall. I made you a promise, an' I'm goin' through with it. Besides, we claim this as part of our range."

Billy found no fault with the fight, but to his last day he persisted in his claim that the opportunity was half wasted, since there was material enough for a second fight, and it had been overlooked. Dave would not take a gun and let him extend the courtesy of the B—B to Clem's companion. While the foreman lifted his beaten adversary and threw him across the saddle, lashing him there with a few deft turns of Clem's own rope, Billy had throbbed in anticipation. It grew when the battered foreman led the horse into the widening of the trail, turned it around, and led it back again. It flared high when Dave motioned to the other man to ride forward; but it flopped suddenly when the horseman turned his animal and rode slowly back to the side of the other horse and its unconscious burden.

"Git!" said Dave, the word sounding a little hashed because of his split lip.

"Hey!" expostulated Billy. "*I* ain't done nothin', Dave!"

"You ain't goin' to," said the foreman. "Don't make me talk no more'n I has to."

Billy sighed, his gaze riveted regretfully on the slowly moving back of the man who led Clem's horse and who was trying to keep the protruding ends of its burden from scraping along the rocky wall. By the time this horseman was going down the far side of the rise, the foreman, attired as he had been before the fight, climbed to his saddle, turned and led the way in silence toward the ranch. Billy sighed again, turned his own horse, and plodded after the boss of the B—B, his look of disappointment gradually giving place to an insistent grin. It had been a beautiful fight, a fight to satisfy the most critical; and he wondered where Dave had ever learned to handle himself like that. The grin became entirely incapable of expressing his emotions and he threw back his head and bounced laughter through the widening chasm and over the waiting hills.

They dismounted before the bunkhouse and saw Red Shea sitting on the bench. There was a bloody groove in one cheek, just below the ear, but it was not more than skin deep. His sister's horse stood dejectedly, head down and panting, a few feet away; and the furrow along its hip was not deep enough to give cause for worry to any one but the horse. Dave walked over to the animal, scrutinized the wound, and then removed the light saddle. Billy stepped inside the house and came out with a can of ointment. In a few minutes they both turned and walked slowly toward the bench.

"If you swapped yore new saddle for *that*," said Billy, grinning, "you shore got stuck." At Dave's significant look Billy rolled a cigarette and then sauntered past the kitchen and on to the fenced-in spring for a cool drink. He remained there, busy with cogitations that furrowed his brow. Old Jim Hankins slyly shoved his head out of the granary door but, at Billy's gesture, frowned indignantly and drew back into his habitation.

Dave was looking down contemplatively at the man on the bench, and spoke first.

"I'm payin' fifty a month, with grub, of course," he said. "You'd be doin' better if you traded in cattle. My offer still stands."

Red touched the groove in his cheek, and shook his head.

"That'll come later," he said, looking frankly in the foreman's inscrutable eyes. "First thing I want to say is this: Alice lets you outa yore promise. She even went so far as to tell me to tell you *not* to hire me. Scrambled all over me like a wild-cat an' didn't give me time to explain." He grinned proudly although somewhat ruefully. "She can fight like hell. Most all the Sheas could. The old man looks peaceable, but it ain't very deep."

"I promised when I knowed I shouldn't," said Dave,

seating himself on the edge of the bench. "A feller can't allus help hisself."

"Don't blame you for promisin', an' I don't blame you for bein' sorry that you did promise," replied Red, crossing his legs. "I was figgerin' on rustlin' yore cattle."

Dave nodded, his eyes on the light saddle lying on the ground.

"By yoreself?" he asked.

"No."

"That why Alice sent me word not to hire you?"

"Part of it. She don't think very much of her brother."

"Neither do I, yet."

Red also gazed at the saddle, and re-crossed his legs.

"Can't say I'm blamin' you; I don't think a hell of a lot of him, myself." He produced a tobacco sack, but failed in his search for papers. He took the thin sheaf that Dave handed him, and carefully made himself a smoke. "Reckon I lost my papers on the way here. Feller bounces a lot sometimes. I was in a hurry."

"Reckon so," said Dave, supplying a match.

The cigarette going strong, Red shifted a little and looked calmly into the foreman's eyes.

"I want a job with you ridin' nights," he said.

"Clem send you?"

"That *would* 'a' been a good scheme, now, wouldn't it? Shootin' at me an' chasin' me like he was mad." Red grinned, and shook his head. "No, he didn't send me; but he was one of the reasons for me comin'.

There wasn't no God-bless-you pinned on my coat-tail. No, nobody sent me *this* time."

"You owe me a watch," said Dave, accusingly.

"If I wasn't aimin' to work for you I'd get you a watch so quick it'd make you laugh," replied Red. "I owe you more'n a watch. Turn me loose nights an' mebby I can pay some of it."

Dave chewed thoughtfully on the end of a match, considering.

"Ridin' nights ain't no Sunday school," he observed.

"Never went to Sunday school," said Red. "I'm figgerin' I ain't got long to live, an' I'm aimin' to cash in with my head an' tail up. You ain't the only man I owe."

Dave removed the match from his mouth and looked curiously at the healed scar running diagonally down his caller's forehead. The match went back again, head first, and he yanked it out, spitting noisily.

"Knife?" he asked, carelessly.

"Bullet," grunted Red. "Had a ruckus in town."

"You know I shouldn't hire you," said Dave, gravely.

"*That* was yesterday; *this* is to-day. I'll shore earn that fifty, an' keep, if I has any luck." Red sat up suddenly, very straight, and swore under his breath. "Dave, you dassn't hire me: I forgot somethin'. I know too much, an' they'll figger I'm tellin'. There's forty men fixin' to raid this ranch to get me an' shut my mouth. If they don't find me here they'll mebby figger I didn't say nothin'. Lend me a fresh hoss."

"Aimin' to tell?" asked Dave, reaching for another match.

"Not a word," answered Red, now on his feet.

"The job's yourn," said the foreman. "Yo're ridin' nights, all over the range. Come inside an' write a letter."

Red stared.

"Write a letter?" he repeated, incredulously. "Who to?"

"Yes. In it you say that you ain't goin' to talk as long as yo're let alone; but yo're leavin' a writin' that'll talk after yo're dead. You also will say that yo're turned honest, an' are workin' for me."

Red considered a moment.

"But if I tell you who to send it to, you'll know what you ain't supposed to know," he objected. "I might just as well talk."

Dave regarded him gravely.

"You leave the guessin' to me, Red. I know who to get it to."

"But that'll only make 'em think I told you!"

Dave shook his head impatiently and motioned toward the door.

"I ain't no blunderin' jackass; don't you reckon I got any brains a-tall?"

Red moved reluctantly forward and the house swallowed him. In a few minutes he came out and handed the foreman a sealed envelope with no address on it. Dave walked over to the light saddle, threw it on Alice's horse and cinched it. Then he fastened the letter to the pommel and led the animal past the end of the building. A resounding slap sent the horse off at an indignant gallop, but it soon settled down to a trot, and headed along the trail leading to its feedbox and stall and much gentler treatment.

Red watched the animal for a few minutes, and slowly turned.

"Dave," he said, thoughtfully, "they're discountin' you in town. More'n that: they ain't even thinkin' about you to call for discountin'. Seems to me you know a hell of a lot for a man that sticks close to this ranch." He hesitated, and glanced at the receding horse. "But suppose they ain't watchin' the trail?"

Dave stopped, without turning. To his mind came the picture of Henry Dangerfield and Alice Shea, sitting on the steps of the little house. They seemed to be very well acquainted. What would be more natural than for Alice, if she found the letter tied to the pommel of her saddle, to discuss it with the gambler? But he was pretty certain that the letter would not remain tied to the saddle for her to see.

"All right; suppose they ain't?" he asked, trying to keep the signs of jealousy out of his voice. "They'll get the information, anyhow." He strode on toward the harness shed to find a saddle for the new rider.

"What you mean?" asked Red, slowly following. He received no answer, but he suddenly slapped his thigh and whistled. He was sincerely glad that it was to-day and not yesterday. "Easy-goin' Dave," he grunted. "Easy-goin' *hell!* Me, I'm a plain an' honest cow-puncher from now on, *an' damn glad of it!*"

A horse roped and saddled, Dave watched his new

puncher ride toward the herd to become familiar with certain things connected with it, and to pay his respects to the riders; and then the foreman walked swiftly toward the granary, motioning Billy to join him. They leaned against the granary wall close to a crack in it, their faces toward the distant hills in the north, where it was possible for a man, if he were armed with a spy-glass, to see distinctly all that went on around the B—B buildings, with the exception of the short distance between the granary door and the kitchen, this stretch being well masked by a corral palisade.

Inside the building old Jim answered to his name and sidled close to the crack. He listened to what his foreman had to tell him and found no pleasure in it.

"But what'll Hank think?" he growled, as though Hank were not dead.

"Never mind what Hank'll think," replied Dave. "There's bigger things than that to think of. Anyhow, I can't figger Red knifin' a man in his sleep. You told me you wasn't plumb shore."

"But that funny scar, runnin' up an' down?" protested Jim.

"If he had his head bent far down, he could get one like that; an' anyhow, we'll find out all about that in the course of time," replied Dave. "Just now I'm tellin' you to hold yore hand. I'll be goin' to the gulch with you some night soon, to talk to them fools that you can't set straight. We'll be tampin' some holes for a big blast, an' we don't want no miss-fires. In the kind of blastin' we're aimin' to do a shot can't be fired over. You let Hank rest for awhile, an' keep on with the scoutin'. There's a couple things more we got to know."

"All right," came the reluctant reply. "You've treated me too well fer me ter hold out agin ye, Dave; but it ain't treatin' Hank right, just the same."

Dave swore and frowned.

"Don't you reckon Hank would rather have the whole damn gang than just a couple of 'em? We got a mighty ticklish game on our hands, an' our only chance of winnin' it is not to let nobody know that we're even thinkin' about 'em. I tell you that Red has changed sides, for he ain't no fool, an' he ain't bad clean through. You let him alone; at least till after we've made our play." He scowled at the distant hills, lying green and fair under the sun. "If they suspect what's in our minds their first play will be to wipe us out."

Billy grunted and shifted his holster.

"It'd cost 'em a lot, but they can do it if they're willin' to pay the price," he growled.

"They won't have nothin' to say about whether they're willin' to pay the price," replied Dave. "They'll get their orders, an' they'll pay. Now, remember, Jim. Hands off Red Shea."

Jim's hesitant and surly reply was a promise, and the two punchers pushed from the wall to go to the bunk-house, satisfied that the old man would keep his word.

CHAPTER XVI

"A MAN'S A MAN——"

BY THE time Red Shea had left the herd the afternoon was spent, and great clouds were banking on the western horizon, an ominous threat. As he rode toward the ranch-house the frown on his face grew deeper, for those gathering clouds whispered facts to him that were not known to any other man on the ranch. He was not so much burning with loyalty for the B—B, although he would be loyal enough, as burning for revenge on Dangerfield and the men who pursued him so hotly earlier in the day. He had no illusions on that score, for he knew that Dave and Billy unquestionably had saved his life. During the last five miles of that hard chase his sister's horse had tired rapidly, having already covered thirty miles at a good pace when he had saddled it. When he had reached the top of the watershed of the B—B valley his pursuers had gained amazingly. It would have been only a matter of a few minutes before they would have forced him to abandon the horse and to hole up on the defensive, to make a losing fight. Back of them, strung out along the trail, had been other riders who would have joined Clem and his companion and made short work of the fugitive.

218

He pulled up at the little horse corral and in a few minutes turned toward the bunkhouse, his saddle on his shoulder, his scabbarded rifle see-sawing in his right hand. Dumping the saddle against the wall where the kitchen joined the bunkhouse, he stood the rifle up and raised his eyes to look into those of the new B——B cook, who was leaning carelessly in the kitchen door.

Red was surprised, but frankly exchanged looks with the old prospector, and grinned with pleasure.

"Well, I'll be cussed! Been here all the time, Jim?" he asked, incredulously.

"Since the night pore Hank was murdered," answered Jim, his eyes beady and his gaze unwavering. "Where'd you reckon I was?"

"Me?" inquired Red, leaning against the wall. Whether from design or not, his knee was touching the rifle; although if it were by design, his choice was a poor one. A thigh gun is much quicker. "Why, everybody reckoned you took to the hills." Something seemed to strike him humorously, for he laughed suddenly. "Good for you, Jim, you wise old fox! Good for you! You've got 'em all guessin', from soda to hock. Good for you!" He sobered quickly. "Don't you let Sheriff Dangerfield know where you are! You lay mighty low, Old-Timer."

Jim stiffened, his jaw sagging in amazement.

"Sheriff Dangerfield!" he snorted. "What you mean?"

The question surprised Red, and then he remembered that he had been so occupied with matters concerning himself that he had not told any one on the ranch anything about the latest news of Cottonwood. He was about to answer old Jim when he saw the foreman pass the end of the building, and he motioned to the latter, waiting until he could tell both of them at once.

"Forgot to tell you, Dave," he said, "that Cottonwood's elected Dangerfield sheriff; an' Colonel Hutton, judge. Reckon I was too busy thinkin' about other things."

Round oaths escaped from the foreman and the old prospector, and they exchanged looks while they listened to the news about the stage robbery and the town's quick back-firing. The foreman did not change expression when Red casually mentioned the hour of the hold-up; but over old Jim's face there flashed a keen and knowing look, to fade out before it was noticed by his intent companions.

"Why should I look out fer the new sheriff?" demanded the old prospector, harking back to Red's well-meant warning. "I ain't done nothin' fer to look out fer nobody; but there's folks as should be a-lookin' out fer me!"

"Jim, I ain't a-goin' to tell you why, because I don't want to hurt yore feelin's," answered Red. "You just take it as gospel, lay low, an' keep yore eyes skinned. There ain't nobody knows yo're here; an' yo're shore wanted."

"I can guess, damn 'em," replied the new cook, anger darkening his seamed face. "They want me fer murderin' Hank Simpson. D'ye hear? Fer murderin' my old pardner of forty years: Hank Simpson!"

His leathery face convulsed and he paid no attention to the foreman's warning scowl. "Sheriff or no sheriff; jedge or no jedge, I'll get them as done it! They would 'a' done a lot better to 'a' got us both."

"Hope you do," replied Red; "but you shore won't if Dangerfield or his deppities get holt of you." He saw the old man's fixed stare, and flushed a trifle as he touched the scar on his forehead.

"Knife?" asked Jim, tensely, knowing it to be a bullet scar.

"Bullet; an' it shore was lucky for me that I slipped," answered Red, smiling grimly. "Ever since then I've been strong in favour of dumpin' *all* the garbage into the street." He chuckled softly. "Don't make no difference, now, where they dump it, far's I'm concerned."

Old Jim, a queer expression on his face, turned swiftly and ducked into the kitchen, his nose warning him of burning food. Red swung about, picked up the saddle and rifle, and frowned at the growing storm.

"You'll need all yore men with the herd to-night," he said, stating an obvious fact without much emphasis. There was no treachery against former friends in such a banal remark; yet, somehow, Dave paid it more attention than he might have done.

The foreman sighed and nodded, leading the way around the end of the kitchen and toward the bunkhouse door, where Billy had swiftly stepped from a window in the end wall of the house. The accepted convictions of three men had been roughly shaken, and Billy's had been shaken the most. Through the grimy window he had studied every change of expression on the recruit's face during the entire conversation, the dirty glass and the dim interior of the house masking his scrutiny. Right now Billy was pretty well convinced that Red Shea had borne no part in the raid on Jim's camp and the killing of old Hank Simpson; but, still, the evidence was strong the other way.

Supper quickly bolted, the inmates of the bunkhouse ran to the corral for fresh mounts, all eyes glancing at the ominous west, where great masses of inky vapour were spreading out to hide the sky and the already low and coppery sun. The men with the loosely held herd would be anxiously awaiting reinforcement, ready to work all night despite their all-day trick. The bunkhouse squad pushed rapidly up the valley toward the cattle, Red turning off toward the eastern hills and their thick brush after a terse argument with the foreman.

Dave had sought to add the recruit to the men with the herd, but Red's argument had won out, not so much because of its value as an argument, although it was good enough, as because of the intensity of his voice. Seven men could not stop that herd if the storm broke. They would be no better than six, for ten times the outfit of the B—B would prove unavailing. The coming storm was going to be an epoch marker for this part of the Territory.

Red pushed up the slope of the first high hill and paused on the crest to look back and down upon the range. The great herd, spread out comfortably, was peacefully grazing, although showing signs of nervousness; the encircling riders were going around it slowly, here and there gently turning back some animal ambitious to gain entire freedom in the brush and brakes, and he noticed that most of the outfit were on the southeastern front, where a man's life would hang on a thread if the cattle broke after dark. His roving gaze settled on the northern hills, where a gash in the skyline marked the narrow chasm which had given him safety earlier in the day. Clem and his companion had turned back, Clem unable to sit the saddle and unfit for hard riding for the remainder of the day, if Billy's account of the fight had been true; but what of the others, the half dozen that had been strung out behind them; what of the scattered gang farther east that had waited long for the signal?

A dull grayness leaped across hill and valley, hastening the coming of night; the air hushed, and every bush stood motionless, not a leaf stirring. A sigh passed over the earth. There came a lightness of the atmosphere that speeded up his breathing; and then there came a salaaming of the brush, like the hollow of some great racing billow of the sea. A leafy wave ran swiftly up and along the hillsides as brush and trees bent before the wind that shrieked over and through them.

Red unfastened the oiled slicker from behind the saddle and slipped it on. He buttoned the collar up close under his chin and jammed his wide hat tightly on his head. Below him the loosely herded cattle ran this way and that, in short, sharp dashes, ending in circles that turned their rumps to the whistling wind, which had become surprisingly cold. The darkness increased swiftly until the herd, the riders, and the valley were vague and indistinct; and then, with the final blackness, there came a partial vacuum which seemed almost to suck the breath from his lungs. He gasped and spurred the horse; and reeled in the saddle under the smashing blow of the wind, closing his eyes to save them from the cutting sting of whirling dust and sand. Bending his head he rode slowly forward, across the crest of the hill and down its eastern slope. Then came the deluge, hissing and smashing, and thunder crashed among the hills. He gave up all thought of trying to guide the horse, content to keep the storm at his back; for the animal had turned tail to the gale and was drifting before it blindly through the resounding blackness. There came a sharp rattle of hail, cruelly punishing; but it did not last, and the rain seemed to sweep past in waves.

In the hollow across the hill east of Red a compact group of six men were also drifting before the storm, which automatically had called them to a rendezvous: drifting and cursing monotonously. Clem Lipscomb had not reached the appointed place by the time they had been compelled to leave it under the irresistible power of the gale; and these men did not know that he could not join them, and that his messenger to them was drifting helplessly, a mile away, lost and powerless to get them the word. They drifted on, wondering how long the tremendous wind and rain would continue. News of Red Shea's defection had reached them just before they had left for the rendezvous, but of more recent events they had no knowledge. The water pouring down the ravine now reached above the fetlocks of their mounts, and the miserable animals angled slightly up the hill and then went on as before; but some of them angled to the right, while others chose the left, and the conformation of the slopes drove them steadily apart.

West of them Red Shea had blundered against an overhanging wall of rock, which provided fair shelter from the raging elements. His horse needed no checking, stopping of its own accord to huddle close against the wall. Red, miserable and chilled, and wet where the slicker had been treacherous, blew out a great breath gustily, rearranged the folds of the raincoat and sat huddled in the saddle, waiting for the storm to ease up. He wondered if he could find wood, and if it would burn after he found it; and his hand searched a water-soaked pocket and came out again phosphorescent and smelling of mushy match heads. A new note came out of the night, the steady uproar of rain and wind becoming gusty, with interludes of gentleness; the sheets of rain grew fitful, and ceased. The gusts steadily lost power, while the interludes lengthened; and suddenly all sounds ceased but the dripping of trees and the musical trickling of uncounted rivulets pouring down the rocky slopes. Overhead the stars blazed in a clear sky, and comparative warmth stole across the hills.

Far to the south of Red, two mounted squads of three men each still pursued their straggling ways, having blundered against no sheltering overhangs to check them. Miserably they watched the storm subside, and became slowly talkative as it died out.

Leaderless and split, both squads argued the matter that had brought them from their various hangouts; and each group came to a different conclusion. The easternmost, farther from the B—B and nearer to their homes, considering that their plans had failed, were glad to return to warmth and lights and stimulating liquor; but the other three, much nearer the fringes of the ranch, and certain that the cattle had stampeded in the right direction, were sullenly determined to wrest some reward for the miseries of the night. A glance at the blazing stars sent them right about face and they rode slowly westward, bearing a little north, their ears tensed for sounds of cattle.

They had guessed right in regard to the herd in the open valley. With the first great flare of the lightning and the roaring crash of thunder the drifting and spreading herd had come to sudden, purposeful activity. Almost as one animal they bolted southward through the pelting downpour, scorning such things as desperately riding men and flaring guns fired across their heaving front. The sting of the short volley of hail was not needed to madden them, but it had done its part. The tremble of their passing died out and left six horsemen riding aimlessly after them in the general direction they had taken. The stampede was thorough and complete.

Two horsemen almost collided, both veering off sharply and reaching under their slickers.

"Who're you?" demanded the foreman, shouting to be heard above the uproar of the storm.

"It's me, Dave," yelled Billy, in quick relief.

They drew together as they drifted south, shouting questions about the others. Such information, in view of the tragic things which can happen during a stampede, was vital to them.

"We'll try to find the rest," shouted Dave. "We can't do nothin' with the cattle till daylight." He tried to turn his horse and felt Billy's knee against his own. "They was too heavy with grass an' water to run far; an' cows ain't naturally runnin' animals. Come dawn, we'll find 'em in the first fringe of brush."

To their left came a brief wink of light, like a firefly in a fog. The sound of the shot was lost. Dave answered the signal and soon became conscious of a thickening in the blackness at his left.

"Cripes!" shouted a boyish voice, that one word so full of meaning that it fully summed up the speaker's feelings about the night's happenings. "Cripes!" he repeated.

"Come on, Bid; we got three more to look for," called the foreman, anxiety in his voice. He hated the thought of what the dawn might show. After a brief consultation they rode southeast, taking turns in discharging their Colts. In ten minutes an answering flash winked on their right, and a moment later Frank Hitchcock and Joe Hawkins joined them.

"Are we all here?" yelled Frank. "Mark? Mark was on the west end the last time I saw him."

"Spread out," ordered Dave, and the short line rode westward, shooting at intervals. Twenty minutes later there came two winking flashes from the northwest end of the line, and they wheeled to ride toward them. Bid had found the missing puncher, limping doggedly for the ranch-houses ten miles away. Mark was cursing steadily and monotonously, soaked to the skin, and his clothing grimed with ingrained mud. It was a miracle that he had not been killed when his horse went down with a broken leg, but unaccountably the tail of the herd had split and swept past on each side of both horse and rider. Mark was too full of wrath and disgust to write down anything on the credit side of the happenings of the night. He ached in every bone of his body, he was almost numb with the cold, his tobacco was soggy and his matches useless, and he had looked forward to ten miles of limping in the storm. Dave's horse made no protest at carrying double, and after a vain search for the wounded horse for the purpose of putting it out of its misery, they turned toward the bunkhouse, fighting their animals to make them face the gale.

They found the kitchen fire out and old Jim missing, which was not out of the ordinary, for Jim's very local reputation was that of a tom-cat: out all night and asleep most of the day. The horses turned into the larger corral, which was attached to the winter stables, the men streamed into the house and in short order a great fire blazed in the bunkhouse stove, while cold beans were getting hot beside the coffee pot. The wet clothes off, a brisk rub, and the grateful feel of dry garments brightened their outlook; and after they had shared the beans and half a pan of cold biscuits, and each had several cups of coffee, they sat back to smoke and to wait for dawn. But full stomachs and the warmth of the room sent them, one by one, to take a few winks in their bunks.

Dave pretended to be cheerful, but he was greatly worried. If there were any cattle-thieves within striking distance of the ranch, this would be an opportunity they could not afford to overlook. He leaned back in a chair, his head against the wall, and waited for signs of the storm letting up. If it moderated before dawn, so a man could find his way about and really be able to do something, he would slip off by himself and let the rest follow at daybreak. They all deserved a rest and a hot breakfast after what they had been through. Dave had not been in the chair very long before the storm ceased, and he tip-toed toward the door. As his hand rested on the heavy latch he heard the rustle of dry straw and glanced over his shoulder to see Billy cautiously leaving his bunk.

"Turn in!" whispered the foreman fiercely, waving the puncher back.

"All right," whispered Billy in reply, but still moving in the same direction. He felt for his boots, and shoved the toe of one foot into the soft leather top. "Ugh!" he grunted. "It's wet as—wet."

"Turn in!" repeated Dave in a louder whisper, shaking his head emphatically.

"*All* right," reiterated Billy, drawing on the second boot. "I'm turnin' in—my saddle." A quick stir in the bunk across from him made him chuckle. Frank Hitchcock, his eyes still closed, and his arm over the side of the bunk, was feeling cautiously for *his* boots. Frank, by a great effort of will, opened his eyes, blinked, in the light of the low-turned lamp, and looked at the grinning Billy, who was now slinging a gun belt around his waist.

"What time is it?" demanded Frank in a loud whisper, which was shattered in continuity by a prodigious yawn. He was now sitting up and lining up his leg toward a soggy boot.

"Time to turn over an' go back to sleep," said Dave, grinning despite himself. He was very proud of his uncomplaining outfit.

"What you an' Billy up to?" inquired Frank with apparent suspicion.

"Takin' a look at the weather," answered the foreman. "After you boys get yore breakfast you can poke cattle outa the brush. It'll be nice, wet, swearin' work, you Siwash."

Frank craned his neck to get a better view of the speaker, noticed the guns at the foreman's waist and the rifle in his hand, and then he squinted at the swiftly moving Billy, and snorted.

"Ain't aimin' to *shoot* it, are you?" he asked very sarcastically. He threw his own belt around him and took an old hat from a peg, whimsically scratching his initials on the dust of the brim. "Go ahead, you two; I want to see how it's done." He swore softly and moved faster. "I got a hoss to shoot, an' the quicker I do it, the better I'll feel."

They slipped out, finding that the rain had stopped, and soon saddled three horses which had kept dry in the stable, and which did not take at all kindly to the cold and wet saddles that were slammed on their backs. Walking the animals for a short distance to avoid waking their tired bunkmates, they pushed into a lope and headed for the vicinity where lay a tortured horse, this act of mercy to be the first thing done.

While they were riding across the open range, Red Shea was pushing more deviously toward that same range. He did not believe that there would be any attempt made to run off cattle on such a night, seeing that it not only had been one to discourage most men, but also that the cattle could not be controlled while in such a panic; but he knew what the first storm was to mean, and as long as he knew the direction of the one which had just passed, he thought it no harm to do a little scouting. Very likely Clem's gang would be hovering around at daybreak, ready to take advantage of the scattered herd.

In Red's circumstances a less courageous man would not have offered himself for night riding; and to ride through the brush, almost every yard of it offering cover to a rifleman, can be classed as foolhardy. It is strange how far an angry and honest reaction will carry a man: twenty-four hours before Red Shea was an undesirable member of society, furtive and secretive in his operations; now he was a bulwark of society, risking his life with every step of his horse; and he knew that to be seen by any of the men he suspected were in that part of the hills would mean that he would be shot on sight. Nevertheless, Red rode steadily onward, twisting and turning as he followed the straightest course he could in the direction of the stampeded cattle. For a month of danger he was to receive, in material things, the munificent sum of fifty dollars and his keep; fifty dollars, when he had made ten times that amount in a single night, and with much less risk. Dave and Billy had saved his life, for he had been forced to flee without a rifle, and a Colt in the circumstances in which he would have found himself would have been practically worthless. He had small faith in the effect of the note that Dave had fastened to the pommel of Alice's saddle; and besides, it would take some time for this saving news to reach all hostile ears.

Dawn was spreading over the earth and blotting out the light of the stars when Red pulled up his horse to listen. He thought he could hear a bunch of moving cattle, and while he waited there came to him the faint rattle of horns on horns. From the steadily increasing sounds he knew that these cattle were running, and after the running they had done during the storm, this was suspicious. He was at the edge of a rocky ravine, its rim fringed with scraggly brush. Behind him a feeding gully sloped upward to the top of this little watershed and there still remained time enough for him to get out of sight; but no thought of escape was in his mind. His sister would not listen to his words, and neither would she have believed them if she had listened; perhaps his deeds would reach her, and be convincing. He rode back a few paces, dismounted, and, taking his borrowed rifle from its water-soaked scabbard, tried the action and then crept forward again.

The sounds of the advancing cattle now rumbled between the rock walls, the clacking of the horns sharp and continuous. The first few animals passed him on a tired trot, their heads low down and swinging; four or five yards behind these came a group of a dozen, bunched tightly together; and now the restrained shouts of the herders arose above the general racket. Red hugged the west wall of the gully, crouching with his Colt ready, the rifle abandoned for this close work. The three riders passed him, urging on the cattle; and then he arose and stepped from the wall.

"Hands up!" he shouted, his gun slanting down.

The three rustlers reacted to the shout instantly and in an unsuspected manner, acting as though they had been well drilled against just such a contingency. Each man abruptly tumbled off his horse on the far side and fired under its neck, sheltered by the body and the forelegs of the animal. Red staggered sidewise, his gun spurting; he saw one man crumple from a bullet that skinned the leg of his horse. Red stumbled and went down, his left shoulder smashed, steadied himself against threatening nausea, and sent his last shot through the head of a rising rustler, the only target that offered. Red was pulling cartridges from his belt when his jaw sagged and he collapsed, his glazing eyes sightless, all his problems solved.

He did not hear the drumming of galloping hoofs coming through the ravine from the west in response to the shooting; neither did he see his remaining enemies frantically mount and flee, all thought of cattle banished from their minds. He did not see Dave Saunders racing at the head of his racing companions, or hear their profane exclamations.

Dave drew rein while his friends shot past him and leaped from the saddle to examine his new puncher; Billy was arising from the dead rustler as Dave struck the saddle again, and together they raced on to overtake Frank Hitchcock.

"Dead," said Dave, his face tense with anger. He glanced at his companion to hear his report.

"Dead," said Billy, his jaw tightening. "Glad he got one of 'em."

Hitchcock nodded grimly and said nothing.

They passed the tired cattle huddled in an enlargement of the ravine, and gave them only a glance. Ahead of them lay the trail of two men, plain in the streaks of soil washed down by the storm, lost on the clean stretches of rock. Going up the slope of the highest part of the hills, they looked down into the little valley beyond, and saw no trace of the men they were pursuing. Spreading out as much as the nature of the ground permitted, they raced on, alert for an ambush, but risking one at every jump. Had the fleeing rustlers known that only half of the B—B outfit was pursuing them there unquestionably would have been an ambush; but not knowing this, they preferred to flee and to hide.

The little pasture-like valley was close at hand when the pursuing three drew rein to hunt for tracks, which they now had lost. They went on again slowly, came to the edge of the valley and saw two tired horses cropping the bunch grass. The three exchanged glances, surprised and disappointed, but greatly enlightened by the horses in a certain matter concerning identity. It spoke ill for the community when cattle-thieves and murderers would so impudently leave tell-tale signs to be found.

"Jumped from their saddles on to clean rock," grunted Dave. "Let the cayuses go, figgerin' they'd head for grass." He looked about him at the great masses of rock, in chaotic piles, which ran westward to the top of the divide, where a score of men on foot might safely hide if they were armed. Away from the few more open ravines horses were useless. He turned and led his companions back the way they had come, closely scrutinizing both sides of the trail. Two hours later, bruised, tired, footsore, and glum from defeat, the three returned to their horses: and found them gone. It was an old trick, but it had worked.

When the pressure of their feelings had been relieved, Dave eased his weight to the other sore foot, and returned to a better brand of English.

"That's what comes of thinkin' of one thing an' nothin' else," he growled. "All right: they've got our cayuses an' saddles, an' they've cleared out; an' it's a safe bet that they took their own animals with 'em. Come on, we've got to make the best of it," and, limping, he led the way toward the ranch.

Reaching the scene of the tragedy the three disgruntled punchers searched for and found the two straying horses which had belonged to Red and the dead rustler. In a few minutes they hobbled on again, leading the animals with their limp burdens roped to the saddles. Debouching from the widening ravine and coming to the edge of the brush, they waved their hats at the three men on the plain, who immediately raced toward them.

After listening to the explanations, Bid Carter took the reins of the two animals and led them toward the bunkhouse, to return as soon as he could with mounts for the three tired men afoot.

"Better lemme trail them skunks," suggested Joe Hawkins. "When Bid comes back with the hosses you can foller me. Mebby we can catch 'em."

Dave shook his head and glanced up at the sky.

"Too late, now; an' mebby that'd please 'em too much, leavin' the cattle unguarded," he replied. "I got another idea, anyhow. The wind's swingin' 'round to the south, an' some of that storm might come back ag'in. If it does, I'll shore give 'em somethin' to think about." He looked over the great, circling stretch of brush. "Poke out as many as you can, Joe; soon's we get cayuses under us we'll turn to an' help."

Bid's return with the horses let the combing of the brush begin in earnest, and it continued all day, the cattle straggling back to the open range in ones and twos and bunches until most of the herd was grazing in plain sight again. In the afternoon the air became cold and a drizzle set in that put a penalty on inactivity; and while the punchers of the B—B regarded it sullenly, their foreman seemed to welcome it. Dave and Billy remained with the herd while their friends went to the bunkhouse for an early and hurried supper; then, relieved from duty by the return of the others, the foreman and his companion rode northward to satisfy ravenous appetites, and to put into effect a plan that Dave had evolved. The drizzle had increased with the coming of twilight and the chill of the air seemed to cut to the bone. If it continued there would be few riders abroad after darkness fell.

CHAPTER XVII

"A LAMP AMID THE DARKNESS"

T HE early darkness found a cold and soggy range. In the larger corral what horses could not squeeze into the restricted space of the stable huddled miserably together for warmth. These days the horse corrals of the B—B were kept well filled with the best riding stock of the ranch, and the enforced grain feeding of so many animals made the foreman grateful for the wagonloads of corn he had had delivered before the present troubles were dreamed of.

Old Jim carried in the last of the supper, grumbling over the number of meals he had to cook, but grumbling only for effect.

"Ridin' in ag'in to-night?" asked the foreman, ignoring the growled protests.

"Yeah," grunted Jim, pouring himself a hot cup of coffee. Forgetting to hold the lid on the pot, it fell into the cup, followed by a rush of coffee and grounds. He yelped and cursed, leaping from the bench to dance around the room. "Why didn't you have the damned thing fixed?" he demanded. "It's *allus* comin' off!"

"It didn't come off until after you busted the hinge loose," replied Dave, placidly eating. He smiled at the old man's outraged stare, swallowed, and continued pleasantly: "If you had the brains of a tick you'd 'a' fixed it first thing."

"I would, would I?" shouted the indignant cook, whose burns were not nearly as bad as he pretended. "Fix it, huh?" he snorted with a vast sarcasm. "S'pose I got solder in my pockets? S'pose I got a iron, an' everythin'?"

"You know where the hammer is, an' the nails, an' the harness rivets," retorted Dave, still placid. "With them three things I can fix 'most everythin' on the ranch; everythin' but yore fool head. Yo're shore helpless. Did you get wet last night?"

"Harness rivets!" snorted Jim, seating himself and fishing the top of the pot out of his generous cup. It had been remarked, *sotto voce*, by the members of the outfit, that there was only one cup larger than the others among the ranch dishes; and that old Jim seized upon it instantly and made it his own. "Harness rivets," he repeated in disdain; "an' raw-hide," he added as an after thought. "Huh! The whole cow world revolves around them two things. Take away harness rivets an' raw-hide—an' the ranch business would go plumb to hell! An' them ranches that has a little balin' wire, besides, reckon they got the world by the tail." He skimmed off a layer of floating grounds, gave it up as a bad job and, too indolent to strain the fluid through a cloth, drank it, grounds and all, catching a fair quantity of the latter against his tongue to serve as chewing material. He looked at the foreman, the last question returning to his mind. "No; I didn't get wet a-tall."

"Do you reckon you can hang out where I tell you to to-night, until we come?" asked Dave.

"Without bein' seen?" qualified Billy, this remark of his making the only break in his steady feeding.

"Could *you?*" asked Jim, studying the foreman.

Dave nodded, and reached for another helping of beans.

"Then *I* kin," said Jim, peering into his empty cup, and sighing.

Ten minutes later the lights went out and the door closed behind three vague figures in the darkness. Jim was one of them and he went toward the smaller corral and not much later was riding a wise old cow-horse toward the hills, contemptuous of the beaten trail leading to town. His tongue was busy digging coffee grounds from between his few remaining teeth, and he spat them out noisily. Biting into a great plug of tobacco, he put it back into a pocket, snuggled down into his loose-fitting clothes, and heaved a sigh of satisfaction, careless of drizzle or cold.

Back near the bunkhouse a curiously shaped blot moved through the darkness, following the trail to Cottonwood. Closer inspection would have shown any watcher that this moving blot was animated by four horses, on two of which the riders, Dave and Billy, sat erect, which was not at all out of the ordinary; behind these two men came the second pair of horses, whose riders lay cross-wise on the saddle-pads, each end drooping down the sides of the animals like long grain sacks partly filled. Like old Jim, these cared nothing for the drizzle or for the cold, but because of a vastly different reason. Old Jim was alive, while these two were not. Dave was taking Cottonwood's dead back to Cottonwood.

There was more than one way to Cottonwood, although the regular trail was the shortest and the best. Having ridden over the country about the ranch for the past half-dozen years, Dave was familiar with it. Halfway between the bunkhouse and the narrow gorge where he and Billy had given timely aid to Red Shea, the foreman forsook the trail and struck straight north to cross the high divide a full mile west of the established route. Grimly and silently, save for the sounds of the horses' hoofs, the two B—B men pushed through the dripping night, squirming in their clothes to warm their skins.

From the gulch itself the town was a scattered collection of blurred lights, each huge and brilliant through the moisture clinging to the eyewinkers of two slowly riding men who now breasted the long slope below the home of Bob and Alice Shea. Behind them, gradually getting lower and farther away, winked the smoky fires of prospectors, here and there one blazing high from prodigal spending of fuel to dispel the misery of the night. Above them and now straight ahead shone one light which should have brought a feeling of pleasure to the cold riders, starting them to talking and, perhaps, to chuckle; instead, it seemed to increase their misery, to deepen their frowns, to make them reluctant instead of eager. Like a beacon it shone out over the gulch, visible as far as its weak flame could hope for, providing food for envious comment and optimistic thought.

Alice Shea had many friends down there along the creek, most of them secretly hopeful although, paradoxically, knowing that they had no chance; and she did not know the name of one of them.

The horseman clambered up the last few yards of the slope and seemed anxious to gain the friendly shelter and the hiding darkness of the stable before dismounting, to get those two following horses out of the range of light from an opening door. They crossed the small yard with a rush, the erstwhile following horses now leading, that they might be sheltered first. As Billy pushed in through the door, his charges safely within the building, his companion dismounted in the yard, warned by quick steps in the house. He let his horse pass in to Billy's waiting hands as the house door swung open and revealed him, sparkling with moisture, squarely in the faint fan of lamplight.

"Who is it?" demanded a brusque voice from the doorway.

"Hello, Bob," said the foreman, stepping forward and pushing his hat back so the other could see his features. "It's Dave Saunders."

"Glory be!" exclaimed the liveryman, moving a hand behind his back. "Wait till I get my hat an' I'll give you a hand. Who's with you?"

"Billy," answered Dave, waiting.

"An' who else?" asked the liveryman, and turned to look impatiently into the room, where his hat was providing a search for his daughter.

"Couple pack hosses," answered the foreman, motioning for the other to join him. Then he swore

softly, for Alice stood in the doorway beside her
father.

"Where did you put it when you took it off?" she
demanded, and then peered out at Dave. "Let Billy
and Father take care of the horses, Dave, and come in
here," she ordered. "You must be wet through, and
chilled to the bone."

"Shore, Dave: come on. You, too, Billy," urged
her father, and then looked at her. "If I knew where
I put it when I took it off I'd be after findin' it myself!"
he retorted, glaring. "You allus say the same thing,
every time: 'Where'd you put it?'" he mimicked.
"As if *that* ain't the one thing I'm wantin' you to find
out: where *did* I put it?"

"You never wore it in this house to-night," retorted
Alice with spirit. "I know right where it is! I can go
an' put my hand on it, this minute!" She faced the
yard again, where the foreman had made no move
toward the door. "Come in, Dave: come in! What
gets into you men at times?"

"Will you please be findin' me hat?" persisted Bob.

"I'll be in as soon as I give Billy a hand," said Dave,
and as she drew back into the house he gestured per-
emptorily for her father to join him.

The liveryman turned and looked at his daughter.
"So you could go out an' put yore hand on it, could
you?" he asked, sarcastically. "Huh! I'll do that myself, an' show you it ain't there, a-tall!" and he slammed
the door behind him and stamped down the steps.

When inside the stable, Dave led the way cautiously
toward the front of the building, feeling before him as

he advanced. Halfway to the front door he stopped and checked his companion, who had grown a little fearful at these mysterious proceedings, although he did not know why.

"Bob," said the foreman, almost in a whisper, "I've brought you bad news; but there's a little mite of it that's good. I'll tell you the good first. It's about Red. I know he's been worrying you a lot, bein' so wild an' spendin' so much of his time with bad companions; but he busted loose from 'em all, clean an' wide. He turned into a man, a real, upstandin' man that nobody need be ashamed of, an' he got a job with me, punchin' cows. Bob, I'm proud of him, this minute."

In the silence sounded a muffled cough from where Billy worked in the black darkness by the sense of touch alone. Bob Shea was breathing heavily through constricted throat, instinctively knowing what he was about to hear. His hands touched the foreman's arm, and closed desperately on it, in his mind a single thought hammering insistently, mercilessly: How could he tell Alice?

He gulped and let his hands fall, standing erect there in the dark.

"Dave, bye," he said, speaking evenly by an effort that made him ache; "did you bring him—back to us?"

Dave nodded, and then realized that the motion could not be seen.

"Yes," he said, "in the night, like a"—his anger did not let him forget how that next word might hurt; and he checked it just in time—"coward," he finished, cheerfully resting under the unjust imputation.

"Dave Saunders is no coward," answered the liveryman. In a moment he spoke again: "Tell me about it, Dave; *all* about it. It may be the mite of good will grow bigger with the passin' of time, as the other will grow less. Tell me about it, bye."

There in the shielding dark, with the soft sounds made by resting horses, and the drip of water sounding from front and rear, Dave Saunders, building on the signs as he had read them, and grateful for a reasonable imagination, told the story of Red Shea's last few hours. He told it slowly and with simple directness, with now and then a low cough from the loitering Billy, or a clearing of the throat of the chief auditor to give his words a weight they could have done well enough without. At last he finished, and a short period of silence ensued.

There came a faint increase of the dim light which blocked out the rear door of the barn; quick, nervous steps crossed the small yard, and the three men turned to see the slim figure of Alice Shea silhouetted against that faintly luminous background as she sped without hesitation into the darkness before her, intuitively fearing calamity: there was only one calamity which hovered over the Shea household, and had hovered for days.

"Dad! Dave!" she called in a voice which sounded unnatural. "Where are you? What has happened? *Dad!* Answer me, won't you, Dave?" A great fear, and not a physical fear, throbbed in her anxious voice.

"Easy!" cautioned her father, reaching out his arm. It slipped around her and drew her close, its mate enfolding her doubly tight.

"*Oh!*" she whispered. "Don't tell me! Don't tell me! I know, *I* know!" After a moment she raised her head from the comforting shoulder. "But I—must know; I must know. Tell me, Dave: how did he—did he——"

"Like a man, Alice; honest an' brave, entirely too brave. Three to one it was; an' he didn't hesitate. He didn't have to make the play; but he made it, just the same. I'm right proud of yore brother; we all are." He cleared his throat, and tried to speak casually, feeling that Red's letter had never reached the town; and in this he was right, for it never had. "I'm glad he worked for me, in spite of the orders he told me about; in spite of what he had been told to tell me. They were honest orders, an' well meant; but I hired him with my eyes open."

Curiously, it was then, after that casual statement, that Alice broke down and gave way to tears, her father having almost to carry her through the barn and into the house.

For a few moments after the passing of Alice and her father there was silence in the barn, and then two unsteady voices muttered profanely. There came the sounds of creaking saddle leather, of slowly falling hoofs, and through the rear door of the barn there issued three horses, the first two bearing upright riders. They crossed the yard, passed close to the smaller stable and plunged down into the wet blackness of the gulch, to turn shortly and follow along the side of the hill which skirted the town on the north.

CHAPTER XVIII

THE BURDEN-BEARER

COTTONWOOD shivered and kept indoors. The fine rain slanted in a cold, driving wind and had a penetrating quality rare for this time of the year, even at that altitude. The street lay muddy and deserted, no lamplight from open doors streaming on it to help an occasional wayfarer avoid the puddles and quagmires. Here and there small groups of horses shivered together, suffering dumbly. They were an overflow from the half-dozen crowded, ramshackle stables behind the buildings. The pale yellow lights of the windows were filtered through fogged and grimy glass, where thin trickles of rain loosed suddenly and flashed downward, draining the areas of heavier precipitation. Despite the weather, every saloon was filled with boisterous, carousing crowds, their uproars scarcely muffled by the thin walls and canvas roofs. The dance halls trembled and shook to the thumping and scraping of heavy boots, their discordant music rising and falling at the whim of the capricious wind.

In the Argonaut a dozen men played silently, grateful for the warmth of the crackling stove. Here and there protesting or exultant mutterings disturbed the silence. In the Argonaut drinks were an accessory to gambling and were not the main attraction, and here, therefore, were those who found in chance their main lure. There was no ribaldry, no drunken singing, but rather a restrained demeanour, thoughtful silence and mathematical cogitation. On such a night as this the Argonaut never held a crowd, frowning as it did on conviviality; its patrons knowing where to go if drink were the chief desire; and on such a night as this the great majority sought drink and furore as an offset against the cold and wet, and once indoors cared little about venturing forth again. Those more restless souls who cruised from saloon to gambling hall and on to saloon again scurried unobservantly from door to door, heads down and collars up, unseeing in their haste and directness.

In the Argonaut the faro table farthest to the rear was a scene of quiet and purposeful activity. Behind it, more to while away the dragging hours than for any need to deal, sat Henry Dangerfield, his long white fingers moving deftly over the ornate silver box. There was no need for his gaze to cruise about the room, no need for his argus eyes to rove from game to game, for to-night his general supervision would be wasted, since the miners had been content to remain in their camps along the creek.

Leaning against the wall at the left of the new sheriff were two rough-looking men, dressed in nondescript apparel, a careless blending of miner and cow-puncher. On their faces a sullen discontent lay heavy and their restless glances roved about the room in useless repetition. Occasionally exchanging a muttered word or two, they would relapse into periods of scowling silence, and evidently found their thoughts poor company.

Outside in the dripping night, keeping well away from those lighted windows after one brief glance inside, a keen-eyed old watcher sought what safe cover might be found against the rain, and swore without feeling against the night and the need for watching, enviously visioning certain campfires down in the gulch, where discreet, old-time miners never failed to make him welcome. To Jim the minutes dragged, the general miseries of the night and his impatient waiting punishingly prolonging them.

Cold and raw as the night was, and blustery and searching the wind, Jim's coat, fastened by the top button, waved open and shut below to let the chill strike in. One hand sought for warmth in a deep and torn trouser pocket; the other, seemingly seeking suppleness from the questionable warmth of his body, lay hidden under the gently billowing coat. Stiff fingers are one of the penalties of increasing old age, and for stiff fingers oft-times the penalty is death. In this watcher's head was the cunning of the fox, the cunning which takes the place of a more trained intelligence; in his heart was a paradox, simple kindness lying side by side with a wolf-like ferocity. The old eyes peered from under their bushy brows to search the surrounding darkness with the keenness of a night-flying bird of prey; the old ears, defiant of that dulling of the senses which stalks old age, were tuned to catch the slightest sounds. Alert and secretive lest he defeat his cherished ends; tensed and furtive against that discovery which would mean a quick and farcical trial, and a verdict adding mortal insult to its mortal findings, he crouched in the whimpering storm in the very heart of his enemies' stronghold, keeping fingers warm, and warming the walnut handles of a gun older than many a swaggering youth in the town.

The ancient cap-and-ball had been transformed in some distant government arsenal, and was a hybrid spanning two epochs of deadly inventive genius. On the seven-and-a-half-inch barrel the wear of years had effaced a famous trademark, composed of a famous name, and the greatest city in all America; while along one side lay the heavy and cunningly contrived extracting rod, its broad thumb-flange hugging the under side of the hexagonal barrel. The original nippled cylinder had made way for a shorter one, the resulting gap filled in by a quarter-inch disk of steel. Reboring had changed the old .36 into a deadly Frontier .38, which snugly held a long cartridge of smashing power. In epochs, both men and gun were straddlers, both born in the Old and living in the New; and both in no way were one whit less deadly because of this.

The watcher turned his head, his questioning ears searching the baffling darkness, his glittering eyes fixed upon one unseen point. Minutes passed without a change in his expectant, ready poise; and then he slipped into the enfolding night, his supple fingers gently closing on satiny wood.

"Jim," came an eerie whisper on the wind, and the

sucking of sticky mud seemed to chuckle in the dark. The wind roared to a boisterous climax, and hushed again. "Jim" sighed the listening lull.

On the brow of the hill two figures waited in the inky dark, one of them bowed grotesquely under a grotesque and ghastly burden. Silently they waited, testing the air currents with eager ears, straining helpless eyes uselessly. Almost without a sound the waiting pair grew to three, and low whispers breathed in hungry ears. The third slipped aside a step or two and magically disappeared; the remaining two moved slowly and with great caution toward the rectangular lines of light leaking around the edges of a closed door. In the lead stole a bow-legged puncher, now oblivious of the rain and the chill, eager to stake his life on a game with Fate; behind him came the burden-bearer, awkwardly advancing in the treacherous mud, his left arm reaching upward to encircle the inert burden on his sloping shoulder; his right arm crooked, its elbow close against his curving side that his free hand might rest on walnut. Slowly they moved forward, doggedly, without hesitation, the serene faith in their united prowess discounting the danger of their hazard. The building reached, a momentary pause was had to recover breath and to poise the burden securely. Then the slowness of their movements turned to speed, their latent deadliness leaped to a greedy readiness, trembling on crooked and straining thumbs holding back one-toothed hammers of death. The barring door moved inward as the foremost puncher slid through the swiftly growing opening and slipped sidewise along the wall, his low and vibrant warning throbbing with sincerity.

"*Don't move!*"

At his left side, through the open door, stepped, like some hunchbacked feline, the grim and ready burden-bearer, on his shoulder the rain-soaked body of a man; at his right side, extending forward beyond his waist, a wet gun glistened in the light of half-a-dozen lamps, its dark and threatening muzzle backed by the shining grease of cartridge ends in geometrical array, a greenish-yellow grease, evil to look upon.

There came the sound of sharply indrawn breaths, and then a strained and astonished silence, broken only by the crackle of wood and the hiss of resinous pine knots in the ravenous stove. The apathetic stud-horse players were apathetic no longer; behind the ornate faro table Henry Dangerfield held his white hands poised above the box, motionless as those of a statue, an earnest of his pacific intentions; at his left, against the wall, two amazed and doubting men forgot their sullen discontent in a sudden blaze of fear, their eyes hypnotically on the advancing burden-bearer, with the tensed gunman against the end wall a threatening background. Their comrade was being brought back to them.

Dave moved straight for the faro table, his inscrutable eyes on the statue-like dealer. Heaving his left shoulder, he dumped the burden across the polished walnut top, where it sprawled with hanging head and feet. With its contemptuous, crashing descent, the relieved bearer drew the left-hand gun, and stepped one pace back.

"Bein' told yo're sheriff now," he said, "an' not knowin' who is the coroner, I'm bringin' *that* to you. I found it in a ravine in the brush lyin' east of our range, with Red Shea's body close by. It had two companions mixed up with it in the attempted stealin' of B—B cows, the theft of three of my cayuses, an' the murder of Red. I didn't see them, but I saw their cayuses. They belong to George an' Sam Glade, who're standin' there ag'in that wall behind you. I'm accusin' both of 'em of hoss-stealin', rustlin', an' murder. When you want me I'll appear ag'in 'em."

Dangerfield dropped his hands on the silver faro-box, stretched out his legs under the table, and smiled as he relaxed.

"You want me to arrest these two men on nothing more than the fact that you think you recognized their horses?" he calmly asked, with a gentle sarcasm.

"I ain't askin' you to; I'm tellin' you to: an' if you don't, we'll take 'em with us to-night," answered Dave, quietly. "Reckon mebby that'll be the best way, after all, seein' all the fuss it'll save." He smiled thinly. "Besides, some of their friends might come down to help 'em, an' give us a chance to do a better job."

There came the sound of steps outside, squashing in the mud. The sounds caused hope to flare up in the habitués of the gambling house, for a shot from the dark, through a window, would relieve the situation of its danger; but Dave's confident smile translated the sounds for Dangerfield, who had no doubt that these two men had come accompanied by their friends.

He was right, for old Jim already was moving into action. For a brief instant a savage face pressed against the fogged and grimy window pane, and at a suggestive sound dropped from sight. A thrown knife, point first, is a deadly thing; but ofttimes the hilt will serve as well: for to stun a man is to render him temporarily harmless. Out in the darkness old Jim slipped up to the victim of his throw, retrieved the unstained knife, and slipped back again, both gun and knife ready for the next.

Languidly Henry Dangerfield turned his head and looked at the two angry and amazed suspects, now standing out from the wall.

"You Glade boys are under arrest," he told them, unemotionally, and waved a deputy forward to disarm and handcuff the two. The sheriff then turned to the foreman, smiling mockingly.

"I'll send you word when you are needed, Mr. Saunders. Meanwhile, you might have the decency to sheathe those guns and act like a gentleman, however far short of that you may fall. You seem to forget that law and order have come to this country and that a public official is entitled to a modicum of respect."

Dave smiled coldly, his two guns unlowered; while back against the rear wall crouched Billy like an angry spider about to spring.

"Law an' order havin' come so recent, since we left the ranch to-night, I'm admittin' that it shore is easy to forget about it. In the last week eight men have been murdered on the trails; but I'm willin' to promise that the law an' order now rampagin' over the country will be copied by the B—B as long as we have guns an' ropes. I'm servin' public warnin', here an' now, ag'in trespassin' on our range. Any upright an' law-abidin' citizen of this here lawful community that is caught in the brush of the B—B with weapons, brandin' irons, or lariat, will get hisself swung at the end of the last named." He laughed softly. "We'll uphold yore law an' order for you, sheriff, till the last ca'tridge is fired."

Dangerfield's flush of anger melted away under the bending of his will, and his face was calm, his voice impersonal, as he answered.

"And *I*'m giving public notice, also here and now, Mr. Saunders," he said, "that I will not tolerate lawlessness and lynchings anywhere in this part of the country. Cattle-stealing and murder, and the summary and illegal punishments of them as well, lie within the jurisdiction of the sheriff's office. It is a burden *I* will bear."

Dave glanced at the figure sprawled on the faro table, and his hard eyes glinted.

"I'm bearin' the burdens of the B—B, as I allus have," he retorted. "I can't see no reason to turn 'em over to a wild-cat court or a bob-tailed sheriff's office: leastawise not till I see how them two murderin' thieves are handled." He sneered. "*That*'s the last burden I'll dump under yore nose, till you show me somethin' more than words."

"These prisoners will be tried promptly, and given justice without fear or favour," replied Dangerfield. There was a quality in his voice that sounded like the ringing of a finely tempered sword-blade.

Dave thought of a graceful bow he had seen executed, and ironically tried to imitate it, with poor success.

"Not long ago you sneered at Texas hosses, Mr. Dangerfield; you won't have no call to sneer at Texas men or Texas ways. I'm sayin' good-night to you, Mr. Sheriff, an' to all these honest gentlemen; an' likewise warnin' all of you that we'll kill the first man that moves a hand, or hops to that back door too soon. Outside, Billy; an' keep it trained."

From the door came a reassuring statement of fact, in a calm but eager voice; and the foreman of the B—B backed slowly toward the opening, his two guns covering the inmates of the room. Bumping against the wall, he slid cautiously along it, felt the edge of the door casing against his back, and suddenly disappeared in the drizzling dark. Inside the lighted room the postures did not change, all eyes turned fearsomely on that rectangle of blackness, or on the gaping and threatening windows; but slowly, timidly the tense expressions softened and at the end of long, stiff silence a querulous, indignant voice broke the tension.

"Judas priest! What cha think of *that?*"

CHAPTER XIX

THE GULCH LISTENS

PERHAPS it was Cherry Creek that first spread wide the knowledge to all ears that in gold rushes all is not gold; and to many who learned first-hand from Cherry Creek, the knowledge was bitter and the price heavy. Fortune is, indeed, a sorry jade; capricious in her favours. A few seekers for the yellow metal are rewarded almost to the height of their dreams, which often touches on the unbelievable; many, less fortunate, find their labours amply rewarded; but there are those who find bitter awakenings, undeserved. To every field there flock the fit and the unfit, the fortunate and the unfortunate, the wise and the ignorant; although of the last two the ignorant may often be first. Gold is where you find it; and fortunate, indeed, is he who does find it. A man may be sober and unceasing in his honest toil, and yet skirt starvation's edge. So it has been in all gold rushes, and so it was in Cottonwood Gulch.

As time went on and supplies dwindled steadily, the fortunate made jests, accusing and indignant perhaps, but still jests, at the prices charged for food in Cottonwood. Yet they could buy, and buying, eat. Time, for them, measured only the distance between the now

257

of their endeavours and the then which visioned their seats upon the southbound coach, headed for home. To others Time was tragic, measuring only the shrinking of their food stocks and their capital. Unlike Time, these material things had an end; and for a score of weary and despondent miners in the gulch, that end had come. Working for day wages, measured in terms of meals, some of these went along, hoping for some lucky turn that would place them, too, on the southbound coach to flee from the accursed place of their disillusionment. Yet there were others whose appetites paced their means to satisfy, and to these the outlook was black and bleak. Some have counted it strange that among the number of these unfortunates the percentum of mortalities from accidental discharges of firearms ran high; and of these there often was one who did not carry out the ghastly pretense of accident. Those who had no accidents found themselves settling to the level of sweeping bar-rooms and doing other odd jobs which lacked dignity.

It was with these slipping men in mind that Dave Saunders and his friend Billy let old Jim Hankins guide them through the freezing drizzle from the warm and indignant Argonaut roundabout into the gulch, whose fires winked invitingly, although half-heartedly, through the slanting rain. Mathematically it has been proved that one may not lose a burden of care on a gaming table; in the long run the burden will grow. Dave was no mathematician, as was his friend Billy in a limited and specialized sense, but he believed implicitly in the above statement. He had rid himself of a burden on that walnut faro table because, easy-going as he was known to be, there were times when pressure must have an outlet.   By that act his burden was to grow; and it was to check that growth that he rode north instead of south.   His name was known among the miners in the gulch: being the only cattle foreman within a radius of two or three hundred miles it was bound to be.   To some it was well known, for his fame had gone before, carried by a grateful old man who had many friends. The story of this old-timer was one calculated to arouse respect and friendliness among stalwart men: they would look with pleasure upon him, and would listen to him with interest and respect.

Old Jim stopped at a certain fire, where nightly gathered the big men of the gulch, the men who could do things if once they started.   Among them were lawyers, doctors, trained men gone wild; men from whose ranks a new country skimmed wisely for the shaping of its destiny.   Here was latent power, sleeping ability.   To old Jim's whimsical yet impressively sincere introduction of Dave they replied by smiles and friendly nods.   They were prepared to accept this well-known stranger on terms of equality, to take his words at full measure.   To them he spoke in his soft words of the South, his very moderation carrying conviction where ranting would have failed.   They hunched closer, hugging knees under chin, their shadows looming large on the canvas sloping down behind them, and larger on the canvas of the pregnant future, had they but known it.

Dave told his story, and his need; made his offer

with neither pride nor humility, and thus offended none. He wanted a dozen worthy men and a cook to add to the fighting weight of his six men and cook. He stated his terms and the obligations going with them. The answer brought a gentle smile to his lean face, and this matter was disposed of. Other matters were broached, matters that tended to crystallize discrete and moving forces. They were forces called thought, than which there is no greater. He made no plea for secrecy, and thus obtained it, being among men; and he gave full credit to the old prospector standing at his side, whose perilous spying expeditions throughout the town and around remote and isolated habitations had acquired a surprising store of strange but useful knowledge. Dave spoke evenly, almost monotonously as he called, name by name, the long roll of villainy, giving to each name its share in the terrorism, coupling each name to its victims. While he spoke to the silent, weighing circle, old Jim slipped away to visit his old camp and new partner; but he would return later to assume a necessary duty.

Having told his story, the foreman tactfully made ready to withdraw and leave discussion to go on unhampered by an alien presence. With a final shaking of hands he left the firelight well satisfied with this full night's work. There came the glint of metal saddle-trappings, the soft *squash-squash* of slowly walking horses, and the miners were left alone again, staring thoughtfully into their leaping and hissing fire.

With the departure of the horses there came no sudden clamour or conversation, but rather a tightening of the silence. These men were thinking with the sureness of hounds on a true scent; they were weighing heavy matters, and mentally pouring acid where doubts arose. Among them were minds that flashed like old Toledo to the mark, striking sparks; and there were those who thought carefully before they set each foot down and shifted weight; but each foot placed was a forward step. So they sat in silence, gravely smoking; and the shadows on the shielding canvas of the lean-to seemed to grow, although this may have been but fancy.

At last a young man rose and spoke, with fiery words and passion, swaying on his spread and planted feet; so these young men have spoken in all times and climes, and so, please God, they will ever speak. Animation moved throughout the circle, some eyes blazing from sparks falling on a tinder almost explosive in its nature; others glowed, but refused to flame until the passing minutes showed that the acids had done their work.

To his feet arose a bearded miner, who needed only reindeers and a sleigh to fill a child-cherished part. Benign wrinkles radiated from his calm blue eyes; but from his lips there came words that showed the working of his soul, a soul naked in the presence of honest men. Lacking fire, he offered practicability; lacking an acrobatic imagination, he offered solidity, and a plan. His simile was not the bundle of sticks, for he knew no folk-lore; but he called on his every-day knowledge, and mentioned a prairie freighting team. First, they must be honest horses; second, they must be broken to harness; third, they must pull one way; fourth, they must have a good driver. Haste, he deprecated; the night and the following day would be well spent if spent in thought; let them turn these matters over well, and meet again when darkness fell. Meanwhile, they had made the Texan a definite promise; let them go among the camps and make it good. And go they did and made it good; so good, that even through the rain and chill and darkness of this same night, thirteen men on borrowed mounts followed old Jim Hankins southwestwardly along little-known and unused trails as grim assurance that a burden should not grow.

Back in the Argonaut, when the B—B punchers had slipped from the room, chilling blasts swept across the floor, gusts of misting rain blowing through the open door. Henry Dangerfield stared unseeingly across the body on his faro table out into the opaque blackness of the boisterous night. Only a moment before a tall, lean Texan had slammed that body down and said his say; only a moment before the Texan had backed warily toward that open door, and through it to effacement. Time passed draggingly, and then there came gentle stirrings throughout the room, low murmurs, whispered conversations; and all eyes centred on the immaculate sheriff-gambler gazing fixedly across the dead.

At his side two handcuffed prisoners moved uneasily, wrath and consternation on their faces, dumbly looking at the man who had caused this swift calamity. One of them cleared a husky throat, and broke the silence:

"You don't mean that we're goin' to be tried for murder?"

"Take them away," snapped the sheriff, his gaze not shifting from the open door.

Colonel Hutton, outraged by the swift and theatrical action which had taken place before his astonished eyes, looked at the miserable two, and nodded.

"You are," he said. "Furthermore, if the evidence convicts, you'll hang. Take them away, and lock them up."

The sheriff, smiling inwardly, made no move; and the bartender walked slowly to the door and closed it. Dangerfield, still staring, was not conscious of the movement. His thoughts, like eager hounds, raced along one trail and then another, each time balked by cold reason. One by one his uneasy suspicions shrank and died, beginning with the most threatening. No; Dave Saunders had no connection with the gulch, no bond with the restless miners; were it otherwise it would be known. Apart from the town and its activities, severed from the yeasty gulch, the B—B was a factor remote and standing by itself. It had been outraged, and had voiced its protest, stalking into a tiger's den to lodge complaint. Had Dave Saunders known those things which would call for his swift elimination, he would have known the Argonaut to have been a tiger's den, and would not have entered it with defiance on his shoulder and contempt in his eye. No: Dave Saunders was a cow-man, his thoughts bounded by his calling. His hostility went back no farther than the natural indignation of an honest foreman: *and a jealous lover!* Here was the note the sheriff had almost overlooked! He remembered the mimicked bow, and his memory took him back to a scene at Alice Shea's. A roar of laughter burst from him, to be swiftly checked; and he turned a smiling countenance to his wondering companions in the room.

"Yes," he said, subconsciously prompted. "If the evidence convicts, they'll hang." He calmly rested a hand on the body before him, and looked at the still gaping bouncer. "Ike," he said, carelessly, "take this out to the shed."

"*Me? Me,* boss?" inquired Ike, his eyes bulging until they threatened to pop from his head. "*Me?*" he repeated, in rising accents of fear.

Dangerfield gently wiped his hand and tucked the handkerchief back into his pocket. He nodded.

"Yes, you."

"*Alone,* boss? In the *dark?*" Terror was marked out by every line of his contorted face. At Dangerfield's cold stare and ominous silence Ike shuffled forward, screwed his courage to the sticking point, and let one finger rest gently on the body. Sweat stood out in greasy beads on his ape-like forehead, and he cast one wild, hopeless look around; and then almost fawned upon the man who was walking toward him to lend a hand. Together they removed the burden and bore it into the masking night.

The front door opened and slammed shut, to reveal a stiffly moving deputy sheriff, whose battered face was purple-mottled, whose swollen lips were thickly scabbed. Clem Lipscomb was not a pleasant sight. He walked slowly to the faro table, and sank gratefully into the chair before it.

"Just met Pete, with his prisoners," he mumbled. "Hear Saunders accused 'em of killin' Red. That so?"

Dangerfield nodded calmly.

"Pete's vocal chords was cross-eyed; what was he tryin' to tell me about Saunders dumpin' Whitey's body on to this table under yore nose?"

He listened to the brief recital, and grinned before he realized it; but at the pain from the stretching lips he killed the grin and muttered a curse. He pictured the audacious play, and grunted his admiration.

"Didn't know Dave had it in him. Sometimes I'm purty nigh proud of him. What you goin' to do about it?"

"You send somebody into the gulch to-morrow morning, to tell our able and zealous prosecuting attorney to get ready to prosecute; and send somebody else to the B—B to notify Mr. Saunders that the trial begins at noon. That's what I am going to do about it. You may tell the prosecuting attorney that the Court desires a panel made up entirely of miners to determine the verdict in this case. A man's intelligence is not developed by close association with cattle."

Clem nodded his understanding of the orders, and leaned forward, his voice sunk to a whisper.

"Reckon most of them B—B fellers will ride in with Dave," he said, avarice licking up in his calculating eyes.

"Loyalty and curiosity might prompt such a move," replied the sheriff. "Two of them are certain to come in with Saunders, both of them being witnesses he cannot do without."

Clem remembered the condition of his lips just in time, and clapped a gentle but firm hand across them; his eyes glowed with more than avarice now.

"You ain't needin' me to-morrow, are you, Sheriff?" he prompted.

"We will have plenty of men without you, if you have anything to do," replied Dangerfield, significantly, and then he raised his voice. "You'd better take a few of the boys with you to-morrow, Clem, and look over that stretch of hills northeast of the gulch. I'll tell you why before time to start."

"All right," said Clem, rising. He wandered about the room for a few minutes, speaking to friends and acquaintances, and then carelessly went out into the storm. Once away from the building, he swung a sore arm exultantly, and hastened as rapidly as he could to his favourite hangout to carry the good news.

CHAPTER XX

TRIALS

THE rider who loped up to the B—B bunkhouse the following morning wore the badge of deputy sheriff, and was about the sheriff's business. His casual view of the range showed him no grazing herd, since swells of the ground hid this from him; and for the same reason he saw no change in the personnel of the ranch. No one being in sight about the premises, he placed the written notice of the trial on the bunkhouse table and rode back the way he had come.

The granary door opened cautiously and old Jim slipped into the bunkhouse, espying the notice as he stepped inside. He looked at it in great disgust, and slowly went to it and picked it up. Apparently he was not curious, since he made no effort to read it, and he replaced it after a brief glance. What should he do? If he took it to the foreman he would have to cross the open range in daylight, something that was extremely repugnant to him. After hiding all these days, and going out only under cover of darkness, he did not purpose to nullify his efforts to remain hidden. Discovered as being one of the outfit of the B—B, he became only a worthless old man, and a grave danger to his friends; if he were not discovered his value to Dave was that of a host of men. Still, he felt that Dave should have the paper, and as soon as possible. While he argued the matter with himself, he heard a distant voice mournfully singing a sad and sorrowful song of the period. It took no look through a window to tell him the identity of the singer.

In a few minutes Bid dismounted before the door, stepped inside, and stopped to look inquiringly at the old prospector, whose arm rigidly pointed toward the folded paper on the table. Then Bid looked at the notice.

"What is it, Jim?" he asked, going to the foreman's bunk.

"Important paper fer Dave," answered Jim, uneasily.

Bid hunted in the bunk, over it and under it, found what he wanted, and went back to the table.

"How'd it get here?" he asked, picking it up and reading it hurriedly. "Gosh! I call that blame quick work! I'll rustle it right down to Dave. What you think of that?"

"What do I think o' what?" demanded Jim, his face stolid.

"Movin' as fast as that. How'd it get here, any-how?"

"Deppity brung it, an' lit out ag'in right quick," answered Jim, his greedy eyes on the document. "What you reckon it means?"

"Means business," replied Bid, folding it once and pushing it down into a pocket. "Dave'll be surprised, a heap surprised."

"Oh, I dunno," said Jim, writhing a little. "What's there in it to s'prise him?" he asked, sarcastically.

"What's there in it?" asked Bid. "Didn't it surprise *you?*"

"Can't say as it did," retorted Jim, after considering for a moment. "There ain't nothin' as would s'prise me, these days. How's it goin' ter s'prise Dave?"

"'Cause I know he ain't expectin' no move like that so soon," answered Bid, turning to go; but old Jim stopped him.

"Did you read it careful?" he demanded, severely. "*All* of it?"

"Shore; why?"

"An' yo're s'prised?"

"Who wouldn't be? I ain't got no time to palaver with you now; see you later," and Bid hastened through the door, mounted, and rode southward at a good pace.

Old Jim stopped in the doorway, on his face indignation and pugnacious disgust. He glared after the hurrying rider and shook his fist. "Damn clam!" he growled, and shook the other fist. "Damn smart-Aleck know-it-all! 'Who wouldn't be?'" he mimicked, his tones full of insult. He looked at the tracks made by the deputy's horse, and turned to look along the floor toward the table. "Said Dave ain't expectin' no move like that, so quick." He scowled at the table, walked over to it and kicked it, and then went back to the granary, uneasy and perplexed.

Time passed and he heard the swelling roll of hoofs coming from the south, and he peered out to discover the foreman riding between Billy and Frank, straight for the corral. They seemed to be in a great hurry, each silent with his own thoughts. They swept up past the door of the granary and flung themselves from the saddle at the corral gate, hurriedly stripping saddles and bridles from the horses, paying scant attention to the old prospector, and ignoring his leading questions.

"Was you s'prised when ye read it, Dave?" asked old Jim, fidgeting.

"Little," grunted the foreman, following Billy into the corral.

"S'prise you, too, Frank?" persisted Jim, his face growing red and his tobacco-stained lips quivering.

"Plumb knocked me into a heap," confessed Frank, swiftly following his companions.

"Got a good mind ter knock ye inter a bigger heap ner that!" growled Jim, savagely. He kicked at the mud, muttering under his breath.

Three horses expertly caught, they were led from the corral and deftly saddled, old Jim making the most of the remaining time.

"Where ye goin'?" he asked.

"Town," grunted Frank, straining at a cinch strap.

"Didn't ye figger that a-tall, Dave?" demanded Jim, anxiously.

Dave shook his head and hauled on his cinch, his eyes turning to Billy.

"Better take some other trail in," he said, suspiciously. "It may be a trap. Dangerfield won't forget last night in a hurry."

"Just what I was thinkin'," grunted Billy, fastening the free end of the strap.

"Why ye reckon he'll mebby ambush ye?" asked Jim with great anxiety. "Did ye read it *all through?*"

Dave flashed him a glance as he settled into the saddle.

"Every damn word of it. What you mean?" he impatiently demanded.

Old Jim wriggled.

"I was jest a-wonderin' how-come it s'prised ye, then."

"Why wouldn't it surprise me?" retorted the foreman, and set off to overtake his hard-riding friends. Had he glanced back he would have seen the new cook of the B—B shaking both fists after him while he danced with rage. More than once old Jim had cursed his illiteracy, but never more heartily than he was cursing it now; but wild horses could not have made him confess his ignorance, and he guarded it with a sly and ever-alert cunning.

The surprise and speed shown by Bid, and the speed and grimness of Dave and his two companions meant that something of importance was in the wind; but what this was, or how dangerous it might be, or what he should do on his own account, Jim did not know; and, not knowing, he stewed in frenzied uncertainty. His curses died out because of their futility and monotonous repetition, and he turned hopelessly back into his hiding place. As he closed the door behind him a sudden and grim determination seized him: there remained just one thing that he could do, and he would do it if the opportunity offered, and do it with an unholy joy; he could sit with a loaded rifle across his knees and make a sieve of any one sneaking around the ranch buildings during the foreman's absence.   Into his mind leaped the names of certain individuals greatly favoured as targets, and the list would have brought consternation to a full score had they but known it.   But like his efforts to obtain information about the paper, his savage waiting was due to be as barren.   The day passed without anything occurring around the ranch buildings; but in two other directions the day was not so uneventful. We will take the less important first, since the telling of it may be brief.

At the head of seven men Clem Lipscomb rode among the hills and through the brush on the east side of the B—B range, working toward a point where the undergrowth ran out in a long tongue, splitting the grass lands.   From this point of concealment they counted on making a quick, sharp dash at the herd, intending to stampede it southward into the brush and broken country, and to cut off enough stragglers to make the raid worth while.   In case of a fight, part of the riders were to fall back and act as a rear guard, covering the retreat of their companions and the stolen cattle.   The country was beautifully adapted for rear-guard actions, and there would be little to fear from the three punchers remaining on the ranch.   Dave and his friends had been watched for a short distance as they rode northward.

Filing through a narrow gully cutting across the last range of hills between them and the range proper, the raiders drew up while their battered leader rode up a slope to get the lay of the land.   They saw him stop, lean forward in his saddle, and remain rigid for a moment. Turning, he rode back toward them, his discoloured face expressing a combination of anger, surprise, and disappointment.

"Damned if there ain't sixteen armed men with that herd!" he called as he rode down the bank of the gully. "Sixteen armed men!" he repeated. "Thirteen of 'em stayin' close to the brush fringe, where they can't be seen so easy from the hills. Where'd they come from? What's it mean?"

"I don't know where they come from," replied one of the raiders; "but I shore know what it means: It means that I ain't aimin' to have no hand in raidin' them cattle. Eight to three ain't so bad, seein' we're the eight; but eight to sixteen, with us on the short end, ain't in my 'rithmetic book." The speaker spurred on a few yards to find room to turn his horse, and as he wheeled and rode back, he looked curiously at his hard-thinking friends. "Anybody ridin' back with me?" he asked, and forthwith found that he would have company, as much company as he had enjoyed on his ride into the hills.

Clem was the last to leave, reluctantly bringing up the rear, his countenance not yet having had time to assume its normal expression.

"Thirteen new men, huh?" he muttered. "Hm! Dave, yo're a long-headed old coyote: *too* long-headed! I'm figgerin' you'll stand a lot of watchin,' henceforth an' hereafter; an' I'm aimin' to do that watchin' myself, seein' as I know you better than anybody hereabouts. Me an' you shore has got to mix, and when we do it won't be with fists, damn you!"

In Cottonwood the street nearest to the southwest trail was well filled with gaping and curious miners idling about, but not in the least idle in their minds. Here and there throughout the little town low-speaking groups of miners stood or wandered uneasily, frankly bearing weapons. They were orderly, but eager; how eager, was only known by certain leaders who as yet were unknown in town, and who had laboured almost to the point of exhaustion to impress the need for holding back. When the line between peace and war had been plainly marked, and the gage of battle definitely thrown down, then there would be no more waiting; but until that time, restraint was to be the rule.

There came a sudden shifting among the miners in that important side street, a nervous ripple of interest, as word ran from mouth to mouth that three horsemen were riding from the gap in the western hills. The word ran through the town like fire across a prairie, and the crowd before the Argonaut moved uneasily, asking many questions. Men broke from it and sought the side streets facing the gap, returning with their expected information.

"It's him, ridin' between that Billy feller an' another of his punchers."

"Huh! I knowed he'd come: he ain't the kind to hunt cover!"

"Texans ain't huntin cover," boasted another, proudly, thereby revealing his native state.

"Ain't no reason *fur* him to hunt none, fur's *I* kin see."

Breasting the slope leading to town rode Dave Saunders, slightly in advance of his flanking friends.

His face was calm and serene, his manner devoid of nervousness, his two guns rubbing gently along his thighs. Among certain of the more observant it was noticed that Billy, also, wore two guns, and that he seemed to be looking for someone not present. Billy's thoughts were on Dangerfield. A lane opened through the miners, and the three rode slowly on toward the Argonaut, the lane quickly filling in behind them. Here and there a waiting group of miners moved out into the street, and went before while others sauntered along on both sides of the mounted trio. Murmurs filled the main street, swelling and dying and swelling again, strangely tense and uneasy; short bursts of laughter were heard now and then, a laughter lacking mirth. The crowd by this time had divided naturally, the bolder in the front, the more timid in the rear; but as yet there was no more significant division, no solid grouping of classes, for miners and townsmen mixed and rubbed elbows; and neither was there division among the townsmen themselves. To the great majority this trial was only a trial of the formal indictment, and care had been taken to keep it so, in so far as the general public was concerned.

Riding carefully through the press before the Argonaut, the three punchers dismounted at the main door and carelessly stepped inside the building. Two men met them, hands outstretched.

"Check yore weapons, gents!"

Billy swelled dangerously, pushing aside the open hands; but the door-tenders pressed closer, their hands outstretched again.

"This is a courthouse; check yore weapons!"

"I'm figgerin' it's the Argonaut!" retorted Billy. He pointed at Dangerfield, who leaned restfully against a wall. "Throw out that faro dealer, an' I'll check everythin' down to my pants!"

"That's the sheriff; check yore weapons!" came the angry reply.

"That's the card-sharp I come near killin' years ago for markin' a deck!" snapped Billy. He raised his voice turbulently. "Hey, *Denver!*"

Dangerfield's lips twitched, but he gave no other indication that the name meant anything to him. Billy started to push into the room, his teeth showing between his sneering lips; but the foreman's hand on his shoulder checked him.

"Let him be," ordered Dave. "You stand right outside this door, on the step, where you can see inside. Keep yore guns on till we call you in. Then me or Frank will take yore place." The foreman pushed his pugnacious friend behind him, outside the door, and gave up his guns. Putting the check carelessly into a vest pocket, he moved toward the open space before a faro table which was covered with a cloth. The room throbbed with noise, jammed as it was with excited men; but so deeply is the germ of order implanted in the average American that with the appearance of Judge Hutton a hush fell and the shifting stopped.

Filling the jury chairs went on with no more hitches than might be expected, several men asking to be excused on the ground of friendship for the accused; and to the uneasy surprise of the dwellers in the gulch,

Dangerfield's statement was made good: the jury was made up of miners. The murmurs of surprise and suspicion, and of indignation, were quickly hushed at the tap of the gavel; and the trial proceeded.

It is needless here to give a verbatim account of this trial of three indictments, the arguments of counsel, the honest and able rulings of the Court; neither is the testimony in detail of sufficient value to be here set down. We will seek our information and satisfy our curiosity in the summing up, and in the charge to the jury.

The prosecuting attorney:

"Your Honour, and gentlemen of the jury:

"The prosecution has undertaken to prove each count of the indictment, but by the nature of the testimony the counts are inseparably interwoven. I am not going to review the testimony of any witness. I am not going to tire you and befog you by reciting the testimony, beyond the indisputable fact that brands indicate unquestioned ownership of horses in this part of the country; that the three witnesses for the People saw those brands plainly and that their testimony successfully withstood all assaults.

"It comes down to a question of veracity. Some of you gentlemen in the jury box found the testimony of certain witnesses beside the point and even, perhaps, wearying; but this testimony had to do with the creditability of the important witnesses. In everyday life you gentlemen bring to bear certain tests to determine whether or not a man is lying. On many things insignificant in themselves you base your judgment as to a man's veracity. If you find that a man will lie in little things, in the ordinary matters of life, and lie endlessly, would you trust his word, under oath or not under oath, in arriving at an important decision? If you knew that a man constantly frequented low dives, and had no visible means of honest livelihood; if you knew that no reputable man had ever seen him earn an honest penny, would you find in that man those things which, in ordinary life, would lead you to conclude that he was honest and dependable? You gentlemen can form your opinions of the matters here before you only by the weight of the evidence; and the weight of the evidence is based unalterably upon, joined irrevocably to, the truth of that evidence. If the evidence is not true, then it is not evidence! And if the witness lies, then his testimony is a lie, and in no way can be considered to be evidence, in no way can it have any bearing whatsoever on the trial of these indictments. We ask no miracles of you, gentlemen; we ask no God-given knowledge; but we do ask that you here in this courtroom bring to bear that same common sense, that same practical knowledge of men, that same power of judging truth and dependability that you use and show in your everyday dealings with men.

"If you have reasonable doubt that a witness speaks the truth, a doubt that you can give a reason for, a doubt which you would employ in your everyday life, then you are bound by common sense and your oaths to discard that testimony except where corrobation has later removed the doubt.

"The prosecution has done the best it can, with the scanty evidence it had to offer, to prove these defendants guilty of each and every charge in the indictment. It has been forced to employ at great length character witnesses, that you gentlemen might be aided in forming true judgments of the value of the glib testimony that we have listened to to-day. You have nothing whatever to do with the imposition of sentence; you swore that you had no prejudices against the death penalty; and you are not asked, not permitted to impose any penalty whatever. Your duty is to weigh the evidence by common-sense standards of truth, and then to base your verdict on the preponderance of trustworthy evidence, one way or the other. I thank you all."

The defence:

"You have heard our learned counsel's lecture on liars and lying, character witnesses and common sense. In his definition of reasonable doubt he took upon himself one of the duties of the Court; but I suppose he had to say all he could, seeing that his remarkable lack of testimony did not leave him very much to talk about along *that* line. I came here to-day prepared to fight desperately for the lives and freedom of these two defendants; but I find that I have been placed in the ridiculous position of the man who loaded up the old buffalo-gun with more powder and lead than it was ever designed to handle, and then found that the tracks he had been following were not made by a grizzly. They were made by a heifer!

"I'll say a few words about evidence and the credibility of witnesses, and sit down.

"Twenty-six witnesses were called by the defense. Eleven of them stated under oath that the defendants had told them that their horses had been stolen, and asked their aid in recovering them. They even insisted on searching Shea's livery barns for the missing animals, as Mr. Shea has admitted. These eleven witnesses swore that the defendants spoke about the missing horses on the day before their supposed crimes took place. Coming down to the day of the supposed crimes, there were nineteen witnesses who swore to having seen the two defendants right here in town before, during, and after the storm, all of them, witnesses and defendants alike, being storm bound. Among those nineteen were some of the first eleven, then engaged with the defendants in hunting for the stolen animals. These witnesses told straight stories, irregularly interlocking many times, and they withstood all the efforts of our able prosecutor to shake them. I'm asking you gentlemen to bring that same everyday common sense to bear, that common sense we have heard so much about, and to ask yourselves if twenty-six witnesses are likely to all lie in the same way.

"I want to say a word or two about the friendship said to exist between the dead man who was found with Red Shea and these defendants. I was a friend of the dead man; the Court was a friend of the dead man; there are many persons in this room who were friends of the dead man; but neither the Court, nor myself, nor the dead man's friends here present aided in the theft of cattle or horses, or killed Red Shea. I believe that will aid you in giving the proper weight to this sly linking of the dead man, through friendship, with these two defendants. It looks as though the dead man was the man who stole the horses belonging to the defendants. You gentlemen have shown a great deal of patience here to-day, and I thank you for it."

The Court:

"Gentlemen of the Jury:

"You have heard the evidence, and the summing up. I am not going to take your mind from the evidence. I am only going to say that if you have a reasonable doubt that these defendants, or either of them, committed the crimes set forth in the indictment, you are bound to acquit. If you find, beyond a reasonable doubt, that they, or either of them, committed any or all of the crimes charged, then you will bring in your verdict accordingly. You must give the defendants full benefit of every reasonable doubt, which already has been defined. You are not to concern yourselves with the thought of the sentence, but entirely with the questions of fact that go to build up the innocence or guilt of these defendants, or either of them. The assumption of innocence at all times lies with the defendants until it is destroyed by the evidence. I find that neither of the learned attorneys has left me anything more to say. Are there any questions? Then, gentlemen, you may retire to deliberate upon your verdict."

Fifteen minutes later the jury returned into court and gave a verdict of Not Guilty.

CHAPTER XXI

SAMPLES

IT WAS generally admitted that no other verdict had been possible under the evidence, especially from the lack of evidence on the side of the prosecution. The increasing excitement in the street died down almost as suddenly as a pricked balloon. Armed and ready men felt suddenly foolish, and hastily sought places less conspicuous than the open street. In a few minutes after the Court had freed the two prisoners every bar in town was lined two deep and every game going full blast. Cottonwood had staged another orderly trial, and was proud of it.

Among the last to leave the courtroom, Dave and Billy surrendered checks to the door-tenders and received their guns, Dangerfield carelessly watching them. Both absent-mindedly and at the same time pushed the cartridges from the cylinders of each gun and filled the chambers from their belts, placing the extracted cartridges carelessly in pockets. Judge Hutton emerged from a rear room, a judge no longer in attitude. He walked slowly toward the front door, outside of which Frank Hitchcock still stood on guard, and stopped before Dave and Billy.

"Mr. Saunders," he said, cordially, "I hadn't the

282

pleasure of your acquaintance before, or that of your
friend. Will you join me at a table?"

Dave looked into the calm eyes and to his surprise
found them frank, friendly, and disconcertingly honest.
Through his mind there flashed a review of the judge's
attitude during the trial, and he nodded. He was
somewhat disturbed, but wisely attempted to form no
judgments there and then. He introduced his companion and together they followed the judge to the rear
of the room, seating themselves at a small table.
There were four chairs at this table, and it was natural
that Judge Hutton, noticing the vacant one, should
beckon to the sheriff.

Dangerfield, smiling inscrutably, spoke softly to a
companion, who forthwith left the room while the
sheriff sauntered to the chair and sat down, nodding
pleasantly to his three companions. Refreshments
ordered, the four men leaned back at ease and regarded
each other gravely. By an effort of will Billy exchanged
a grim smile with the sheriff, and then gave his attention
to the conversation.

"What do you think of the verdict, Mr. Saunders?"
asked the judge.

"I don't see how any other verdict could 'a' been
brought in, considerin' the evidence an' the expert
perjury that the jury swallowed," answered Dave.
His glance flicked at Dangerfield. "What's puzzlin'
me is the hell-rushin' hurry of the whole thing. I dump
a dead man under the sheriff's nose an' accuse two men
of murder an' rustlin'; an' the next noon the trial is on.
It ain't dark yet, an' it's all over. We didn't have no

time to search that trail in the hills on the long chance of pickin' up more evidence. Ain't such all-fired speed sorta onusual, Judge?"

"Here is where you show me up in my true light," laughed the judge. "I'll have to admit that up to a few days ago I knew very little about courts and, for that matter, still know very little about them. But, speaking as a layman, as I really am, I must admit that I never before heard of such speed in bringing about a trial. I have known judges who would have been utterly dumbfounded at such a smashing of precedent. The speed of this trial resulted from a suggestion of our sheriff. We'll let him explain it."

Dangerfield looked calmly into the faces about him and nodded gravely. There was about him an air of furtive expectancy, almost concealed. It would not have impressed itself on any mind not already acutely suspicious.

"Judge Hutton acted upon my suggestion," he said. "As peace-officer, I had to consider the unrest of this population of ours. Every man in these diggings seems suspicious of delay. If they would keep their suspicions to themselves this would not be so bad, although it would tend to bring the court into disrespect; but, Mr. Saunders, they do not keep their suspicions to themselves. They add to them, and pass them on. The ferment grows, and let me tell you that ferment in this kind of a society is a very dangerous thing. We are no more than an island in a sea of lawlessness, only a short step removed from lawlessness, and one false step will overwhelm us and destroy our efforts. Why,

Mr. Saunders, you yourself are an example in point. You are a level-headed man with responsibilities. You have something at stake, something that needs every safeguard of law and order that can be found and thrown around it. You have perishable wealth under your care, great wealth and very perishable. Am I right?"

Dave admitted the truth of the remarks by a nod, too busy with suspicious conjectures to give all his attention to the words.

"And yet, sir, what is your attitude?" quickly demanded Dangerfield, leaning forward over the table and bringing a closed fist down upon it with a crash. "I'll tell you, sir! Last night, in this room, you told me that you would bear your own burdens, and shoot or hang any man you found unlawfully on your range! Did you not, sir?"

"I did; an' I will," answered the foreman, quietly, his glance leaving the front door. "If the cattle was mine I might gamble with 'em. Not bein' mine, I ain't gamblin' with 'em. I've just added thirteen men to my outfit, which I reckon is already known in town, an' my orders were short an' sweet. An' what's more, they'll be obeyed."

Judge Hutton gasped.

"Is all that necessary, Mr. Saunders?" he exclaimed, staring at the placid foreman.

"My best judgment says it is. Red Shea was workin' for me less than one day when he was murdered because he protected our cattle," retorted Dave, coldly. "When it comes to killin' I aim, from now on, to let my men do it first. An' verdict or no verdict, you can tell them Glade brothers that if I catch them anywhere in the brush on my side of the hills they'll be shot on sight. You know, an' we know, that they're guilty on all three charges."

Judge Hutton nodded gravely, and sighed.

"I'm afraid they are, Mr. Saunders; I'm afraid they are. But you heard the evidence."

"Heard it an' smelled it," answered Dave. "Understand me, Judge," he said, placing a hand on the other's wrist. "I ain't findin' no fault with the verdict. The verdict was all right. We didn't have no time to get enough evidence, or train enough liars to make evidence. You had nothin' to do with that. That's somethin' outside yore part of the proceedin's. I should 'a' had more evidence before I shot off my mouth. That verdict ain't yore fault, a-tall; it's mine. But that don't change things a bit, so far as we are concerned; an' them Glade boys will find it out right sudden if we catch 'em hangin' 'round the ranch. An' if there's any liars with 'em, they'll get the same dose."

"You know what that will mean," said Dangerfield, sadly. "We are determined to stamp out this lawlessness no matter whose bull is gored. If your men kill anybody for hanging around in the brush, they'll have to face their trial for murder."

Billy sat up in his chair, looking at the sheriff.

"Comin' after 'em yoreself, Denver?" he inquired, with childish curiosity. His gaze was direct and unwavering and he did not wink an eye; neither did he by any sign reveal the warning pressure he felt on his knee.

Dangerfield whitened a little, but smiled and fidgeted.

"If I do come I hope it will be you I'm after," he replied in a calm conversational voice.

"If it'll help that along I'll get down on my knees right now," retorted Billy, starting to rise.

Dave quickly placed a hand on his friend's shoulder, shaking his head, and then turned a proud and smiling face to the surprised judge.

"That's the kind of men work for old Ben Benson, Judge; law an' order are very fine when you've got 'em; but there ain't nothin' on this earth that can stack up alongside loyalty. If the sheriff comes or sends to the B—B for any man of us on account of us protectin' our own property, he wants to come with enough deppeties to take every last man of us!" He chuckled. "Then he wants to keep an eye skinned for the delegation that Benson'll shore as hell send up here to ask a lot of questions. Ever meet old Benjamin Dash Benson?" He chuckled again. "He's worth close onto a quarter million dollars, an' allus runnin' for Congress, back in his state; but he'll spend every dollar he's got, an' tell Congress to go plumb to hell the minute one of his boys needs any help. So far I ain't writ nothin' to Ben about what's loose up here, an' I don't want to."

Billy was a forthright individual, but he believed in backing up his foreman. If Dave wanted to keep the peace, then Dave should have help; but Billy was greatly puzzled by the intermittent pressure on his knee. At first he had taken it to be a warning against him starting trouble; now he was wondering just what it did mean. He glanced toward the watchful Hitchcock, and then at the judge; and to make more time for himself he chuckled and spoke.

"Judge, ever hear about Benson an' his middle name?" he asked; "or why our brand's the B Dash B? That dash ain't no bar; no, sir!" The polite denial made him grin at his foreman. "You better tell it, Dave."

"Tell it yoreself: you started it," retorted the foreman, laughingly. He moved in his chair, facing a little more toward the street door, and composed himself to listen.

"Yes; by all means," urged the judge, motioning to the bartender.

"Well," said Billy, plunging into his task. "The old man's full name is Benjamin Marmaduke Benson, though if you tell him that I let it slip he'll shore as hell fire me, an' skin me to boot. Ben's a craggy old cuss an' hates all kinds of doofuldangles. When he got old enough to figger about that there name he shore soured on it. Said it was bad enough bein' born an' havin' to hustle for a livin' all the time, even with an even break, without havin' no Marmaduke burned onto him. Said if his fambly had stayed in Boston, where Marmadukes mebby ain't so scarce, it wouldn't be so all-fired bad; but they didn't stay there. They moved to Missouri first, an' after Ben had fought an' licked about every human bein' wearin' pants in that part of the country, they moved ag'in, over inter Kansas. Ben had to do it all over ag'in. Then he lit out for the

solitudes an' finally located up here. Gettin' inter the
cattle business meant that he had to have a brand, an'
he was sorta proud of the Benjamin an' the Benson ends
of his name. He told me he tried to keep the two
B's for a brand, but the more he thought about the
Marmaduke part, the madder he got. It made him
swear every time it come into his mind. Now, in
polite society like they has back in Boston, swear words
are stood for by a dash. An' Ben said if Marmaduke
wasn't a swear word, it shore oughta be; an' anyhow,
it made him swear a-plenty. So he branded his cattle
B Dash B, an' he signs his checks with the dash included."

As the laughter died out there came a battered face
at the front door, where Clem Lipscomb paused for a
moment to look around the room. He stiffened a little
when he caught sight of the friendly group at the table,
their faces still wrinkled by laughter; but, catching
Dangerfield's eye, he almost imperceptibly shook his
head, and then went out again. Frank Hitchcock, still
on guard because no one had thought to tell him otherwise, now was inside the room, leaning against the wall,
and he did not leave his post to watch Clem after that
person had left the building.

After a few minutes more of careless conversation,
Dave and Billy arose, pushed back their chairs, and
leaned slightly forward to extend their hands to the
judge, the front of the room in their arc of vision.
At that moment Clem returned and moved swiftly
toward the table, the two men who followed him stopping when a few paces from the door; silently through the

back way came Sam and George Glade, lately freed from a charge of murder. They had been drinking, as had their two friends in the front part of the room. Their burning eyes were on the man who was responsible for their trial, and they moved slowly apart, hands on guns, in their liquor-inflamed hatred intent only on the foreman and his grim companion. As Billy shook hands with the judge he heard Dave's low exclamation, and looked behind.

Sam Glade's gun covered the foreman, point blank; his brother's weapon rested easily in the hand that held it, ready to swing up and cover Billy. Both punchers had been caught unawares from behind, for both had been watching Clem and the two men with him, watching out of the corner of their eyes while they said their good-byes to the judge.

Slowly turning, Dave fixed a cold gaze on the man behind the menacing gun; and then swiftly leaped sidewise, his hands dropping to his belt. Deafening roars filled the room, the several shots coming as one. Through the smoke Dave could be seen crouching low, his guns on Clem's companions; Billy, blood welling from his neck, had his back to a wall, one gun on Clem and the other on Dangerfield; near the front of the room Frank Hitchcock was leaning to one side, the better to see through the swirling smoke of his own shots, intently watching the Glade brothers in case they needed more, but the whole room was under his eyes. His spasmodic snap shot at Sam Glade had been aided by luck, and his second at the brother had cut only skin deep; but it had thrown George off his aim and given Billy that fraction of a second that was all Billy needed. Clem Lipscomb had made no move to draw, not thinking it would be necessary; and when the need arose he found himself looking into the smoke-wreathed barrel of Billy's left-hand gun. Clem had all the qualifications, save one, which make a gun-fighter; and the lack of that one nullified all the others in a crucial test: his courage was not equal to his viciousness.

Sam Glade stirred and rolled over, clawing to hands and knees, his gun ten feet from him; his brother, bent over and hugging his right arm close against his body, looked hypnotically at the alert Hitchcock and the slightly upraised gun; the two men behind Clem Lipscomb were slowly raising their hands under the threat of the foreman's guns. Clem, his face pale, held his arms well out from his body, his dangling hands two feet from his belt. Not a word had been spoken between the swirling action and this grotesque and statuesque posing. Hitchcock moved swiftly forward, sliding his feet across the floor, straight for the first of Clem's companions. In a moment he had rendered both of them weaponless, and had turned to watch the door and the eager and curious faces in the street.

Dave sheathed his guns and motioned to his friend Billy, whose left-hand gun now turned from its mark and was free to strike in any direction, while its mate peered with Cyclopean eye at the middle button on the sheriff's vest. Through it all Dangerfield had not moved, for there was that in Billy's eyes that made movement dangerous. Judge Hutton, his mouth gaping, sat like a man in a trance, unable to collect his scattered wits. His gaze had settled on Dave and remained there, unable to leave. Dave glanced at him, and smiled gently.

"Judge," he said, "there's the man that tried to talk me inter helpin' him steal old Ben's cattle. I told him I was goin' to thrash him every time I saw him. I'm seein' him now."

The foreman walked unconcernedly from the judge's side, straight for the ridiculous Clem, his gently swinging hands brushing the handles of the low-swung guns; but still, there was something about him that told Clem that he would not shoot instantly, that he would hesitate; and in gun-play he who hesitates is lost. Clem, himself, was hesitating, wishing to reassure himself that he read the foreman right; and then Clem's hand flashed downward toward walnut.

Dave covered the intervening distance by a bound, his right hand swinging out and forward from his side. It landed flush on the point of Clem's jaw just as Clem's gun was swinging free from the holster. All the sinewy weight of a heavy and well-conditioned man was behind the blow and it was a miracle that it did not kill. Clem left the floor like a bouncing ball, his feet flashing upward, and when he struck the angle of the wall and floor he lay as limp as a gossamer veil.

Dave turned and bowed to Dangerfield, showing his teeth; he had an understanding smile for Judge Hutton, whose expression would have made an idol smile. Drawing both guns, the foreman motioned with them toward the front door, and Billy slid along the wall to join his friend Frank at the portal.

"I'm goin' back to sixteen armed men, an' to law an' order," said Dave, grinning. "Cottonwood stinks; stinks near as much as *you*, Dangerfield. We've just had a sample of you an' yore law; an' you-all shore have had a sample of *us*. There's plenty more samples on the ranch. Good-day, gentlemen; good-day."

The foreman of the B—B turned and walked confidently to and through the door, the heavy guns dangling from his hands. Billy and Frank fell in behind him without a backward glance, mounted after him, and after him rode down the street, their narrowed eyes looking for targets. Of these, none offered; and three cowmen swung out of town to cover fifteen miles at a gentle lope, pleasantly eager to return to the law and order promised by a garrisoned ranch, although they all had thoroughly enjoyed themselves in town.

CHAPTER XXII

SETTING THE TRIGGERS

FOLLOWING a brief lull in the robberies and murders came a swelling increase in outlawry close on the heels of the acquittal of George and Sam Glade. Justice, preening itself upon being blind, had been blind, indeed. Ribald jests were whispered about the town, guffawed throughout the countryside, mocking the useless court and its helpless and honest judge. There was some great jest that bore the stamp of secrecy, that was vaguely referred to at the bars and gaming tables, heavy winks exchanging among the initiated, who slapped their thighs and roared with laughter. Daily the town grew more turbulent, its streets less safe even than before. Nightly the outrages grew, volleys of lead through futile canvas walls murdering the well-to-do as a preliminary to their robbing. Honest men slunk like furtive coyotes, not knowing when their time would come. Cherokee Jim, taking offense at a storekeeper's just and polite demand for payment, dragged the unfortunate merchant into the street and blew out his brains in sight of twoscore gaping men; and walked carelessly away, fearing neither law nor man. The stage-coach, now running empty of passengers and treasure on its southbound trips, aroused the ire of cheated desperadoes, who had held it up in vain on each oᵣ ᵢₜs last three runs. It stood before the rough board office, ready to make its barren trip, its six proud horses champing restlessly. There came a rush of heavy feet, a scattering volley, and those six fine animals never more would prance and dance.

The Court was busy, striving hard to keep up to a hard-working sheriff's office. Three trials a day gave it a record in criminal jurisprudence, and another record in acquittals. At last Judge Hutton, tired of playing buffoon, sick of the ridiculous figure he cut behind the judicial bench, flew into apoplectic rage and closed his doors to justice, his speech of resignation an epic of the bench.

Standing before a jeering, hilarious crowd, he tore the covering from the disguised faro table and hurled it from him. Quivering with rage, white-faced, with bloodshot eyes staring out like glowing coals, he gave up his office with a choking shout that echoed back in screams and howls of laughter:

"I'm *through*, you —— —— buzzards!"

Expecting death in the crack of some ready pistol, he shook his clenched fists around the cheering circle and hammered out a path to the privacy of his sleeping quarters, choking with curses. Instead of death he received three hearty cheers; and a wolf-faced desperado, leaping lightly to the faro table, called for a standing vote of thanks, adding that the judge had done his best to entertain them.

In the gulch, robbery and death crept farther within the confines with the passing of each new night. Solitary prospectors were found at daylight lying in their blood, their meagre possessions ripped and scattered, their caches unearthed. Sluices were robbed in broad daylight, their owners helpless under threatening guns; and if they raised a voice of protest they were fortunate to stay alive.

On the B—B, of all that crime-cursed country, there was peace and security—the peace and security earned by unceasing vigilance, stern readiness to shoot to kill. The bunkhouse now was dim even in the brightest daylight, the thick planks that closed its small windows letting in only faint streams of light where ominous loopholes had been roughly cut. No longer were the herds bedded down on the open range; no longer rode the night shift, crooning reassuringly. Grazed during the daylight hours and watered on its way up, the herd moved northward with the sinking sun, to be split and crowded into the corrals and the remainder held between the two big pens. Trenches and their earthworks guarded each lonely corner, while inside the house the waiting shifts slept on their arms.

Drawn by this carnival of crime, desperate strangers flocked to Cottonwood like vultures to a kill, and turned the town into a rioting, carousing shambles. These newcomers, searching quarters, turned Bob Shea's livery barn into a lodging house, forcing him and his daughter to flee down the hill as the swaggering vermin cheered, to seek protection in the heart of the muttering gulch. That same night an even dozen grim and heavily armed horsemen, riding roundabout, escorted them by devious trails to the sanctuary of the

B—B ,where old Jim grandly offered them his granary, and thenceforth swaggered openly, for watching eyes to see.

The following night, as was his hard-held custom, old Jim made his nocturnal pilgrimage; and returned a full hour before dawn, trembling with eagerness, unholy joy, and great excitement. He burst into the bunkhouse with a yell that made many a head bump resoundingly against an upper bunk. There in the light of the evil-smelling, dancing flames of kerosene lamps, the off-shift men crowded close around him, one of them dashing into the paling night to bring back the foreman.

Dave pushed inside and placed a hand on the old man's shoulder.

"Let's have it, short, brief, an' without no trimmin's," he ordered, and old Jim began anew. The miners had ceased their bickering, buried their jealousies, suspended their mutual suspicions and had agreed on teamwork, organization, unquestioning obedience to orders, and now clamoured for a leader who belonged to no faction. They were drilling in the darkness beyond the gulch, with sentries posted.

"Huh!" sneered the foreman. "They've said all this before. Let 'em sizzle over their own fire."

"Dave, yo're wrong!" shouted the old prospector, dancing in anxiety. "I know when men air in earnest, Dave! I could *feel* it to-night! Like bloody wolves, they air, that disprit they'll do anythin'! They want ye to lead 'em, Dave! There ain't a man of 'em as won't go through hell fer the sake o' peace, fer the sake o' sleepin' nights without the fear of their throats bein'

slit. They mean it, Dave, An' I promised 'em you'd
come. I promised, Dave! I told 'em you'd come to-
morrow night."

"Then you can tell 'em, to-morrow night, that you
talked without bein' told to!" snapped Dave, and turned
at a whispered word in his ear. "Mornin' shift, turn
out," he said, and went to the door, trying to hide his
eagerness.

Huddled in a blanket, Indian-fashion, Alice Shea
stood against her father, his arm tightly around her.

"Dave," she said, pleadingly, "we've heard enough
to guess the rest. You can't turn down such a duty."
She moistened her throat as she pushed from her
father's arm, and placed a coaxing hand on the shoulder
of the stern cattleman. "I know it means great
danger, Dave; I know it means risking all you guard.
I don't want you to be in danger. If you are killed
I—— Dave! Dave! Don't tell them *no!*"

He gripped her and held her back from him, bending
down to read her eyes in the faint light of coming day;
and then a smile broke across his face, and he stepped
quickly back one pace, and nodded slowly.

"All right: I'll tell 'em *yes*," he promised calmly.
"An' when we've cleaned out this hole of hell I'm
comin' back to find out what word *you'll* say to *me*."
He swung on his heel and stepped to the bunkhouse
door. "Jim!" he called.

The old man turned at the hail and moved toward
the opening, on his anxious face a gleam of hope.

"What ye want, Dave?"

"I'm goin' to the gulch with you to-night. I'll take

that job of cleanin' up. Soon's we have our breakfast we'll complete the lists an' figger out a plan of action. It's somethin' that's plumb easy to start; but God only knows where it'll end."

Alice impulsively moved closer to him.

"You don't mean that you have any doubts about succeeding?" she asked, somewhat breathlessly, now that the magnitude of the affair began to face her; the magnitude, and the tremenduous danger which would come from failure.

Dave faced her squarely, his eyes flickering with grim amusement.

"Coyotes hardly ever toe the scratch," he answered. "You show me a bully an' a murderer, an' I'll show you a coward at heart. Mebby it's well hidden, but the taint is there. I ain't sayin' they're goin' to get much of a chance to toe any mark." He paused, and his expression became tense and anxious. "Have you figgered what it means to send to death a score or two human bein's? To be responsible for the death of so many men? We know they deserve it; but playin' hangman is shore new to me. An' there's one I got to hang that will haunt me all my life. *Why* did he come up here! Oh, God: *why did he come?*"

To Alice there came a sudden understanding, a flash of light that swept away every doubt that hung its head in the most secret places of her heart; she stiffened suddenly and crossed her hands tightly on her breast, in her staring eyes an agony of questioning. How stupid she had been not to have understood before; how utterly stupid! Her impulse was to throw herself into his arms, to fold him to her and to mother him in the face of his ordeal; but she found that she could not move.

"We'll pay up for Red," said her father, soothingly, misreading the cause for her emotion; and then he swore under his breath as he thought of the tumult his reassuring words had caused. He caught her, petted her, trying to pacify her, to stop her streaming tears. Over and over again he told her that her brother had died like a man. After a few moments she mastered herself and pushed from his arms, wildly looking around for Dave; but Dave had disappeared. Again her father misread.

"Don' you worry about Dave Saunders," he said, proudly. "It looked bad that time when Clem faced him like that; but I'm beginnin' to understand Dave. Don't you worry about him a bit, not a bit."

"Yo're beginnin' to understand him?" she cried, and fled around the corner of the kitchen for the sanctuary of the granary, laughing hysterically.

The herd moved eagerly up the valley toward the grazing ground, well guarded by punchers; an outer ring of quiet and ready prospectors moved at equal pace, the muzzles of their rifles pointing toward the brush-covered hillsides. Thus through the long pageants of the history of the West have such men always moved, it seems. They flanked the many moving bodies, thrown out to face and hold back danger, pushing doggedly onward in spite of man and nature; to the bones of Indian and buffalo they added a goodly quota of their own, as though to hold down for all eternity that ground so dearly bought. It was all in the day's work; but we who come after them can find no words to pay our tribute; we may pay it in just one way: to safeguard and keep sweet that which they have won for us.

In the kitchen three men sat closely about a grease-stained table, their elbows on it, their heads close together. Under their eyes lay sheets of paper and in their clumsy fingers stubs of pencils awkwardly moved from time to time, determining the fate of many men. They debated earnestly and moved a name once in a while, from one sheet to another; and in that move, although he knew it not, some man died. There were three groups of sheets, ranking in direct and infamous order. The first, and largest, which was a pity, contained the names of those men whose murders and robberies had been well witnessed; those hardened criminals who boastingly, swaggeringly, had made their plays without concealment, scorning secrecy. The second list contained the names of those whom three or less eye-witnesses stood ready to accuse, if in their accusing there was no threat of death to hold them back. The third paper held the names of those who were strongly suspected, and both of these latter lists would yield a harvest to be given trial before a miners' court. On that second list stood a name that burned into Dave Saunders's heart and soul like a white-hot iron, that again and again drew his sorrowful gaze back to it, to torture him anew. Jealously he guarded his throbbing interest in it, trying to give no sign; even when he had stubborn-ly insisted that it be moved from the first to the second list, he had tried to steel himself from revealing more than ordinary interest; but his confrères, refusing to look either at him or at each other, knew his interest, and ached for him. On the second list it went, and there it remained, although Jim and Billy would have consented to move it farther; and remaining there without protest, it gave to both these men a deeper respect and a warmer sympathy for their foreman; and made them sad.

Dave arose, feeling a leaden weariness which was strange to him. He looked down at the three lists, picked them up, one by one, slowly folded them, and even more slowly put them in his pocket.

"When the herd's in the corrals we'll leave for the gulch," he said, his voice sounding unnatural and from a distance. "The new men stay here, on guard; the outfit rides with me, to give them miners a few leaders they won't question. We'll settle the details when we get to the gulch. Tell the boys to bring their ropes."

His companions watched him leave, watched his stooped shoulders; listened to his heavy-footed, slow steps passing around the kitchen.

"It's a shame," said Billy, drawing a deep breath.

Old Jim looked at him curiously, and understood.

"Yer right: it is," said the old prospector, grim resolution emerging through the composite expression of his face like a granite rock through a lowering tide. He unconsciously felt at his belt, and also drew a long breath. "There's one feller on that second list as ain't goin' ter hang; an' hang he will if I don't cut in," he said in quiet determination, thinking of the disgrace coming from such a death, a disgrace not dying with the dead.

Billy was half out of his chair when the old man's words exploded in his mind, and he remained half out, frozen in the posture, his unwavering stare probing deep into the other's eyes and soul. Slowly his hand moved out and rested on his companion's shoulder, its grip like that of some great pincers.

"I'll go with you, to make it dead shore," he said, almost in a whisper.

Old Jim stubbornly shook his head, determined that what he should say to that listed man should reach no other ears. The whole outfit, including Dave, knew the old man's well-founded suspicions and had faith in the accuracy of his eyesight; but unless they knew actual proof there would always be a doubt; and this doubt should be a gift of the old prospector to his good and loyal friend, the foreman. There would be little profit in saving the dishonour of a hanging if the reason for the hanging lived afterward as a fact, to drag its slimy tail over the present generation and into the next. The old prospector's skillful spying would be a gift to the community at large; but this one thing should be his gift to Dave.

"Yer goin' whar Dave sends ye," replied Jim, with great indignation. "Dave's shore countin' on you, an' ye ain't goin' ter be no brake on his wheels. With the best o' luck I ain't got many more years ter live; an' if I fall down, then ye can do what ye please; but yer goin' ter pick yer own quarrel, by yer own self. Don't it jest beat hell, Billy?"

"There ain't no word for it," growled Billy, going out, as thoughtful as he had ever been in all his life.

"There ain't *no* word for it," he repeated in unconscious reiteration. He had an impulse to return and shake old Jim by the hand; but he flushed with gentle shame at the thought of such a show of sentiment, this being a measure of weakness in a man.

CHAPTER XXIII

RETRIBUTIVE JUSTICE

SEVEN horsemen rode single file through the night, grim and wordless. They pushed due north, preferring the natural dangers of a rough and little-used trail to the comparative smoothness of the regular route to Cottonwood and probable spying eyes somewhere along it. They remained seven horsemen until the trail pitched down into Cottonwood Gulch, the lights of the miners' fires directly ahead of them, and the lights of the town at their right. As the last man crossed the divide he stopped his horse and let the jogging line go on without him. This was old Jim Hankins. He had won the position of last man by cunning subterfuge, gradually dropping back from his place behind the leader; and now the six riders moved on without him, not knowing of his temporary desertion. From now on the attention of the six would be on the trail ahead, and already they were bunching into a compact group.

Old Jim watched them disappear, almost instantly swallowed by the darkness, except where a head or two momentarily bobbed up against the faint radiance of the distant campfires. Then they moved into a lower level and were lost to sight and hearing.

Turning a little to the right, the old prospector rode off at a tangent, heading straight for the lights of the town, whence came a low murmur, like that of an angry sea breaking on a beach. Horsemen came and went from the side streets, looming up in heroic silhouettes against the yellow glow behind them. Drunken choruses, ribald laughter, venomous curses, and a shot or two, provided high lights against the general background of noise.

Mounted silhouettes were picturesque, but posturing had no charms for old Jim Hankins. When a full quarter of a mile from the town's outer fringe of shacks, he slipped from his horse, picketed it in a brushy hollow, and went on afoot at a half crouch, toeing in atrociously. No stalking animal of the wild could have moved less conspicuously, for his progress was as cautious as his old-school training could make it. Not for nothing had he crossed the Blackfoot country when such crossing was full of peril; or made his way into the Bayou Salade, the wintering ground of the Utes, for a season's hunt.

Reaching the ragged environs of the town, he slunk in the deepest shadows, testing his surroundings by eye and ear and nose. Deviously he moved forward, but to a definite objective, in his hand a double-edged knife in preference to the clamorous but not more deadly gun.

At last he paused again, a longer pause. The ramshackle building loomed above him, lamplight seeping here and there through cracks and partly stopped knotholes. Sounds of tinware told of a tardy cook finishing his work. From the other corner of the building came the noises of a low bar-room and the composite odour of cheap liquors. Jim stood pressing against the side of the building, his head slowly going back until the window above him was in his line of sight. The window was dark, and open, and no sounds came from it. Its sill was not very far from the ground, the low ceiling of the lower floor accounting for this. At his side was a packing case, standing against the wall; and directly under the open window was an empty alcohol barrel, standing on end.

He slipped to each corner of the wall, hurried back again, and silently climbed on the barrel, the great knife gripped by his teeth. Again he listened, this time for sounds of breathing inside the room; and then, grasping the splintery sill with both sinewy hands, he drew himself up and through the opening, and slipped sidewise along the wall that he should not loom up against the straggling stars. Several moments passed before he moved again, and then he set each cautious foot on the floor with care and slowness, putting his weight on it gradually so that the floor boards should not creak. At last his seeking hand touched the closed door, and he turned until his back rested near the hinge side, and against the wall. Here he waited, calm and patient, with no increase in the beat of his pulse. This last has a great significance, being an indisputable measure of this man. About the only sign he gave of being a sentient being was the brief smile which wreathed his lips when a well-known voice rode, for a moment, on the crest of the loud conversation below.

This voice, angry and profane, roared out on the tail

of a burst of laughter. The speaker stood within the bar-room door, dripping with greasy water, his face convulsed by rage. From the verbal deluge, his companions gathered that he had been passing a kitchen door just as some dishwasher had emptied his well-filled pan into the darkness. They also gathered that there was a temporary vacancy in that kitchen; temporary because a man can't always shoot straight while his eyes are full of grease and strong lye soap. Their merriment now took the form of wit, and sent Clem Lipscomb stamping to the flimsy stairs and up them, where dry clothes were scattered about his room.

Growling and muttering, Clem shoved open the door and slammed it shut again behind him. There came the greenish-yellow flicker of a sulphur match, boiling and stinking before it seized upon the wood and changed colour. Lighting the small lamp, Clem jammed the smoked cihmney into place and jerked open his vest, turning carelessly as he flung it down. He froze in rigid immobility, his left hand on the flannel shirt it was about to unbutton, his right held unnaturally from his body, its fingers opened for a clutch it dare not make.

"—— ——!" he whispered, wondering if a backward kick would reach the lamp, whose disheartened radiance picked out two narrow streaks of glistening steel where a whetstone had diligently ground. Evidence of the intruder's intention was further given by the made-over cap-and-ball that pointed squarely at Clem Lipscomb's stomach.

"Keep to whisperin'!" said old Jim, ominously.

"What you want?" asked Clem, obeying.

"Want ter pow-pow a little, an' save ye from a hangin'. Set down on the floor, an' then you can be as careless with that right hand as ye want ter be."

"Set down on the floor?" inquired Clem, his active mind racing along several possible courses of action. Not being able to decide upon one of them in preference to any other, Clem decided to mark time in hope that the situation would develop something of value to him.

"Don't want no curious folks ter see ye standin' thar like that," explained Jim, ingenuously. He was thinking that a falling body makes quite a crash, especially on such a flimsy floor. Theory is invaluable, but there is nothing like experience to guide a course of action.

"Ain't takin' no chances, are you?" sneered Clem, moving one step to the side so he could rest his back against the bed, under the blanket of which lay his extra gun. He flung his left arm carelessly on the covers, his body partly hiding it from his companion. His attitude was one of seeming indifference, although it somewhat suggested that he was bored.

"Yer helpin' me considerable," replied Jim, his imagination painting a vivid picture. He had little to fear from the tell-tale floor-boards now, for a man in that position would not fall: he would slump like a sack of flour.

That Clem's attitude of mind was a pretense was shown by his sudden snarl.

"What you want?" he again demanded, showing his teeth as his nervous lips parted.

"I want the snakes that murdered my old pardner," said Jim, without emotion, but again telling himself that

a knife would be not only silent, but peculiarly retrib-
utive. At that distance there could be no doubt about
its efficiency. "Yo're one of 'em," he stated, matter of
fact.

"Yore pardner? Who was he? What have *I* got to
do with him?" asked Clem, preserving remarkable
control of muscles and nerves. For that left hand to
move so slowly, so smoothly that its motion could not
be seen, was a great test, considering the tremendous
strain he was under. He had no illusions about the
meaning of the presence of this leather-faced, icy old-
timer; no doubt whatever as to his intentions.

"Ye must have quite a sizable string o' dead uns,"
said Jim, "if ye don't know which man I mean." His
voice was mildly congratulatory, almost envious.
"How'd Red Shea git that thar scar he had on his forehead, Clem?" he asked, easily wandering from the main
thought.

Clem's face wrinkled with savage suspicion. His left
hand was still moving with damnable slowness toward
the weapon under the blanket. Better to cover its
stealthy reaching he squirmed a little, shifting his
body as though for comfort's sake, and he sought to
engage the old man's interest in this new subject.

"He slipped on some potato peelin's, down in the
street," he truthfully answered. "It saved his life, too,
the lucky blunderer, The other feller fired as he
started to slip."

"Who was the third man with you an' Dangerfield,
when Hank Simpson was murdered in the gulch?"
asked old Jim, keyed for high-speed action. The

unnatural position of Clem's left shoulder had caught his attention, and was being considered.

"Not bein' there, I can't say!" snapped Clem, the muscles of his left arm almost numbed because of its strained position.

"Yer a squaw dog liar!" retorted Jim, his eyes glinting. "I *saw* you an' Dangerfield an' the glitter o' the knife in one glance. I'm here to square up yer part in the murder o' Hank Simpson, Clem *Saunders!*" His gun moved forward an inch or two, by its movement becoming more threatening than the knife, and taking Clem's attention from the other weapon. Then, unbelievably, at a sudden uproar in the room below, the gun wavered and partly slipped from the hand that held it, its muzzle for an instant leaving its target, a temptation and a chance which a gunman would not overlook.

Clem writhed sidewise, his left arm moving quickly; but across the poorly lighted room there came a second movement, and a glittering length of heavy steel split the air. Persistent, thoughtful practice spread out over forty years will give a man amazing accuracy; an accuracy that even the jumpy, spasmodic muscles will not spoil. Old Jim arose, put out the lamp with one whisking, downward swing of his hand, and moved unerringly through the darkness, the visual image of everything in that room persisting for an instant. Noiselessly he retrieved the knife, crept to the window, dropped from it with a cushioning motion to the barrel top, and moved away in the darkness, setting a direct course for the hollow in which he had left his horse.

It has been said that an Indian never forgets an injury or a favour; and old Jim Hankins was as close to being an Indian as any white man could be. Clem Lipscomb would neither be hung nor reveal his relationship to the detriment of his brother, Dave.

CHAPTER XXIV

A BUSY NIGHT

WHEN old Jim reached the outskirts of the camp in the gulch he was challenged from the darkness, gave his name, and passed on through the line. The first tent he came to was closed, its fire burning low and fitfully; then came two more tents, mere lean-tos, their fires dead but their ashes warm. From a distance a watcher could not have told whether they were occupied or not; but one searching look under the canvas showed old Jim that they had been deserted for the night. This seemed to give him satisfaction, and when other tents proved to be empty he grunted grimly. With no hesitation he turned and followed the stream northward, down its course, where no lights showed in the darkness; but after a few minutes of swift walking he could hear the low murmur of many voices. The sound grew steadily and he knew that not far in front of him almost the entire population of the gulch was assembled in the dark. Again he was challenged, and again passed; and as he went by the inner sentry a group of five men pushed past him, talking in low tones and keeping in step. There came the ring of metal striking metal, and it was instantly followed by a sharp reproof. A few minutes later the steps died out and the sound of walking horses grew less in the distance. Another squad moved past him, this one silent, and also keeping step. The fruits of hard drilling were showing in more ways than one, and old Jim sensed a curious feeling of power in those moving squads, a power not to be denied.

He went on more slowly in the faint starlight and soon caught sight of a black and restless mass, from which came low conversation, the sound of steel, and the moving of many feet.

"Frank Hitchcock!" called a voice well known to the old prospector.

"Here!" came the answer.

"Jim Badgley, Tom Jennings, Joe Schneider, George Watkins!" said the voice, and the men answered in turn, stepped out from the crowd, and fell in behind the first named. "You know what you've got to do, Frank? All right, then. March!"

The squad stepped quickly forward and was soon lost to sight.

"Joe Hawkins!" said the voice, and Joe Hawkins stepped forward to face the speaker. "Jim Schroeder, Al Ripley, Harry Thompson, Fred Ives!" The quadruple movement ceased. "You've learned yore list, Joe, an' know where you are goin'? Good! March!"

"Mark Luttrell!"

"Right here," came the answer as a man moved out from the mass.

"Al Thompson, Sid Notter, Ike Smithers, French George!" Again there came swift movement, and again it stopped. "You boys know yore orders? Got yore lists, Mark? Then march!"

Five more men stepped with a swing toward the creek and to their waiting animals.

"Billy!"

"Right in front of you, Dave," came the answer.

Four more names were called off, four more men left the dark mass, answered satisfactorily, and were swallowed up by the night.

"Jim Hankins! Thought you'd got lost, Jim," said the B—B foreman, not realizing the humour of the remark. "Get yore men together an' time yore move like we planned. You take the south side; an' don't forget."

Old Jim's low voice called off a score of names from memory and a few minutes later he led his group southward along the creek, not bothering with horses. Three more large groups followed at intervals, to turn off when nearer the town and to take the sides assigned to them. The remaining group split up into threes and marched more slowly along the creek, rehearsing their parts as they went along. The birth of law and order is sometimes accompanied by strange convulsions.

South of the town the relay stage station bulked vaguely in the night, dark and silent. Toward it rode five men in grim silence, bunched almost knee to knee. When within half a mile of the building they turned from the road, dismounted in a hollow, picketed their horses, and went forward on foot, spreading out as they advanced. One by one they reached the station from different directions, and on different sides. When once more together they slipped around the building and stopped quietly in front of the door. A sulphur match sizzled under a coat, the wick of a lantern was lighted and swiftly turned down, the lantern hidden beneath a coat, and then a slowly moving hand pushed open the door, and five armed and determined men stood within the building in the light of a high-held lantern.

"Not a move!" snapped Frank Hitchcock, leader of this grim squad, the lantern light falling on ready weapons covering the two bunks.

"What 'n hell is this?" roared a blinking man from his bedding, staring in amazement at these ominous visitors. "What you want here, Hitchcock?"

Hitchcock held a paper close to the lantern, and answered:

"I want Cherokee Jim for the murder, in broad daylight, in the streets of Cottonwood, of Nelson Cope; for the murder, in front of twenty men, of Little Sandy; for the murder, in sight of the whole town, of Frank Harper. What you got to say, Jim?"

"Yo're a good guesser; but who sent you?"

"The Vigilantes. Got anythin' to say, Jim?"

"Yo're damned shoutin' I has!" roared the accused, his face pasty white at mention of that dread name. "I want a trial. You turn me over to the sheriff, —— —— you! What business you got ——"

Hitchcock nodded, and two men sprang forward, throwing themselves on the snarling, fighting desperado. Hitchcock turned and faced the other bunk, whose inmate still kept his hands above his head under the threat of a steady gun.

"Big Jack," read Hitchcock from his paper. "We want you for the murder of Dutch Goetz. You blew him near in two with a shotgun while a dozen cowards looked on. Got anythin' to say before you die?"

"Yo're a —— —— liar!" snapped the accused, his hands slowly lowering. "He pulled a gun on me."

"You shot him in the back, an' after he fell you shot him again. Any word you want to send back home?"

"If I had half a chance I'd send you to hell!" shouted Big Jack. "Where's Dangerfield, the —— —— ——?" He stopped to listen to the sound of hammering which came from the stable, and his face blanched.

"Dangerfield has got troubles of his own," replied Hitchcock. "You got any message to leave behind?"

The shouted answer was as insulting as rage could make it, and after a flurry Big Jack was stood against the wall with his partner in crime, both bound hand and foot. A Vigilante hurried in and spoke to the leader.

"We had to rig an arm from the top of the stable," he reported. "There wasn't nothin' else high enough. It's plenty strong, for we tested it."

"How much of a drop does it give?" demanded Hitchcock, determining to be as merciful as possible.

"Near four feet: that enough?"

"Plenty," answered the leader, and again turned to the doomed men. "I'm askin' you ag'in: got any word you want to leave? We'll deliver it faithfully."

"Who else is on that damn list?" asked Big Jack, his face calm.

Hitchcock hesitated a moment, and then read the names. There was no danger of either of these two men passing along any warnings.

Big Jack nodded grimly.

"Who else is goin' to hell to-night besides them on that list?" he asked, and after Hitchcock had mentioned a dozen names from memory, the desperado nodded again. "Ain't made no mistakes so fur," he said. "How'd you learn all this?"

"Old Jim Hankins, scoutin' nights," answered the leader, impatiently.

"The —— —— ——!" snarled Big Jack, looking at his bound companion. "What the hell do ye think o' that, Jim?" he demanded.

"Shut yore damn face!" snapped Cherokee Jim. "What you askin' so many damn questions fer? Let's have it over with quick!" His face wrinkled with rage at sight of a Vigilante moving toward him with a handkerchief ready for binding over his eyes. "Take that damn thing away! How can I see what yo're doin' with that thing over my eyes?"

"Any word you want to leave?" again asked Hitchcock, and remained unemotional under a burst of epithets. He sighed. "Take 'em out," he said, leading the way.

Fifteen minutes later the five horsemen left the stage station and pushed into the night, leaving behind them hideous warning for the dawn to disclose. They stopped near a ramshackle hut built against a rock wall, and went noiselessly up to it on foot. Hitchcock crept up to the door, his men moving silently at his heels. Gently touching it, he found it tightly closed; the latch string moved under his cautious hand, but in vain. Turning, he crept away, leaving his men behind him. The minutes dragged slowly past, and then the waiting squad heard the swift galloping of a horse coming straight for the hut with no play for secrecy. The rider rode clatteringly up to the door, hammered on it, and called out impatiently.

"What you want?" growled a voice from within.

"Git a move on you," replied the horseman, vexatiously. "Sheriff wants you *pronto*. I'm goin' after Lefty Hooper an' can't wait!"

"Where's Dangerfield waitin'?" asked the voice in the hut, and swore as he heard the horseman gallop away. He moved toward the door, jerked the bar loose, and stepped one pace across the sill, shouting after the horseman. "Hey! Hey, you damn fool! Where's Danger——"

He did the best he could under the unexpected assault which amounted to practically nothing against the concerted efforts of four determined men; and when the struggling pile disintegrated he was securely bound, his panted curses unavailing. The galloping horseman —it was Hitchcock—was now coming back, and in a few minutes he stopped and dismounted before the hut. From his pocket he took a paper, but he did not need to consult it, since he repeated his information from memory.

"Boone Trotter," he said, slowly, "we want you for murderin' a stranger in broad daylight, in front of the Argonaut. Near a dozen men saw you do it, and one of our men heard you confess it, and laugh about it. Got anythin' to say?"

"My God!" cried the prisoner, sagging against the wall of the hut. "What you mean? Who are you? What you goin' to do with me?"

"We're Vigilantes; we want you for murder, an' we're goin' to hang you," answered Hitchcock, implacably. "Got anythin' to say? Any word you want to leave? Any messages to send?"

"But you can't do it!" shrilled Trotter, who had once confessed to cannibalism; who had killed a companion when winter-bound in the mountains, and lived off the body. He choked, and burst into supplication, asking them to think of his mother, and what it would mean to her.

"Yore mother's bein' thought about too late," answered Hitchcock, not unkindly. "Is Boone Trotter yore own name, yore real name? . . . All right: then she'll never know how you died. Near a dozen men have sworn that they saw you kill this stranger. Did you?"

"Yes, yes, yes!" shouted the desperate man; "but, my God, boys, I didn't mean to do it! I tell you I didn't mean to do it!"

The short, grim episode was tersely recalled to his memory, in vivid and ugly detail, and again he was asked if he had any word to leave. Blubberingly he answered and gave his mother's name and told where she could be reached, and asked that they tell her he had died from an accident.

Hitchcock stepped inside the hut, lighted the lamp, and motioned the miserable man toward the table.

"You got five minutes to write," he said; but those shaking hands could not guide a pen.

"I can't! I can't write! My God, boys, have pity!"

"You must reckon we like to do this job," said

Hitchcock. "Well, we shore don't. You tell me what to write, an' I'll send the news on later."

"Tell her I was killed—by a—a rock slide!" sobbed the condemned.

Hitchcock made a pencilled note opposite a name on his list, and put the paper back in his pocket.

"That's a lie that I'll be proud an' glad to send," he said, thinking of a mother's sorrow. "Get up!" he ordered.

The bound man grovelled and shouted, writhed off the chair and tried to wriggle under the rickety table. He was picked up in four stalwart pairs of arms and was carried, writhing and yelling, through the door and toward a tree on the edge of a little grove. There he was placed on a horse and held in the saddle while the rope was adjusted, screaming and cursing until the restless animal was led from under him.

It still lacked an hour of dawn when Hitchcock and his squad surrounded another hut which stood in the heart of a thin stand of timber. The door was open, and a lamp, turned down low, burned on a box in the middle of the room. Snores sounded from the bunks, where two men lay sleeping, oblivious of the death that was drawing near to them. They awakened with curses and fought frantically, and then strained and tugged at the tight and cutting cords on wrists and ankles.

Hitchcock read the accusation of murder to each of them in turn, and a second accusation of highway robbery, and asked the usual questions. The first named sullenly refused to talk; the second sneeringly admitted the crimes, and demanded to know what the accusers were going to do about it. Evidently he regarded these men as a sheriff's posse, and was thinking that there would be another farcical trial under the direction of a judge friendly to them.

"We're goin' to hang you," answered Hitchcock, calmly.

"Oh, shore; when's it due to take place?" sneered the prisoner.

"In about five minutes," said Hitchcock.

"By what authority?" shouted the doomed man in sudden fear and rage.

"By the authority of the Vigilance Committee of Sixty," answered Hitchcock. "Got anythin' to say?"

The words aroused a frenzy of fear in the doomed men, and they screamed curses and denials, struggling against their bonds until limp from weakness.

"I want a fair trial!" yelled the other man, saliva flowing down his unshaven chin. "I tell you I want a fair trial! Where's Dangerfield? Take me to Dangerfield!"

"Yo're gettin' near the same kind of trial that you gave Old John in Tim Healy's dance hall; only we're substitutin' a rope in place of the gun, an' actin' from a just cause. Any word you want to leave?"

A string of curses answered, and the leader turned to the second prisoner. In a few moments the two men walked unassisted to the nearest tree, from a limb of which two ropes dangled.

"My God, boys!" begged the weaker man. "Be

shore you break my neck first thing! For God's sake, don't let me hang there an' strangle!"

"Shut yore mouth!" snapped his companion, contemptuously. "Lookit the drop we'll have!" His eyes were on the two horses standing near the ropes. "Got a bottle on you?" he asked his left-hand guard. "You ain't? Yo're a lyin', stingy —— —— ——! You won't give a man a last swig, you —— —— ——!"

"Shut up!" said the guard on his right, and held a pint flask to the cursing mouth, and kept it there until it was nearly drained.

"Good likker," sighed the bound man after drawing a deep breath. "Much obliged; I hope somebody does the same fer you, friend." A sob caught his ear, and he turned his head to look at his companion in misery. "Like a yaller pup!" he snorted. "Better hang him first, so I can watch him kick inter hell."

Dawn crept through the little stand of timber, and seemed to pause. The gentle wind sighed and shivered, and hushed as it stole softly past two gruesome objects which slowly turned first one way and then the other at the ends of bright yellow ropes.

On all sides of the town of Cottonwood there had been direct movements in the darkness. Ravines, hillsides, little clearings had been visited by squads of Vigilantes; faint paths and well-beaten trails had sounded to the impact of swiftly moving hoofs; mysterious sorties on foot had surrounded cabins, tents, and huts; and left behind them grim warnings to greet the light of the coming day. Not a word had leaked out; not a visit had been in vain. The country around the town had been carefully gleaned before the dawn, and not a desperado had ridden in to carry warning or to give succour to his companions in crime who slept in town.

The Committee of Sixty had many members who had gone through this same kind of work in other camps. There had been shrewd planning, and perfect co-ordination of effort. Not an innocent man had died; and not a guilty man whose name was on those first lists had been overlooked or had got away.

While the fast-riding squads had swept the country clean around the town, Cottonwood had not been neglected. From the four points of the compass as many lines of men moved quietly in the darkness to and through the environs. Here and there two or three men dropped out of the advancing line and slipped aside to perform the task assigned to them, the others going steadily onward.

In the main the town was asleep, only two lighted shacks on side streets giving signs of wakefulness. Maudlin voices came from these, incoherent, sagging into sleepy lulls. The door of the Cheyenne Saloon was flung open and two more deserters from its noisy crowd staggered into the street. They clung together while they said their blubbering good-nights, and separated, each to seek his bed. One turned a corner and ran his head into a blanket, swift and heavy hands rendering him both silent and helpless. The other grunted under the impact of a club and dropped to the earth. The shadows around the Cheyenne Saloon became animated, indistinct movements going on close to the ground. A roar of laughter from within the building died out quickly and gave way to a stunned and curious silence, and hands shot or wabbled heavenward under the threats of rifle barrels in windows and doors. Across the town the same thing was occurring at the Goldpan, where a gasping hush put an end to riotous noise.

In the Cheyenne the owlish group stood with their backs against the wall, blinking at the tall foreman of the B—B who was looking them over and checking their names on a paper in his hand, their identities made known to him by some of his men. Over his head the boards creaked, where two of his force, having silently entered the room by its window, were emerging by the door. They clattered down the trembling stairs, surprise on their faces.

"That Lipscomb feller was dead when we found him," reported the foremost. "Somebody knifed him."

Dave closed his eyes for an instant, and then crossed off a name. For a moment he stood rigid and silent, then drew a long breath and stepped out into the night, standing bareheaded as he looked up at the brilliant stars. He turned slowly as a hand fell on his shoulder, and saw old Jim Hankins silhouetted against the light streaming through the open door.

"Buck up, Dave," whispered the old man, squeezing the sloping shoulder. "Can't quit now; the big fish ain't been caught yit!"

Dave stiffened, nodded, and put on his sombrero; but his legs seemed to be tired, his feet leaden as he stepped back into the saloon. He viewed the sullen and frightened line-up with small interest, but went through with his part. Looking at the ball of paper in his hand, he opened it, smoothed it out, and read four names, motioning the owners to step from the wall.

"You four bums will be turned loose at daylight," he told them. "See that you never put foot in this country ag'in. If you come back you'll mebby get yoreselves hung." He let his gaze rest on the fifth, now standing alone. "Hammond, you got five minutes to live. Make the most of it."

Hammond sobered under the shock, his vacant eyes slowly filling with terror, and he scarcely heard the terse and deadly charge read to him. As the full import of his position made itself known to his liquor-stupified brain he moaned and sagged to the floor.

Around the corner the Argonaut stood like a smudge of soot in the gray darkness, at each window an armed man; at each door, two. Down the street rode a horseman, his life promised him if he played his treacherous part without a slip. Leaping from his horse in front of the silent building, he knocked on the barred door, knocked softly and in a set rhythm. From within there came a protesting, gentle creaking, and a low voice asked a question through the door. The parley was short, and the sound of wood sliding back through iron grated loudly through the night. The door opened, and Sheriff Dangerfield stepped back, that the messenger might enter; and at the sudden rush of bunched figures leaping through the doorway Dangerfield snarled a curse and had time for one shot before he went down like a broken reed, overwhe'med by numbers. Some-one struck a match, and in another minute one of the great lamps of the gambling hall threw its rays over a struggling heap, writhing and slithering across the floor. It crashed into a wall and started back again, and then broke up into rising units softly cursing, in their midst a dazed and helpless man, his hands tied behind his back, his legs wound round with rope. The breathless squad placed him in a chair, to turn angrily toward a night-shirted figure that stood in the door of a sleeping room and cursed them steadily.

Dangerfield opened his eyes and looked at the enraged colonel, slowly gathering the sense of the wordy torrent pouring from the lips of the one-time judge. A smile trembled about the gambler's lips.

"You should wear an abdominal belt, Colonel, even when you sleep," he said, and chuckled.

The indignant colonel folded hairy forearms before the hanging paunch, and wrapped himself in dignity, his tirade checked by this personal insult.

"Sir!" he cried, his florid face the colour of a poppy. "What do you mean, sir?"

Dangerfield turned his eyes from the misshapen figure in the bedroom door, and looked with great satisfaction at a figure sprawled motionless on the floor. The contorted visage, stained crimson, stared at him with glazed eyes. The sheriff nodded pleasantly, and laughed.

"So be it always with traitors," he said, and then glanced sidewise at the man who had just entered the room. "Ah, my good friend, Mr. Saunders! You are the only mistake I've made in years," he said, and then shook his head, and looked at the dead man on the floor. "No; you are one of the two mistakes I've made. Now," he said, looking back at the foreman, and smiling a little, "suppose you tell me the meaning of all this? You must admit that my curiosity is natural, and justified."

"You'll hear the formal charge in court," answered Dave; "but I'll tell you, now, that yore gang's busted up, an' most of 'em hung. Yo're wrong about only makin' two mistakes, Mr. Dangerfield. You made the third when you knifed old Hank Simpson instead of his pardner, Jim."

"I don't understand you; but I suppose that is not my privilege," replied Dangerfield. "Then I am to have a trial for something or other, and not be frankly murdered?"

"A trial before a miners' court, with Judge Hutton on the bench, if we can persuade him to preside."

"Ah, Judge," drawled Dangerfield, smoothly, as he smiled at the red-faced and tongue-tied colonel, whose forearms remained as he had placed them. "It is a mistake to incur the unnecessary enmity of the Court. May I say that I spoke, just now, without thought, sir? That there was no intent to offend? I hope you'll pardon the slip of the tongue of a man who was somewhat dazed and shaken. Nature her way will hold, in spite of hell and high water; and if a man will swizzle and gorge, he must expect to look like a tub. Judge, I humbly beg your august pardon," and his burst of ironic laughter boomed in the great room.

Colonel Hutton flushed a deeper shade, whirled, and slammed the door behind him, swearing under his breath. Then he fumbled for a match, to light a lamp and dress as speedily as he could. Past his shaded window there went the measured tramp of feet, and scared voices arose in a swelling murmur from some point near. He went to the window and drew aside the curtain, the room flooding with the light from leaping, towering bonfires. There were four of these fires enclosing an area about eighty paces square, and between them paced sentries with rifles resting on ready arms. Within the space marked out by the fires and the patrol was a number of men seated or lying on the ground, ropes around their wrists and ankles. Intermittently from the street in front of the building came the sound of booted feet, moving in creditable unison. Sharp commands rang through the darkness, and once or twice a gunshot sounded. The colonel opened the door again and stepped into the main room of the Argonaut, now ablaze with light.

Henry Dangerfield, with two alert men guarding him, rested indolently in a chair, his re-bound hands lying on his knees. He appeared to take a calm interest in the bustling scene around him, but his calculating eyes rested most of the time on the face of Dave Saunders, who was seated behind a faro table, where he received reports and issued orders. Behind him, and a little to the left, where he could watch the movements of every man who came and went, and where the whole room lay before his keen old eyes, sat old Jim Hankins, frankly holding a made-over gun across a knee. Dangerfield's every movement was answered on the old prospector's face by a glint of eagerness, and the gambler amused himself occasionally by experimenting. The ex-sheriff smiled grimly to himself; there was no need for him to face the ordeal of a miners' trial, to be stared at by a mob hungering for his life.

He raised his head and spoke to the B—B foreman, calmly preparing for his own death, thoughtfully avoiding the disgraceful hangman's knot.

"You spoke the truth, Mr. Saunders," he said. "The third mistake was the worst; although, of course, it was no fault of mine. I intended to kill both Hank Simpson and his partner, Hankins. We both stabbed the same man." He chuckled grimly, looking at the floor where a traitor's body had so recently lain. "That skunk I shot a few minutes ago was the blundering fool to get his men mixed, and stab a man already dead."

"Yo're a liar!" growled old Jim, raising his ancient weapon. "Clem Lipscomb was the buzzard as stabbed when you did!" His eyes gleamed. "Clem's waitin' fer ye in hell, this minute!"

Dangerfield raised inquiring eyebrows, smiling slightly.

"That right, Saunders?" he asked. "Lipscomb dead?"

Dave nodded, his eyes on Colonel Hutton, who stood motionless against the wall, doubting his ears.

"Dead as hell," growled the old prospector, letting the gun settle carelessly back on his knee; but its muzzle lay in line with the ex-sheriff's heart, a line as true as though it had been sighted.

Dangerfield laughed gently, looking at old Jim.

"Then as long as my good friend Clem is dead, there is no use in trying to shield him. He was too nervous, too flighty, for work like that; and, besides, the light was very poor. I see that I am the last of the three: that traitor I killed a little while ago was the third. He didn't have any nerve at all."

"You better save yore talk," warned Dave, coldly. "You'll be faced with everythin' you say when we get you on trial."

"Who've you hung, so far?" asked Dangerfield, and when he was told he nodded emphatic congratulations. "Every one of them was guilty. I suppose some of them talked a good deal?"

"Some of them did," answered Dave, indicating a bunch of papers sticking out of his pocket. "I ain't got what you might call a weak stummick; but some of the things they said fair sickened me."

"Who are being held for trial?"

Dave carelessly read the list, and tapped the papers in his pocket.

"We saved 'em to try 'em along with you, to give 'em plenty of time to remember things, an' talk."

"They will, too; most of them," said Dangerfield. "The best of them are dead." He gently shifted in the chair. "State's evidence?" he asked, and at Dave's nod, the ex-sheriff laughed grimly. "Saving their necks at the price of mine, eh? I don't like that, Saunders; I don't like it a bit. I hate a bleating turncoat. I'm going to make their evidence worthless, and let them swing, by confessing. They think they hold winning cards; but I've cold-decked many a game that was better played than theirs. I was at the head of the gang. I planned scores of hold-ups and murders, and all the stage hold-ups. When that big-paunched fool over there," he glanced at the colonel, "nominated me for sheriff I could hardly believe my good fortune."

Dave cut in harshly.

"I'm warnin' you, Dangerfield," he said. "You'll be faced in court with everythin' you say here. It'll all get to a miners' jury, near word for word."

"Thank you; but I said that I am going to poison the feast of a pack of coyotes," explained Dangerfield. He shifted the position of his feet by drawing them closer to him, under the chair. "I'm as good as dead now, and no one is going to get free by testifying against me. This gives me a great deal of satisfaction, Mr. Saunders; almost as much satisfaction as I received when I stuck ten inches of cold steel into that filthy old Hank Simpson." Out of the corner of his eye he saw old Jim stiffen, and the blood recede from the leathery old face. "He smelled like a hog in a sty——" and the speaker moved like a flash, leaping with both feet bound firmly together, straight for the open window at his side.

There was a spasmodic movement on old Jim's knee, a stabbing lick of flame, a rolling burst of black-powder smoke, and the roar shook the room. The leaping prisoner seemed to turn a complete somersault in the air, and was dead before his body touched the floor.

Dave was on his feet, leaning far over the table, a gun in each hand; the two guards near the vacant chair held their weapons on the quiet figure under the window;

Colonel Hutton was stiff with surprise, his mouth agape. Old Jim calmly turned the smoking cylinder around, poked out the empty shell, and slid a fresh cartridge in its place. He arose and walked slowly to the door, his eyes straight ahead, to stop and stand in the street, under the paling stars, and tell the spirit of Hank Simpson that at last the slate was clean.

"Well!" ejaculated the Colonel, looking at the thoughtful foreman in amazement. "The man was a fool to make such a hopeless and desperate play."

For a moment Dave thoughtfully regarded the quiet figure, and then he turned a gently smiling face to the Colonel.

"Think so?" he asked, and became busy with a pile of papers on the faro table.

CHAPTER XXV

BRIGHTER DAYS

TEN days had passed since old Jim had cheated himself out of a greater vengeance, had he but known it. The grim miners' jury had signified their verdicts; the Judge had passed his sentences, six of them for execution and the rest for banishment from the town, camp, and country. Now the jury had been dissolved, and the Court was idle. The Committee of Sixty, having cleaned up the country, had disbanded at the insistent demand of Dave Saunders, who was imaginative enough to know that such an organization, having functioned properly and performed the work to be done, was very likely to become an instrument of injustice and tyranny, through which personal grudges would work their unclean courses.

The town of Cottonwood, at first greatly reduced in population because of the Vigilantes' activities, was steadily growing beyond the limits of its previous census. The gulch worked openly, without fear of robbery and murder; the stage ran three days a week without molestation. In the streets of the town honest women, newly arrived, walked fearlessly, marketing for their husbands. The threat of death had passed, taking with it furtiveness, and drunken brawls and shootings.

With such a lesson still raw in their consciousness, the harmless ne'er-do-wells remained harmless, careful of how they stepped.

Across the intervening ridges and valleys the range of the B—B lay green under the sun, the cattle wandering at will and no herd formations to be seen. Gone were the armed guards back to the peaceful gulch, with money in their pockets to tide them over. In the ranch kitchen a humbled and contrite cook resumed his duties, while his erstwhile substitute panned for gold and wrangled with his new partner, a partner who regarded him with a vast respect; yet, somehow, seemed reluctant to spend good dust for a funeral long delayed.

From the smaller corral of the ranch a dozen sleek three-year-old steers issued in single file, choice meat fattened on a bunch-grass range. Billy swung through the gate behind them and headed the animals toward a gap in the distant hills, loosing a bellowing shout in the direction of the bunkhouse.

"Dave! *Hi, Dave!*"

Dave Saunders, wearing one gun now, and that more for the sake of ornamentation, stepped through the open door and swung into the saddle, turning his head at a hail from the kitchen.

"Dave!" called the thirsty cook, strong in his belief regarding the hair of the dog. He shoved his towsled head far out of the window. "Bring back a bottle o' good corn likker for me," he requested.

Dave took a memo slip from his pocket, placed it on the pommel of the saddle, and gravely made a pencilled note to purchase a bottle for "Stub."

"You want the yaller label or the red?" asked the foreman.

"What you mean yaller or red?" demanded Stub, with burning curiosity. "I don't care what's on the bottle as long as it's geniwine bourbon on the *in*-side."

"This here that I'm figgerin' to get is geniwine sarsyparillar," enlightened Dave, folding the memo and putting it back in his pocket.

"Sarsyparillar?" barked Stub, his face turning red. "Who the hell ast ye to git any sarsyparillar, you cross-eyed cow?" While he choked under the insult, and searched for words exactly suited to the occasion, Dave replied:

"A damn fool by the name of *Mister* William H. Norris."

A shout of laughter came from the bunkhouse, followed by inspired remarks and the makers of the same.

"You done forgot the Exquire, Dave," said one of them, peering around the corner for a sight of the indignant cook.

"You better play safe, Dave, an' bring both of them there colours," said the second, hitching up his belt. "He'll drink both of 'em if it takes *all* of us to help him do it. I've done dosed many a hoss, but I ain't never yet dosed a jackass; here's where I get my chance to try it." He joined his friend at the corner and looked hungrily at the scowling cook, licking his lips in keen anticipation. "You look good for two quarts, mixed, Stub."

"You go plumb to hell!" politely retorted the cook, and then leaned so far through the window that only a miracle kept him from falling out of it. "Dave! *Oh,* Dave!" he shouted in a voice which must have sent a shiver through Cottonwood, fifteen miles away. "Never mind no bottles, Dave! Don't bring nothin' a-*tall!* I ain't got no money fer to pay fer 'em."

Dave turned a serious face and looked back over the rump of his moving horse.

"I'll treat you to 'em," he called, and made a gesture with one hand which seems to be eloquent in any clime.

From behind the bunkhouse a wailing, boyish voice sang one of the latest songs to work that far westward:

> *When the corn is wavin', An-nie de-ear,*
> *Oh, meet me by the s-t-i-l-e.*
> *I long to hear yore voice a-gain,*
> *An' greet yore winnin' s-m-i-l-e.*
>
> *The moon is on the hill, de-ear,*
> *An' the stars do brightly shine;*
> *Oh, come, my love* ——

Bid stopped his feet and his vocal cords at the same instant and suspiciously regarded the scowling cook and the two grinning tormentors. His hand sought a pocket and came into sight again with two ivory cubes, yellowed by age and stained by use.

"Shoot *any* body two-bits," he offered, not knowing that in him and his offer stood Peace personified. The cook let loose his hold on the window frame, fell through it and arose to a sitting posture, his hand outstretched; the two loafing punchers amicably squatted where they stood, silver gleaming in dirt-grimed hands.

"Turn her loose, cowboy," grunted Hitchcock with avarice in his heart.

"Ride her," grunted Joe Hawkins, hypnotized by the rolling dice.

Along the easy trail jogged Dave and Billy, following the steers and silent from sheer contentment and the joy of being alive. Slowly the green miles unwound, to reveal Cottonwood perched cockily on its little hill. Blue streamers of smoke arose like plumb lines from the gulch, where human ants laboured cheerfully. Leaving the cattle in a flimsy corral, newly built behind Tom Buckner's store, the two punchers wandered in through the rear door and reported the delivery. Loitering here until tired of pestering the proprietor, they sauntered to the front door and out into the street.

"Hey!" said Billy in a loud whisper, his elbow smashing the foreman in the ribs.

Dave looked, and turned his back on the grinning Billy. Hat in hand he walked briskly across the street where Alice Shea, flushing a little, waited for him. They engaged in low-voiced conversation, taking up more than their share of the new sidewalk, and were oblivious of the knowing grins of passers-by, who gladly took to the dust of the street.

Billy watched the pair, saw them turn without thought, and start toward the domicile of one Bob Shea, walking very slowly. The smiling puncher lifted his sombrero enough to scratch gently under it, and then asked a question loudly:

"Shall I wait for you, Dave?"

There was no reply, and Billy ironed out the grin,

crossed the street, and overtook them. He placed one hand on the foreman's shoulder while the other removed his hat.

"Beggin' yore pardon for cuttin' in like this, Miss Alice; but I gotta ask him an important question. Dave, shall I wait for you?"

Dave's expression revealed vexation, Christian charity and self-restraint, and a vast disgust.

"Shore, Billy," he answered, enunciating with deliberate exactness. "Shore; you wait for me; but do it on the ranch, you bow-laigged chump!" The foreman's right hand dropped heavily on the top of his friend's hat, while his left gallantly took hold of Miss Shea's arm and led her from the annoyance of possible other gibbering idiots.

Billy forced the hat upward, first by one side and then by the other. His mouth came in sight, then his nose, and then the lifting operation ceased for a moment as one eye emerged from cover and gazed at the backs of two people who were unaware that the earth was populated by something like a billion and a half other individuals. The hat resumed its walking-beam motion and the other eye gave aid to vision; but corroboration was not needed: he had seen correctly with the first.

Billy loafed around town, burning with curiosity, and finally drifted up to the front of Shea's livery stable, where its proprietor leaned back as of yore, his kindly eyes twinkling.

"Seen Dave?" asked Billy, stopping to lean against the building.

"I have that," rumbled Bob Shea, trying to sound

fierce; "but he didn't see me! Damn near stumbled across my feet, the pair av them. It's a fine howdy-do when a man's not let enter his own house, Billy; a fine howdy-do!"

"Yeah," grunted Billy, smiling down into the cheery face. "Yeah," he repeated, pushing from the side of the building and starting carelessly up the street. "I'm shoutin' it's fine!"

THE END